ALL THAT I WANT

THE HESITANT HUSBANDS
BOOK TWO

GRACE HARTWELL

For Cris, whose sense of humor during a conversation at a cafe in Iceland bestowed upon me the name Charles Devereaux. Thank you for your friendship, and a most entertaining afternoon!

And for Jamie, with love from Aidan.

CHAPTER 1

*L*ady Elaine Lockwood was in hell. And if this wasn't hell, surely it was a close second.

All around her rang the normal sounds associated with a dinner party…the clinking of silver on china, the happy buzz of conversation, the gurgle of wine being poured into crystal goblets…but the smacking sound emanating from her right sent a shudder through Lainey that reached all the way down to her toes.

Thhhttt!

Lainey closed her eyes and breathed deeply, squelching the urge to simply slap the man seated next to her. It was bad enough she had to suffer through the Viscount's boorish conversation, did he really have to suck his teeth at the dinner table, too? But since violence against another guest was generally frowned upon, she took another healthy swallow of wine and glared across the table at her brother instead. Aidan regarded her with sympathetic amusement, pressing his lips together to hold in his laughter as he looked away. She narrowed her eyes further at him until they were mere murderous slits.

"I say, Lady Elaine, do you enjoy horses?" Viscount Molesworth asked, shaking her from her thoughts of fratricide.

"I do indeed, my lord," she responded, brightening. Finally, a subject in which she was interested!

"I have quite the impressive stable, you know," he boasted. "Some very fine horseflesh indeed." He leaned a little too close to her and dropped his voice, along with his gaze, which he flicked back up to her face when she gave a discreet cough. "Perhaps you'd enjoy a visit one afternoon?"

Lainey's lips thinned. *Not a chance in hell.*

"Perhaps," she said demurely.

"Tell me what else the lovely Lady Elaine enjoys doing with her time," he said abruptly, straightening in his seat and sawing at his meat. "I envy those with such a free schedule. Ah, what would it be like to have the time to sit with friends all afternoon, enjoying tea and sharing gossip?" He smiled and popped a piece of pheasant in his mouth, unaware that Lainey's grasp on the stem of her wine glass was tightening to a dangerous degree. "A ride through the park at the fashionable hour?" he asked around the food in his mouth. "Shopping on Bond Street? Embroidery, perhaps?" He chuckled as though he has made some sort of joke, completely unaware that it wasn't funny in the least.

It was all she could do not to dump her remaining wine over his balding head. But that would be a waste of a really good claret. She pasted what she hoped was a polite smile on her face. "Actually, I'm afraid I am abysmal at embroidery, and quite honestly, I don't truly have the time to practice it. My charity work keeps me terribly busy, you know. And while I do enjoy a ride through the park, I prefer to gallop across an open field at dawn when the dew is still fresh and the morning mist has not yet burned away. And, given that my father began a successful business importing fabrics, which my brother now runs to perfection, I'll admit that a love of fashion is in my blood. But while I do adore a good clothes shopping trip, I'd rather spend my day in a book shop. I've acquired a nice library thus far, but I'm always interested in new books."

"Books?"

"Yes. For reading."

"I know what books are for, Lady Elaine. I've just never met a female so interested in them."

"Perhaps you need to broaden your horizons," she said sweetly, attacking the pheasant on her plate with a vicious stab of her fork.

"What sort of book do you enjoy, then? Don't tell me you are hooked on those dreadful gothic novels." He gave a derisive snort before sipping his wine.

Lainey calmly put down her fork before an unfortunate accident occurred and turned to face him. "Actually, my lord, though those are diverting, I mostly like to improve my mind."

"Egad, your brother didn't tell me you were a bluestocking!" He speared a large lump of potato and stuffed it in his mouth.

If he choked on it, would she even try to save him?

"I am not a bluestocking," she bit out. "And even if I were, what is wrong with that? What is wrong with acquiring knowledge? I like to read. I like to learn. Does that worry you?"

"Course not. I just think that men are better suited to—"

"Pray, do not finish that sentence, my lord," she interrupted, a warning note in her voice. "I do not wish to spill my wine on your snowy, white shirt. Accidentally, of course," she added, widening her eyes in feigned innocence. Dear God, would this dinner party never end?

He pursed his lips and studied her for an interminable

moment, then nodded as if he'd come to some sort of conclusion. "You have spirit." He chuckled and lowered his voice in a conspiratorial whisper. "I like that in a girl." He waggled his eyebrows at her and turned back to his meal. Lainey's stomach roiled. Was he actually suggesting—

Thhhhtttt!

The viscount sucked a piece of wayward potato out of his teeth. Lainey squeezed her eyes shut and downed the rest of her wine. How had her life come to this? A burp from the right reached her ears and she willed herself not to scream. Sighing, she turned to the elderly gentleman on her left. This was going to be a long night

THE CARRIAGE DOOR swung closed and Lainey leaned back against the squabs with a sigh of relief.

"Tough night?"

Her brother Aidan, Earl of Ashby, grinned at her. His new wife, Elizabeth, sat beside him, shaking her head in sympathy.

"Aidan, you know I love you," Lainey began. "But if you ever put me through a hell like that again, I will do you bodily harm with no regret."

Aidan burst out laughing. "I'm so sorry, Lainey! I had no idea what a blowhard the fellow was. I kept waiting to see if you were going to quietly stab him in the thigh with your fork."

"I wanted to do more than that," she replied dryly.

"Oh, my dear," Elizabeth said, reaching forward to squeeze her hand. "You are a good friend for suffering through these dinners for me."

Though Elizabeth had come from a good family, she'd been separated from them at age fourteen, and had lived a hard existence until she'd saved Aidan's life six months ago. Aidan hadn't intended to fall in love, but fate had other ideas, and now they were happily married and introducing Elizabeth to society. It was a slow process as not all were accepting of Aidan's choice to marry so far beneath him, but it was their hope that the more Elizabeth socialized, the more people would forget about her questionable past and enjoy the person she had become. Lainey loved her to pieces and was doing everything she could to help, including being the sacrificial female when a single eligible gentleman (and she used that term loosely) graced the table. However, she was reaching the end of her rope.

"You know I would do anything for you, Eliza."

"Yes, but…let's just say you've been extremely patient."

Lainey gave an unladylike snort and let her head fall back. "It *would* be nice if at least one of these men were open-minded and slightly less obnoxious. But then, I suppose that is why they are still unmarried." The women laughed.

"Speaking of unmarried," Aidan began, and Lainey rolled her eyes.

"Aidan, can I at least recover from this evening before we talk about this?"

"I just want to see you happily settled, Lainey. I know you desire a family, and love and companionship. I want you to have those things. You're my little sister and I love you. It's been just you and I for so long, but it's time to live our own lives. You will always be welcome to live with us if that is what you choose, but I don't think it's really what you want."

Lainey gazed out the window. As much as she hated to admit it, Aidan was right. He was a married man now, and would be starting his own family soon. She loathed being the spinster relation who lived off the generosity of her brother. Watching the two of them fawn over each other all the time…she was so happy for them, but it was hard to quietly sit by knowing they had what she so desperately desired for herself. Lainey knew she would always have a home with them, and they all got on well, but she wished for a home of her own, and children she could spoil and love, with cousins their age with whom to play and grow together. She wanted a husband who loved her, or at least liked her, and accepted her for who she was and wouldn't try to change her or clip her wings.

Because most of all, Lainey needed a purpose. She wanted to do something with the life she'd been given, to make a difference in the world around her. When Elizabeth had come into their lives, her desperate situation had awoken something in Lainey. She'd always done her bit with charity work and such, but she'd never really felt fulfilled. What good was money and prestige if she didn't *do* something with it?

So, she had begun thinking about how she could change the direction of her life and do something important, something fulfilling, something that would *matter*. And a plan had begun to take shape in her mind.

Unfortunately, her plan would require a husband.

It was too bad that the only man she'd ever really loved simply didn't want her.

CHAPTER 2

The next morning, Lainey began putting her plan into motion. Seated across from her in the carriage, Elizabeth pinned her with a hard look.

"Where exactly are we going that I had to be so secretive about?" she demanded, folding her arms across her chest while she waited for Lainey's reply.

Lainey, for her part, at least had the grace to be chagrined. "I'm sorry, Eliza, but I knew if I told him he wouldn't let me go." Elizabeth raised a brow and remained silent, her jaw set in a stubborn line. "All right, I'm sorry I made you lie to your husband. I don't like lying to him either, but this is important."

"For heaven's sake, would you just spit it out?"

"We are headed to the docks to look at some real estate."

Elizabeth snapped to attention. "Real estate? Whatever for?"

Lainey grinned. "I am going to open a Center for the Betterment of Underprivileged Women!"

Elizabeth just stared at her, her jaw slack.

"Well, I rather thought you'd be a little more excited than that," Lainey said dryly.

"You're going to do...what?" Elizabeth's brow furrowed with doubt.

"Don't look at me like that, Eliza. I can do this. I want to help."

"But...how? Do you know anything about running a charity?"

"I know enough. I've learned quite a bit from my work at the Sommerset House, and I've friends there who will help me get started. I'm a smart and capable woman. I can figure it out."

"Well, of course you can. But this is a vast undertaking."

"That's why I'm planning on enlisting help. Aidan and Gavin manage to run a successful business. I can't imagine they wouldn't offer some advice when I get stuck. Who better to learn from than those two?"

Elizabeth grinned. "You do have a way of bending everyone to your will without them knowing it."

Lainey assumed an innocent expression. "Do I?"

Elizabeth's brow furrowed. "But a lady in business, Lainey? Aidan deals with enough prejudice as a working peer, and he's a man. Do you really think those same doors will be open to you, a female?"

"If anyone tries to close a door in my face, I shall simply have to wedge my foot in it. Besides, this isn't a trade, it's a cause. It's different."

The carriage rolled to a stop. Lainey peered out the window, a sliver of doubt sneaking its way into her stomach. There were a lot of people outside, many of them openly staring at the carriage. She'd taken the unmarked one, but still, it was finer than what was normally seen in this area. She'd dressed plainly but smartly, and she knew they would attract attention as soon as they descended. She'd brought their burliest footman just in case there was any trouble, though she doubted there would be. The land agent had assured her the location she was surveying would be relatively safe. Still, her confidence faltered a little as they were handed down from the carriage onto the dirty street. Lainey linked her arm through Elizabeth's and hung on tightly as they set off to meet the agent, the big footman trailing behind them. Elizabeth regarded her friend. "This is not going to be an easy task, Lainey. Why do you want to do this when you could just continue working with your current charities?"

Lainey covered Elizabeth's hand with hers. "Because I met you." She turned to smile at her sister-in-law. "I know women land on the street for all manner of reasons, but I'd never personally known any of the women I help more than casually. But you…you were living in my house, and you were bright and funny and loving, and by all rights, you should have had a beautiful life. You should have had gentleman callers and glittering balls and a circle of friends who love you as much as you love them. Instead, that had all been taken away through no fault of your own, and you lived a dark and dangerous life. But you didn't let yourself grow bitter. You kept fighting for a way forward. Unfortunately, that way almost got you killed, but your selflessness brought you here, back to the life you should have had all along. And then you brought us sweet Betsy, who is as hard-working and loyal a woman as I have ever met, and she deserves her chance at a better life too." Lainey paused, remembering the moment she'd first laid eyes on the half-starved woman who'd been the only person Elizabeth could trust during her time on the streets. Betsy had risked her life for her friend, and there was no way Lainey was going to return her to her squalid living conditions. Instead, the Lockwoods took her in and began training her for a new life. And Betsy had proved eager to learn. "The charities I work for...they provide basic aid and comfort, but they don't *teach* anything. They don't provide the skills women need to get better jobs so they can support themselves. I want to change that. I want to change *them.* I am in a position to do something about their situation. What kind of person would I be if I ignored that?"

Elizabeth pulled Lainey to a stop and stared intently at her, eyes brimming with tears. She took both of Lainey's hands in hers and gave them a squeeze. "Lady Elaine Lockwood, you are the most wonderful woman I have ever had the honor to know."

Lainey blinked rapidly against the sting in her eyes and gave a little gasp as Elizabeth threw her arms around her. Lainey's heart was full to bursting. Here was someone who, without a doubt, understood who Lainey was inside, someone who would always stand beside her. How fortunate was she to have Elizabeth for a sister?

She stepped out of Elizabeth's embrace and took her by the shoulders. "Now. As you said, this is a big undertaking, and I am going to need help. Do you think you and Betsy might be willing to be part of my team?"

"I would love that! Oh, Lainey, this is such a wonderfully exciting thing you are doing! Aidan is going to be so proud of you."

A shadow flickered across her face. "Let's hope so."

"How could he not? Come, show me what you've found. I can help you decide if it's the right place or not. Location is going to be very important."

"And that, my dear Eliza, is exactly why I brought you with me!"

～

As it turned out, site number three was indeed the charm.

"Just think of what you can do with all this space!" Elizabeth gushed. "It can be sectioned out into classrooms large enough to hold the equipment you need to teach life skills, this area can be turned into a beautiful reception area with your office just over there, and the location can't be beat. It's accessible enough to the poor without being completely unsafe. I don't think you are going to find a better spot, Lainey."

"It is rather perfect, isn't it?" Lainey tried to hold in her enthusiasm, but it bubbled and oozed like warm apple pie filling escaping the crust. She was really doing this. She was going to make her mark on the world, leaving it better than she found it, and it was going to start here. Of course, she needed to make an offer that would be accepted, but she didn't see that as a problem. How many people would want a building like this? Her real problem was accessing the capital she needed to buy the place. That was going to prove a little more complicated. "I don't think I need to see any more, Eliza. Let's go home and draw up an offer."

Elizabeth clapped her hands, bouncing up and down. "This is so exciting!" As they exited the building, she asked the question Lainey was dreading. "I don't mean to pry, but how exactly are you going to pay for all this? I mean, I know you will fundraise, but you need to be able to purchase the building now. Do you think Aidan will easily agree to paying for it? I can influence him if he gives you grief," she said, winking.

"I have no doubt you would be a strong influence on my brother, but actually…erhm…" How to put this? "I don't want Aidan's help. I am going to buy it myself."

"But how? I thought your money was in trust until you marry?"

"It is." Lainey scratched behind her ear, not meeting Elizabeth's eyes. "I am going to get married. The sooner the better."

"What?" Elizabeth was dismayed. "But I thought you hadn't found a love match yet."

"I haven't. It's time to be practical."

"Oh, Lainey. No."

"I am twenty-four, Eliza. Soon to be twenty-five. I want children and a home of my own. And a husband who isn't marrying me just for my money," she added wryly. "For heaven's sake, you saw yourself last night what my options are like. I have to find someone who isn't frightened or offended by the fact that I want to work, and there isn't a lord alive who will accept that. At least, I certainly haven't found him. Plenty of women make happy marriages without being over the moon in love. Not all of us are as lucky as you and Aidan."

Elizabeth grinned. "And he didn't even want love!" She looped her arm through Lainey's as they headed toward the carriage. "Are you sure about this? It seems a little…impetuous."

"I've been thinking on it for a couple of months, and I believe it's the right decision. I have enough to make a down payment, and I'm sure I can negotiate some time to pay the balance. I hope I can count on your support. I know Aidan is not going to be happy with me."

"Of course I will support you, as long as it is truly what you want. But how do you plan to go husband hunting with the season over?"

"About that—"

A shout drew their attention, and Lainey turned to see Gavin Mayfield flagging them down from across the street. Oh, bother. She had almost made it to the carriage without being seen by anyone she knew.

"Ask and ye shall receive," Elizabeth murmured.

"No," Lainey said firmly. "Absolutely not."

"Why ever not?"

Why not indeed? Lainey looked at Gavin and her heart gave a little flutter, as it always did when she laid eyes on him. Cursed organ. Gavin Mayfield was Aidan's best friend and business partner, the neighbor she'd grown up with, and the man she had secretly loved her entire life. She'd even managed to talk herself into believing that he felt the same about her but was just being respectful of his and Aidan's friendship. So sure was she that Gavin would be thrilled to have her for a wife, she'd confessed her feelings to him one mortifying evening two years ago in the hopes of making him feel safe enough to offer for her. What she got instead was a humiliating rejection.

"Because if he'd said yes, we'd be married by now," Lainey muttered under her breath.Her skin tightened as she watched Gavin jog across the street with ease, that winsome smile on his face, the sun glinting off his thick blond hair. Hair that made her wonder if it felt as silky as it looked.

Rein yourself in, Lainey. He doesn't want you.

"Hello, Countess, my lady. What on earth brings you to this part of town?" Gavin asked when he arrived in front of them. "You shouldn't be down here by yourselves."

"We brought Big Jack," Lainey impatiently informed him, indicating the footman behind them.

"Still and all, I'd rather you had brought an escort. What are you doing here, anyway?"

"Research, not that it's any of your business. And we are perfectly safe." On any other day, she'd be her normal, friendly self with him, but she was nervous Gavin would ferret out the truth from her and then go tattle to Aidan. This needed to be a short conversation.

But before she could try to extricate herself, a dirty, bedraggled man approached, staring hard at Elizabeth. Gavin tensed, ready to defend the women, but then the man burst out with, "Blimey! 'Zat you, 'Lizabeth?"

Light dawned on Elizabeth's face. "Douglas! I'm so glad to see you!" With no regard for her fine clothes, she hugged the wizened man, then turned to introduce him to her companions. "Lady Elaine, Mr. Mayfield, this is my friend Douglas. Douglas was my defender and champion here when my life was a little rougher."

Lainey nodded and said hello, but Gavin, blasted saint that he was, reached out and shook hands with the dirty man and gave him a genuine smile. "You don't say? Thank you for protecting her."

Flip, flop went Lainey's heart. She mentally rolled her eyes.

Stop. It.

"Aw, she's a treasure to be guarded! I can hardly believe 's you, Lizzie! Lookit ye!"

"I know! Things have changed for the better. And with a little bit of luck, things will be changing around here for the better, too!"

Lainey's eyes widened and she shook her head. Aidan would kill her if Gavin heard of her plans first.

"Oops, sorry, Lainey, I'm getting ahead." She fished in her reticule and pressed some coins into Douglas's hand.

"Now, Lizzie, that ain't necessary—"

"I insist. It's the least I can do after you were so kind to keep an eye on me all those years."

Douglas turned red under the smudges of dirt on his face and shuffled his feet. "Twern't nothin', Lizzie. Right happy to help. I'll be going now. Ye take care of yerself."

"I'll see you again, Douglas," Elizabeth said as he wandered away. She watched him go, an inscrutable expression on her face. She turned to Lainey. "Whatever your plans are, I am with you," she said with conviction. "I want to help these people who helped me."

"Plans? What plans? Do tell," Gavin said, curiosity tinging his voice. "Though I think it best if we remove to a safer locale."

Lainey sighed. "Why don't you come over for tea this afternoon and we'll discuss it. I have to beg a favor of you, I'm afraid."

"Name it and it shall be done, my lady." He gave her a gallant bow, complete with hand flourishes. She giggled in spite of herself.

"Stop with the charming nonsense and hand me into the carriage, will you?"

He obeyed, and once the ladies were settled, he tipped his hat. "Until tea, then."

"Oh, Gavin," Lainey called, poking her head out the window as the carriage began to pull away. "You'd better be careful about agreeing to favors before you know what they are!"

CHAPTER 3

Gavin pondered Lainey's parting remark as he ambled toward the Lockwood home on the outskirts of town. The day was fine, the dappled sun creating spots of light that danced on the sidewalk at his feet. He'd sent the carriage on ahead of him, choosing to walk the rest of the way so he could enjoy the late summer breeze…and to have a little more time to prepare himself for whatever awaited him.

Lainey's reception down near the docks had been unusually frosty. Something had changed in her since Aidan had married, though if he were being honest with himself, she'd been different since that disastrous night when she'd given her heart to him and he'd rewarded her by slicing it to ribbons. Turning her down had been the hardest thing he'd ever done, but he'd done it for her…though he doubted she would see it that way even if he told her the truth of it.

She'd been distant after his rejection, which was certainly understandable, but he'd rather thought she'd come round once she'd started speaking to him again. Although they put on a good show of their old friendship, it had become apparent to Gavin that a divide had opened between them, one he despaired of ever fixing.

Her behavior earlier today had been deuced odd. And what on earth had she been doing in that section of town, anyway? That was certainly no place for a woman to go wandering. She was up to something, and she'd been none too pleased to run into him. He couldn't wait to hear what scheme she was cooking up now. Lainey always had her hands in more than one pie, and he secretly admired her for it. If only he could feel as useful.

He knocked on the door, dazzling Tibbs with a smile when he opened it. "Good

afternoon, Tibbs."

"Good afternoon, sir," the butler replied, swinging the door wide. "His Lordship has requested your presence in the study before you go in to tea."

"Thank you, Tibbs," Gavin said, handing him his hat and gloves. He strode toward the study and found Aidan seated behind his desk. "Working inside on this beautiful day? For shame."

Aidan looked up, his face creasing into a grin. "One of us has to be the grown up." He rose and shook Gavin's hand. "How did the scouting go?"

"And here I thought you wanted to see me because you missed me at the office today," he said, dropping into a chair with a cat-in-the-cream smile. "I think I may have found our new warehouse site. Perfect location, good price. We'll want to move quickly, not that I think we'll have any competition, but why risk it?"

"That's excellent news, precisely what I was hoping to hear. I trust your judgement. I'll have the papers drawn up tomorrow." Aidan paused, regarding his life-long friend. "I'm proud of you for spearheading our expansion. Thank you for bringing to my attention the fact that you are ready to be in charge of this venture. I can't think of anyone I trust more, and I know you will be successful at it."

"I thank you for the opportunity. I've been feeling..." Lost? Restless? Like he was missing something? Gavin couldn't quite put into words what was bothering him lately. He just knew he needed to do more, stay busy. "...ready to take on more responsibility within the company," he finished, not wanting to look too closely at those feelings. "Oddest thing, though. I ran into Lainey and Elizabeth down near the docks."

Aidan's brow slammed down. "What the devil were the ladies doing there alone?"

"Exactly what I said."

"And?"

"And your sister told me it was none of my concern and then invited me to tea to ask a favor of me."

Aidan stared at Gavin. "I have no idea what goes through that woman's head sometimes."

"I gave up trying to guess long ago. Perhaps we should go in? I'm dying of curiosity about this favor."

THEY ENTERED the drawing room to find the ladies seated, their heads close together. Lainey laughed at something Elizabeth said, and Gavin's breath caught in his throat. It was such a melodious sound, like water tripping over pebbles in a brook. It never failed to bring him a sense of peace.

"So nice of you to join us, gentlemen," Lainey said as Gavin sat down across from her. He winked at her and a smile tugged at her lips as she looked away. Elizabeth handed him a teacup.

"What did we miss? I can tell the two of you are plotting something," Gavin observed, taking a sip of his tea.

Lainey slid her gaze to his. "Oh, we are that transparent, are we?"

Aidan snorted. "Any time the two of you have your heads together, I know there is going to be trouble."

"I rather resent that, husband," Elizabeth said wryly.

"Do you?" he replied, eyes dancing. "Am I wrong?"

Elizabeth primly stirred her tea. "No. It's just rude of you to point it out."

They all laughed and tucked in to the tea sandwiches. Gavin was impressed that Aidan did not immediately demand what the women were doing down at the docks. He could be a little overbearing sometimes where his family was concerned. The companionable silence didn't last for long, however.

"Well, ladies? Are you going to let us in on your secret?" Aidan asked. Gavin watched as Lainey and Elizabeth exchanged a look. Something was definitely up, and he suddenly had the feeling he wasn't going to like what they were about to say.

"Very well," Lainey replied. "If you must know, Elizabeth and I were discussing having a house party."

Gavin *definitely* did not like what they had to say.

"A house party?" Aidan grimaced, dismay tinging his voice. "Is there a special occasion for such torture?"

"As a matter of fact...," Lainey shifted uncomfortably, setting her cup on the table and smoothing imaginary wrinkles out of her skirt. "I would like to find a husband. And Gavin, you are going to help me."

The tea that had been flowing smoothly down his throat a moment before now threatened to come out his nose as Gavin choked on both his surprise and the tea. The cup rattled precariously in its saucer when he lurched forward in a desperate attempt to free his hands for a handkerchief before he coughed tea out all over the Aubusson rug. An alarming clatter sounded and tea sloshed over the side of the cup as he fairly tossed the fragile china onto the table, groping in his pocket. He stared at the woman seated across from him while he forced the tea down and raised his handkerchief to his lips. Lainey, blast her, hardly even blinked.

"I (cough) beg your (cough) pardon?"

"Oh, Gavin, don't be so tedious. It will be fun!"

"Fun for whom?" he asked, incredulous.

"All of us! Between your recovery, Aidan, from the incident with, well, you know..." The incident to which she referred involved Gavin's brother, Garrett, who had nearly killed Aidan last spring. "...and then the wedding, it's been a whirlwind. September is the most wonderful time of year to enjoy Rosecroft, and it's time the two of you did some old-fashioned relaxing."

"Exactly how is a house party relaxing?" Gavin's voice cracked. "The season is bad enough, I'm not sure I can take four days with very determined, marriage-minded ladies. A man can get trapped at parties like this!"

"Actually, I'd like to invite everyone for a week."

"A week!" Aidan squawked. "Lainey, no one does that anymore."

"Well, I'm doing it. I want to get to know my potential suitors, and a Friday to Monday just isn't enough. Gavin, do stop panicking," Lainey said calmly at the look of terror on his face. "I will do my best to protect you from the ladies, but I need your help to invite the right kind of men."

"What are the right kind of men?" Aidan interjected. "I've been introducing you to men for years. You never want any of them!"

"Precisely why I need Gavin's help, brother."

Gavin picked up the dangerous teacup again. It was a risk, but he really was thirsty. "I'm not following you, Lainey."

She sighed and looked at her brother. "Aidan, there are no

words that can express the depth of my love for you, but you have terrible taste in men." She ignored Elizabeth's poorly concealed snort of laughter and continued. "You want me to marry a peer, but they aren't interested in me for the right reasons. They want my money or my connections. They all think a woman's place is at home and want me to sit and do embroidery or painting all day while being a gracious hostess in the evening. That isn't the life I want, Aidan."

"So how do I fit in?" Gavin asked.

"I'd like you to invite some of your business friends," she said, turning to him. "Ones who aren't afraid of women who want to do something with their lives, who would support me in my endeavors rather than trying to keep me from them. There must be someone you know who is interested in a partner in life, not just an ornament to it."

"Lainey, I don't know about this…" he hedged.

"Gavin, please? You have so many connections. There must be a few men you would consider. And you know them better than Aidan. You're the one they talk to. Aidan is too scary."

"I beg your pardon," Aidan demanded. "I am not scary."

"Well, not since you met Elizabeth. You are much less terrifying now."

Aidan scowled. "Lainey, this is all rather sudden. You haven't been all that interested in marrying since Danby broke your engagement. Which leads me to wonder, what is really driving this decision?"

Lainey looked uncomfortable as she toyed with the cucumber sandwiches. Gavin waited with bated breath to hear what Lainey would cite as the reason for her change of heart, because for the life of him, he couldn't think of a single good reason for her to give up on love. She was too special for a marriage of convenience.

"Well, you know I have always loved my charity work…"

She seemed to gather her resolve and straighten her spine a little when she looked at her brother.

"Yeeees," Aidan prompted.

"I would like access to my inheritance so that I may start a school for the betterment of underprivileged women," she said in a rush. There was a moment of stunned silence during which Gavin's esteem for Lainey went a notch higher.

"You want to establish a business?" Aidan said, doubt tinging his words.

"Yes, and I can hear what you are thinking. I can do this, Aidan. I want to do this. Did it not bother you to see first-hand the circumstances your wife and Betsy were living in before we found them?"

"Well, of course—"

"I will admit I didn't give it quite as much thought until I met them and realized that these are women who have simply been beaten down by things out of their control. I want to do what I can to help them. Elizabeth and Betsy cannot be the only ones worth saving."

"Yes, but Lainey, you don't have to marry to access capital," Aidan insisted. "I can give you whatever you need."

"I knew you would say that, and I am so very grateful for the offer. You have done so well taking care of me over the years, but you have a wife now, and perhaps children will come next…I need to do this on my own. I want to do this on my own. I can't rely on you for the rest of my life. And since a love match does not seem to be appearing for me, then I will settle for a happy life with someone who appreciates my ambition."

"You cannot throw away your dream—"

"My work fulfills me, Aidan. I wish to make a difference for people who can't change their lives on their own. I am merely trading one dream for another."

There was an awkward silence as Lainey's declaration

settled in. The sandwiches Gavin had consumed were turning to lead in his stomach. Lainey was a woman who normally weighed decisions carefully. Leaping into a marriage to someone she barely knew was completely out of character for her.

"I don't like this, Lainey," he said, leaning his elbows on his knees. "This isn't like you."

"I don't like it either," Aidan chimed in. "It is ridiculous for you to marry just to gain access to your trust fund when I can supply what you need."

"Then you aren't hearing me. I want to be in charge of my own life, Aidan. I want children. A partner. I want to build something through hard work with my own two hands. I want to do something with the time I've been given other than embroidering handkerchiefs."

"And you want Gavin to help you instead of your own brother, the one who is responsible for you?" Aidan sounded put out.

Lainey smiled. "Of course I want your help, too. I just thought perhaps Gavin may have some connections that you don't. He has always been welcome in polite society, but he moves in a different circle as well. I will still need you to be my big brother and scare away anyone inappropriate."

"That I can do." Aidan sighed. "Lainey, I wish you would think about this more. Running a business is not easy, and once children come along, they will need you."

"I've already spent months thinking about it. That disastrous dinner the other night just proved to me it is the right time to put things into motion. My hope is that by the time children come along, I will be well established enough that I can step away when needed. I already have two staff members."

"Who?"

Both Lainey and Elizabeth fidgeted with their teacups,

silently daring one another to be the first to break the news. Aidan's eyes narrowed.

"You cannot be serious." He speared Elizabeth with a dark look. "You are partnering in this endeavor? Without even consulting me first?"

"Before you get indignant, I didn't even know about this myself until today. And yes, when your sister told me of her plan and asked for my help, I immediately agreed. These are my people, Aidan. I wouldn't be alive if it weren't for some of them. If there is some way that I can help them, then I must. I would hope you would understand."

Aidan looked at her for a long moment, then sighed. "I do understand. And I admire you both. But Lainey, you do not need to rush a marriage in order to do this. That part I do not comprehend."

Lainey smiled patiently at her brother. "You don't have to comprehend, you just have to support me. I think, given time, you will come to see my way of thinking. And by having the two of you handpick my potential husbands, I should think I will have a good chance at a happy marriage."

Gavin leaned forward, studying her. "Lainey, you are *sure* this is what you want?"

Lainey met his eyes while several seconds ticked by, and Gavin suddenly felt a kinship with those butterflies that were pinned to white cotton and displayed under glass. She dropped her gaze and stirred her tea that did not need to be stirred. "It may not be *precisely* what I've always wanted, but it will do."

The seemingly innocent comment zapped him all the way down to his toes. Blast it, even after two years…

Well, by God, if this is what Lainey wanted, then Gavin was going to do everything in his power to make it happen for her. It was his chance at redemption. "Aidan?"

He looked to his best friend for his blessing. He could see

Aidan's unhappiness warring with the desire to back Lainey's decision.

"Can we avoid the house party?" Aidan asked hopefully.

"Absolutely not."

He sighed. "I guess you'd better start drafting a list then, Gav. It appears my baby sister is getting married."

Lainey grinned. "Thank you, Aidan. I will make you proud of me, you'll see."

"I've always been proud of you. I want you to be *happy*."

"I believe I shall be."

"Well then," Gavin said, rising. "I trust you will send me all the details for the party, Lainey. I will do my best."

"I know you will," she replied. "I will see you out."

Once at the door, Gavin turned and studied Lainey for a few heartbeats. "Sweetheart, you are sure? You deserve to be loved fiercely and to love fiercely in return."

"Yes, I do," she replied, squarely meeting his gaze. "But being rejected first by you, and then shortly after by Mr. Danby, certainly has a way of stripping a girl of self-confidence and making her believe she needs to settle for less."

Gavin's heart squeezed. "Lainey. I never meant—"

She held up a hand. "It was a long time ago, Gavin. I've made peace with it, and it's time to move on. Perhaps a love match just isn't in the cards for me, or perhaps you'll introduce me to the love of my life. Whichever it is, I will be content. I cherish your friendship, and I appreciate your willingness to help me with this even though I sprang it on you."

He recognized the determined look in her eyes. Lainey had truly given this some thought; this was not as impulsive as it seemed. Still and all, this decision did not sit well with him. If only he could marry her himself...but he could not, and Lainey could not know the true reason or she'd never look at him the same way again. But helping her find a good husband just might earn her forgiveness.

Gavin flashed her his most winsome smile, hoping to pull some of their old closeness to the surface. "I am here to assist, my lady."

The corners of Lainey's mouth turned up, but it appeared more resigned than happy. "Very well then, Mr. Mayfield, off with you! Go and find me someone who isn't a dead bore."

Gavin winked and donned his top hat. "Your wish is my command."

CHAPTER 4

"Why hat do you *mean* someone else has bought it? It just became available!" Lainey stared at her land agent, flummoxed.

"I'm sorry, my lady, sometimes things move quickly."

"But I only just viewed it three days ago!" Lainey cried.

"We received a cash offer for the full amount and accepted it. My lady, forgive me, but without actual money to purchase the property, there is no guarantee it will wait for you."

"No, of course not," Lainey conceded with a sigh. "It's just that it was so perfect for my needs."

"I understand. Were none of the other properties you viewed satisfactory?"

Lainey frowned. "Not nearly so as that one," she said, dejected.

"Have faith, my lady. When you are ready to purchase, the right property will come along. If you'll allow me, I think you are setting yourself up for disappointment until you have funds available. Once you have those in place, then begin your search."

Lainey deflated in her chair. "I suppose you are right."

The rounded man leaned forward, light reflecting off his balding head. "I think it's an admirable thing you are doing, Lady Elaine."

"You do?" Lainey straightened up again.

He nodded. "I do. Not many women would take a project like this on by themselves...or even with help, for that matter. You have backbone, my lady, and a generous spirit. I've always admired you for that."

"Well, thank you, Mr. Seawell. That is nice to hear. My brother thinks I am addlepated."

Seawell chuckled. "Oh, I doubt that, my lady. He's just overly protective. He's afraid if you knew how proud he is of you, it would go straight to your head."

Lainey laughed, then stood to go. "I don't suppose you can tell me who made the offer on the property?"

"Not until all the paperwork is filed."

"Of course. But perhaps once things are finalized, you'll be so kind as to send me a note with this person's name? I will be spending the next few weeks at Rosecroft. I intend to be married soon, and then I'll be in a position to make him a generous offer to sell to me. He may find he doesn't need this specific property after all!"

"I will do that, my lady, but don't get your hopes up. People don't generally buy properties like this with the intent of letting them go."

"Well, we'll just see about that, won't we?"

LAINEY SLUMPED BACK against the squabs in the carriage. Blast it! She wanted that property. There wasn't anything else comparable that was available, and the other two just weren't in safe enough areas. She would need staff that felt comfortable coming to the center, and she wanted the women who used its services to feel safe there as well. Plus, it had the perfect amount of space she would need when she was ready to expand.

She stared blindly out the window and wondered for the hundredth time in two days if she was doing the right thing. Mr. Seawell was correct, she'd gotten ahead of herself going to look at properties when she couldn't make an offer on them. She'd just been so excited! But that was typical. Once she made a decision, she leaped in with both feet without looking.

"If you weren't so stubborn, you could just ask your brother for a loan, you dunderhead," Lainey scolded herself. But it wasn't just her stubbornness. She needed, for once in her life, to do something—to have something—that was hers and hers alone. Something she could be proud of, a legacy to leave behind.

And the women of London desperately needed her help. After Betsy had appeared on their doorstep and the issue with Elizabeth's safety had been resolved, Lainey had gone with Elizabeth to the lodging—if one could call it that—she and Betsy had once shared to collect the few possessions that remained. Lainey had been horrified to see firsthand the conditions in which her friends had been living. She knew right then that she simply had to do something. She'd spent months pondering the best way for her to help, and the little seedling of an idea had grown until it burst into full bloom at that wretched dinner.

Perhaps she *was* being a bit hasty and rushing into marriage. But honestly, she was tired of the whole circus surrounding the marriage mart. She was nearly twenty-five, for heaven's sake! If she hadn't found a love match by now, then maybe she just wasn't meant to find one. She'd had suitors, but none of them had measured up to—

There you go again, Lainey.

She really, really needed to find a way to get Gavin Mayfield out of her system. It had been easy when she'd still been so angry with him, but once the anger had worn off, the yearning reappeared, much to her annoyance. She tried to maintain her distance from him, but it was hard when he was around all the time! As Aidan's best friend and business partner, there was truly no escaping him. So, Lainey had lived in torment for the past two years.

But no more. If this party was a success, Lainey would find a suitable match, perhaps even someone she could grow to love as much as Gavin. She was convinced that if she could find a replacement for him in her heart, then she would stop mooning over him every time he walked into the room. She just needed a new place to focus her love, be it on a husband or her children.

Lainey smiled at the thought of children. She was so jealous of her friends who already had them…she lived for the moment she would hold her new baby in her arms. Oh, wouldn't it be delightful if she and Elizabeth had little ones at the same time? Lainey grinned. It may not have gone exactly as she'd planned, but her life was going to be good.

"Are you excited?" Elizabeth asked as she and Lainey ascended the stairs of Rosecroft Manor, the country home of the Lockwoods. It had been a hectic month of planning, sending out invitations, and coordinating travel, but they were here at last, in the final stages of prepping for the house party. Betsy had travelled with them and was already in the kitchen with Cook, excited to learn how a grand country estate is run. Betsy had been a remarkable addition to their household, with an insatiable thirst for learning, and Elizabeth had been glad of a friend nearby as she embarked on her new life.

Lainey picked up her skirts a little higher after she stumbled for a second time. "I think so…I'm not really sure, actually. It's rather unnerving throwing myself at the feet of eligible bachelors, particularly after my last experience."

Elizabeth nodded sagely. "Ah yes. Aidan told me about Mr. Danby."

"Danby?" Belatedly, Lainey realized Elizabeth hadn't meant Gavin. Sometimes she forgot only John Danby knew about that night. He'd found her crying in the garden and Lainey had poured out her woes in a torrent of sobs on her poor friend's shoulder. She cringed at the memory. Her behavior that night still embarrassed her to this day. Lainey sighed. "Yes, of course. He did cause quite the scandal, but I bear him no ill will. John's heart simply belonged to someone else. He was marrying me for the money he desperately needed, and I was—" She broke off suddenly, realizing she'd almost let slip the real reason she'd accepted Danby's proposal. His attentions had soothed her wounded pride. "I was…young and impetuous, I suppose. I thought he was what I wanted, but in the end, I'm glad he broke it off. He was a good man, but I didn't love him and he didn't love me. He's happily married now, though still living a very modest life. He chose love over financial security and I admire him for that." Lainey couldn't help but think he'd felt sorry for her and that was the real reason behind his proposal. What a disaster that would have been if she'd married him.

"I imagine that was rather difficult to bear." They reached the top of the stairs and continued on down the hall, Elizabeth looping her arm through Lainey's. "I do wonder though…"

"Yes?" Lainey drew out the word, curiosity setting her on high alert.

"Well, it's just that Aidan told me the reason you haven't been interested in finding a husband is because you were heartbroken."

"Ah…yes."

"Yet you just told me that you didn't love Mr. Danby."

"Er—"

"So that would lead one to wonder…who *actually* broke your heart?"

Elizabeth eyed her shrewdly, and Lainey's stomach plummeted to her toes. Elizabeth couldn't know, could she? Lainey had thought she'd fooled everyone.

"Well…er… no one. I just…I just said that to save face."

"Mm hm. And saving face kept you off the market for two years?"

"I just didn't meet anyone that interested me, that's all. At least, anyone who was interested in more than an ornament for their arm."

"I see."

"Ah! Here we are!" Lainey said brightly. She opened the door they were standing in front of and ushered Elizabeth inside. "Your room is one of my favorites in the house."

Elizabeth glanced around, an appreciative smile lighting her face. Between the rush of the season, Aidan's recovery, and the wedding planning, Elizabeth had not yet been to Rosecroft, and Lainey was enjoying seeing her beloved childhood home through Eliza's eyes. "It's darling!" Elizabeth exclaimed. "But don't think you have successfully diverted me away from our conversation." She laughed.

Lainey rolled her eyes. "You are too astute, my dear friend."

"So, I am right!"

Lainey sighed. "If I tell you the truth, do you swear to keep it to yourself?"

Elizabeth clapped her hands in glee while bouncing up

and down like a child who's had one sweet too many. She grabbed Lainey's hand and dragged her over to the bed, and they collapsed together, laughing. "I swear."

Lainey tugged at her skirts, tucking one leg beneath her. "There was someone before Mr. Danby."

"I knew it! Were you very much in love?"

Lainey's face softened. "Well...I was. Unfortunately, he didn't feel the same."

"What happened?"

"I poured my heart out to him, and he turned me down flat."

"What?" Elizabeth was dismayed. "For what reason? You are a spectacular catch!"

Lainey chuckled. "Thank you for thinking so. Apparently, he did not agree."

"Did he say why?"

"Some ridiculous business about not being good enough for me," Lainey replied bitterly. "But I think he was just using that as an excuse so he didn't have to admit he didn't care for me."

"Are you sure, Lainey? I don't get the feeling most men would immediately own up to being unworthy," Elizabeth said wryly.

"As I said, it seemed a feeble excuse. He was plenty worthy of me." Lainey was surprised at the stab of pain in her chest. Even after two years, the memory of that day still hurt more than she liked to admit.

"Lainey..." Elizabeth chose her word carefully. "I'm sure there will be many suitors from whom you can choose this week, but I wonder..." She trailed off, irritating Lainey's last nerve.

"Out with it, Eliza."

"Well, I'd just wondered whether perhaps you might take a second look at those you already know."

"What do you mean by that? I haven't had a single offer I'm interested in accepting."

"Perhaps he hasn't offered because he's unsure of how you feel."

"Elizabeth, who on earth are you talking about?"

"Gavin."

"*Gavin?*" Lainey nearly slid off the edge of the bed.

"Hear me out. I think there is something there that he doesn't want to admit to out loud. I've seen the way he looks at you."

The way he looks at her, indeed. Lainey had seen those looks too…all they said to her was please forgive me so can we go back to being dear friends. "I think your romantic heart is imagining things."

"I don't agree. There is something between the two of you. I can feel it every time you are together. I'm just suggesting that you should consider him as well. He's kind, and handsome, and you already have a life-long friendship as a base for love to grow on. He's not a bad option."

"Eliza, Gavin does not want to marry me, I assure you. We are friends, that is all. He'll never see me as anything other than Aidan's little sister, and I don't want to muddy our friendship with something as messy as love. Things are just fine the way they are. I shall just have to choose from the men he and Aidan have assembled for me this week. Who knows, I may find my great love match after all!"

"Lainey, are you sure? I really think—"

"Dearest, you've known him barely six months. I've known him practically my whole life. Trust me when I say Gavin and I are not a match. Now," she said, hopping off of the bed. "I am going to change out of these dusty travel clothes and supervise the unpacking. We still have lots to prepare before the guests arrive tomorrow, so I will see you at tea and we can hatch a plan for the week." She bussed Elizabeth's cheek. "Thank you for being a good friend. I'm so glad Aidan married you." She squeezed Elizabeth's hand and left the room.

She hadn't made it but a few steps down the hall when Elizabeth's words came floating back to her. *I see the way he looks at you.* Could Elizabeth really see something that Lainey had been missing?

"Pull yourself together, Lainey," she muttered, quickening her steps. "You are not going down that road again."

But her steps slowed the more she thought. Could there have been another reason Gavin had turned her down? He'd tried to explain that he didn't think he was good enough for her, but she'd known that was just an excuse, although life had definitely changed when her father had inherited his title all those years go. Still, Gavin and Aidan had remained close. If he was good enough for a future earl, then he should have been good enough for Lainey, too.

She sagged against a hall table. It had to be that he simply was not attracted to her and didn't want to say so. Just because she'd fallen head over heels in love with him didn't mean he was going to do the same. Lainey had attracted plenty of men who wanted her dowry or her social connections, but none that seemed to want to know *her*. Even John had changed his mind. So, the problem must lie with her. Although…

Gavin didn't seem interested in marriage at all, now that she thought about it. He'd never spoken of finding a wife, and he effortlessly dissuaded all the young debutantes who swooned over him. What if…what if Elizabeth was right, and Gavin was worried about something else that was preventing him from offering for her?

Lainey raised a hand to her brow and squeezed her eyes shut. *Stop it, Elaine Lockwood. What's done is done. It's time to move forward with someone else.*

"Lainey? Are you all right?"

Lainey catapulted herself away from the table with a yelp and stumbled backwards a few steps when her eyes rested upon the person who had inquired after her well-being. "You nearly scared the life out of me! Gavin, what are you *doing* here?"

CHAPTER 5

"I'm sorry, I didn't mean to scare you," Gavin replied, concern etching his face. "You just looked as though you were unwell."

"I'm fine," Lainey said, exasperated and a little embarrassed at having been caught lost in thought about *him.* "But why are you here? The guests aren't arriving until tomorrow. I didn't expect company today."

"I've been visiting my father and Kate, and I had a meeting with Aidan this morning, so I arrived early." He gave her a mischievous smile. "I'm sorry if that doesn't fit in with your plans, but I'm afraid you are stuck with me this evening."

She rolled her eyes. "Well, that is just fabulous," she said, her tone laced with sarcasm, but a smile belying her words.

"You are not unwell?"

"Not at all. I was just…thinking."

"Oh? Anything I can help you sort out?"

Ha! "No, I don't believe so. But thank you for offering. If you'll excuse me, I need to get out of my traveling clothes. I do hope you will join Eliza and myself for tea?"

"You know I never miss an opportunity to eat."

"It's a wonder you aren't as large as a house."

He chuckled. "Give me time."

Lainey remained for a moment, looking up at him. His brows drew together in question. "Lainey, are you quite sure you're all right?" he asked, gently grasping her elbow.

A tingle ran down her arm and her breath caught. She gave herself a mental shake. "Yes, I'm fine, thank you," she said brightly. "I will see you shortly." She escaped down the hall before her over active imagination got the best of her. It was absolutely maddening how her body reacted to his touch. Honestly, had she no self-control?

Although, it really would help if he weren't so devastatingly attractive.

GAVIN WATCHED LAINEY GLIDE AWAY. How odd. He could have sworn she'd looked at him…well, like she used to before everything went to hell. He missed the closeness they'd had. Perhaps having someone else to focus on might help heal her pride and they could go back to sharing the bond they'd once had. If it didn't kill him to watch her fall in love with someone else.

He wandered down to Aidan's study, where he found the earl seated behind his enormous desk. "The ladies have arrived," Gavin said, lowering himself into the chair across from Aidan. "The guests descend tomorrow. Are you ready for this?"

"God no." Aidan's mouth was set in a line. "What was I thinking?"

"That you love your sister and want to see her happy?"

"Ah. Yes. There's that." Aidan set down his pen. "What do you make of her sudden change of heart about marriage? I was beginning to despair of her ever getting settled, but now that she's approaching all this with such practicality…it doesn't feel right. I'm worried that she's rushing into this."

Gavin nodded. "It certainly seems that way. I don't agree with her choice, but Lainey has always been like a dog with a bone once she gets an idea in her head. And if I know her at all, she's given this a great deal of thought, even if she hasn't shared those thoughts with you."

"I suppose." Aidan leaned back in his chair and swiveled to stare out the window. Two birds were doing a merry dance, darting in and out of the remaining flowers, and Aidan watched them for a moment. "Have I done right by her, Gav?"

Gavin sat up straight. "Aidan." The earl drew his attention back to Gavin's face. "You were barely a man yourself when you had to assume the role of both mother and father as well as big brother. Lainey is a beautiful, kind, and compassionate woman. She has wanted for nothing, but that hasn't made her spoiled. She is tremendously independent, well-liked, and stands up for those who can't speak for themselves. You have done an amazing job raising her, and you should be proud."

"She is an extraordinary woman," he conceded. "But she hasn't seemed herself since that damned broken engagement. I can't quite put my finger on it, but she's different. Less self-assured. She was always so vivacious and confident, but somehow that sparkle has dimmed."

Aidan may as well have kicked Gavin right in the teeth. Gavin had everything to do with dimming Lainey's sparkle. He'd spent two years trying to put it back.

"She claims her heart was broken," Aidan continued. "But here's the thing. I didn't think she was all that much in love with Danby to begin with…in fact, I was completely surprised when he came to speak with me. I'd always thought they were simply friends, so I don't understand why she's seemingly shrinking in on herself."

"Well, she did have to weather the ensuing scandal. That weighs heavily on a person."

Aidan gave his friend a sympathetic smile. "You can certainly understand that, I know." He gazed out the window again, lost in a memory. "It was not easy for her to be whispered about and cut out of social engagements. That first year was devastating. Completely ruined her following season and any hope for a match. It amazes me that somehow she was made out to be the guilty party even though Danby is the one who broke it off. Yet my sister became the pariah! None but those who knew her best would associate with her. And of course, this year I was too busy falling in love myself to notice if anyone had caught her eye."

"You know she would have told you if they had."

"Things have settled down now and it appears she's been forgiven, but do you think that's why no one has offered for her?"

Gavin pursed his lips. "To be honest, I'm not entirely sure that no one has. I've noticed several men show interest in her, but she seems to be the one who is reluctant."

"Then why the devil the big rush? Six months ago, I couldn't get her to go out riding with a man, now she wants to marry a total stranger? It makes no sense."

It didn't make sense to Gavin, either. Lainey had wanted nothing more her entire life than to be loved fiercely, and it angered him that she was going to settle for companionship instead.

"This whole Center for Underprivileged Women took me by surprise," Aidan continued. "I had no idea she was planning any of this. She's always been involved in charities, but I didn't realize her passion had gone so far."

"Nor I. But I think it's an admirable undertaking."

"It is indeed. But why can't she just let me loan her the money she needs? Why is she insisting on doing this all on her own?"

"I think..." Gavin said slowly. "I think that is the point."

Aidan sighed. "I suppose I have to let her be her own woman someday, don't I?"

Gavin smiled. The bond between Lainey and Aidan had always warmed his heart, especially since he hadn't had that kind of relationship with his own twin. Garrett had been a despicable man with a black heart that could hold no love for anything, and Gavin...Gavin had just wanted his brother's love. Although he had always envied the Lockwoods their closeness, he was also so very grateful their familial love had encompassed him as well. If not for them, his childhood would have been very bleak indeed. "She's an intelligent woman who knows what she wants. It doesn't matter if we agree or not, we aren't going to be able to talk her out of this."

Aidan nodded. "I know. I just want what's best for her."

"Maybe being her own woman *is* what's best for her."

Aidan regarded his friend. "When did you get so bloody wise?"

"I'm going to be heading up the new millinery division. I have to sound like I know something about life!"

Aidan laughed. "Speaking of which, I have the papers here for you to sign. I'm pleased we were able to move on that warehouse so quickly. You're right, it's ideal for our new location. This is the final contract here, so once you sign, I'll courier them to London and it will be ours."

Gavin took the offered sheaf of papers. "Do I need to read over these?"

"Not unless you don't trust me." Aidan winked. Gavin

grinned and reached for the fountain pen, signing with a flourish.

"Congratulations! You are now general manager of our millinery division…and equal partner."

"I'll drink to that!" Gavin had worked his whole life for this moment, in so many ways. He could scarcely believe it was finally happening. He headed to the sideboard and glanced at his pocket watch. "Is eleven too early for scotch?"

"Are you kidding? Not with the week we are about to have!"

Gavin chuckled as he handed Aidan a glass with a small amount of amber liquid in it. "Here's to new adventures."

"In more ways than one," Aidan replied, raising his glass. "Cheers, mate."

"So," Gavin said, taking a healthy swallow. "I think we've managed to compile a decent guest list for your sister, no?"

"I hope so. I want her well cared for. I've certainly managed to bore her to death with my choices for husbands. Perhaps you'll fare better."

Gavin gave a shout of laughter. "Sometimes I did wonder if you actually knew your sister."

Aidan's gaze grew speculative. "You do often seem to know her better than I do. I didn't think that was possible, but somehow you manage."

"We are great friends, Lainey and I. Or at least, we were," he added under his breath. He rushed on at Aidan's sharp glance. "Sometimes it's easier to talk to friends than it is your family."

Aidan studied Gavin for several heartbeats, an unreadable expression on his face. "Perhaps you are right," he finally admitted, sitting forward. "Plus, apparently, I was scary." He looked down at the list to his right. "Oh, I forgot to mention, it seems we are adding one more guest to the list. Pritchard wrote me asking if he could bring a gentleman who is staying with him for a few days. Some distant cousin who has apparently inherited an estate north of here. Pritchard offered him lodgings while he was in London taking care of some business. New money, looking for a wife. One Charles Devereaux. I don't know anything about him, do you?"

"Can't say as I've heard of him. But Pritchard is a good sort, and he adores Lainey. I doubt he'd bring someone unsuitable. He probably just wants to introduce Devereaux around."

"Probably. Well, what's one more at this point? Though I'm afraid it's going to mess with Lainey's numbers. She is not going to be happy about that." Aidan consulted his pocket watch and gusted a sigh. "Is eleven too early for a *double* scotch?"

CHAPTER 6

The first carriage arrived at noon the following day. Lainey re-rolled the same ribbon she had been working on sorting for the last ten minutes and crammed the whole pile into the basket. Her head snapped up when she heard voices in the front hall, and a little butterfly let loose in her stomach. She put her hand on her abdomen to still it.

"It's not too late to change your mind," Gavin observed from where he sat reading. His smug little smile made Lainey stiffen her resolve.

"I am tired of waiting for my life to begin," she replied, rising. "It is time to take matters into my own hands." She smoothed her skirts and patted her hair, not that she could see if anything was out of place. She just needed something to do with her hands or they were going to flail about of their own accord. Gavin stood and put his book aside.

"I don't mean to tease, Lainey. I just want you to be sure of your choice. I wish for nothing but your happiness."

Her happiness, indeed. He didn't seem to care about that two years ago. "Thank you, I am sure. I promise I won't marry anyone who doesn't suit me well."

The door opened and in walked Aidan, followed by Mr. Pritchard, a fabulous milliner who was a long-time client of Aidan's. He was in his early thirties, rather plain-looking yet not unattractive, with brown hair and unremarkable features. Lainey had known him by acquaintance for some years, but hadn't realized he was looking for a wife. He worked long hours and seemed happy as a bachelor. Perhaps he was tired of waiting as well.

Then the door opened wider and Lainey's heart tripped and fell all the way down to her toes. A tall, angular, and sinfully handsome man Lainey had never seen before followed Pritchard into the room. His wavy hair was the exact color of the wet sand on the beach, and somehow it managed to appear wind-blown and arranged to perfection all at the same time. Confidence radiated off of him as he glanced around the room with an engaging smile. Elizabeth appeared to be having difficulty keeping her jaw from gaping open, and Lainey stifled a giggle. Beside her, Gavin stiffened when the stranger's eyes came to rest on Lainey, assessing her with an appreciative gaze.

Good, Lainey thought. *Let him look. Serves you right, Gavin. What's it like to not be the most handsome man in the room anymore?*

Aidan approached with the men following in his wake. "Allow me to make introductions. Mr. Pritchard you already know, of course."

"Of course. How lovely to see you again, Mr. Pritchard," Lainey said as he bowed over her hand.

"And you as well, my lady. Thank you for inviting us to your home."

He moved aside as Aidan said, "And this is Mr. Charles Devereaux, newly arrived to England. Mr. Devereaux, my sister, Lady Elaine Lockwood."

"Very pleased to meet you, my lady," Devereaux said,

taking her offered hand. "I apologize for crashing your party. It was kind of you to allow me to come." His voice was smooth and rich, a fine French brandy flowing through her veins. Lainey suddenly wished for a fan as he bent his head to kiss her hand. His hair had highlights of gold threaded through it, that caught the light like the subtle embroidery on her favorite ball gown. He looked up and met her eyes with a smile that bordered on sensual.

Sweet, merciful Lord in heaven.

"I'm so glad you could join us." Did she sound out of breath? She was mesmerized by his intensely green eyes that held flecks of amber.

Someone's throat clearing snapped her out of her reverie, and she turned to see Gavin looking pointedly at the hand that was still in Devereaux's grasp. She removed it so the introductions could continue.

"This is my business partner and good friend, Mr. Gavin Mayfield, and this, of course, is my lovely wife, the Marchioness of Ashby."

Devereaux shook and kissed hands where appropriate. Lainey noted Elizabeth's flushed cheeks. At least she wasn't the only one affected by the man's stunning good looks.

"Thank you for allowing me to bring my cousin at the last minute, Lady Ashby," Pritchard interjected. "He has just arrived from France and I felt it in poor taste to leave him behind, as I did not want to miss your party."

"We are happy for the extra company, Mr. Pritchard," Elizabeth responded. "What brings you to England, Mr. Devereaux?"

"My father has died and I have inherited his estate."

"Oh! I'm so sorry for your loss."

A shadow flickered through his eyes. "Don't be."

Lainey hesitated for an awkward moment, unsure of what to say.

"Forgive me, Lady Elaine." He turned to her, shaking off whatever had haunted him. "That was uncouth. I am afraid there was no love lost between my father and me."

"Well, I am sorry to hear that, too. How long were you in France, if I may ask?"

"Six years."

"That's a good, long while. But are you sure you won't mind leaving France behind?"

"It's true I've grown fond of France, but it is good to be back on English soil." His eyes bored into hers. "And though I am anxious to travel on from here to return to my family home, I suddenly find myself with a reason to linger," he said softly, flashing her another one of those smiles that seemed almost inappropriate.

Lainey's pulse stuttered under his assessing gaze. Oh, this man was simply too much.

"Right then," Gavin boomed, clapping his hands together, practically startling Lainey out of her skin. "I'm sure you must be tired from your journey. Perhaps you would like to be shown to your rooms?"

Lainey's head slowly swiveled toward Gavin. He raised his brows in innocence.

"Quite right," Pritchard replied. "Let us get settled, and we will return to you post haste."

"Thank you again for allowing me to attend," Devereaux added.

"It will be a pleasure to get to know you," Lainey said.

"It will indeed," Devereaux agreed with a ghost of a smile before following Tibbs and Pritchard out of the room.

"Oh, my heavens," Lainey said, her hand going to her throat.

Gavin snorted. "He's rather full of himself, isn't he?"

"That isn't at all what *I* was thinking," Elizabeth murmured, staring after Devereaux.

"Oh, come off it, ladies. Are you really going to fall for all that charm he was oozing?"

Lainey perched her hands on her hips, exasperated. "And what, exactly, is wrong with that? Am I not hosting this party to be charmed and wooed to my heart's content? If you and Aidan are going to disparage every option I have, then there isn't much point to this, is there?"

"Hey, I was perfectly nice," Aidan said, affronted. "But he is certainly someone I'm going to be keeping a close eye on, Lainey. We don't know anything about him, and he seems somewhat…overconfident."

"Oh, for heaven's sake, my love," Elizabeth chimed in. "Let your sister have a little fun for once."

"Thank you, Eliza."

"He's going to be trouble, mark my words," Gavin grumbled.

"Gavin, you sound like a jealous little boy," Lainey scolded. "Perhaps some sunshine and fresh air would do you some good. Would you like to take a turn in the garden?"

"As you wish," he replied, offering her his arm. Lainey shook her head.

"I meant by yourself," she said flatly, crossing her arms over her chest.

Gavin glanced at the faces around him, the ladies most definitely scowling and Aidan trying to contain his laughter. "Fine," he ground out. "Perhaps a short walk will clear my head of the nonsense Devereux just spouted." He strode out of the room.

"Lainey, don't be too hard on him," Aidan said. "He's only trying to help."

"If glowering at every eligible gentleman is what you consider helpful, then I fear I may be single for life. The two of you had best behave yourselves and not scare off any of my prospects. I'm serious about this."

"He did find you most of the men who are attending, don't forget. He is taking your husband hunt seriously as well. He's just trying to protect you. As am I."

Lainey threw her hands up, exasperated. "I am a grown woman, Aidan. I do not need to be protected. I can make my own choices when it comes to husbands."

"I know that, Lainey." Aidan's expression softened. "Sometimes it's hard for me not to see you as a lost eleven-year-old anymore."

Lainey sighed. "You've done so much for me, Aidan. Don't ever think I don't appreciate you." She laid a hand against his cheek and locked her eyes with his. "You are an excellent big brother, and I wouldn't trade you for anything. But please, *please* try not to be overbearing this week." She moved her hand and poked him in the chest. "I've met one man and the two of you are behaving like he's going to trap me in a closet and have his way with me the first chance he gets."

"That really wouldn't be a bad way to pass half an hour," Elizabeth mused. Two heads swung in her direction. "What?"

Lainey burst out laughing and Aidan ran a palm over his face.

"I don't know how I am going to survive this week."

GAVIN VICIOUSLY KICKED a stone out of his path. What had triggered such an appalling response in him? Lainey was right. This party was being held specifically for her to meet men, yet the moment one paid her the slightest bit of attention, he turned into a surly child. He was going to have to gain better control over his emotions if he didn't want to give everyone the wrong idea. But he couldn't seem to help himself...seeing Devereaux fawn over Lainey like that had set his teeth on edge. The man was too perfect. Gavin knew

Devereaux would have the ladies falling all over him, and he wanted to make sure no one was being taken advantage of, especially Lainey. She was entirely guileless, a trait someone like Devereaux could exploit if he had nefarious purposes.

Gavin sank down on a stone bench. He didn't want to examine too closely why he was reacting the way he was to seeing Lainey garner such attention. She was not his, he had to remember that. If things were different…

But they weren't. Lainey was a jewel for some other man to treasure. So, for her sake, he was going to tamp down his feelings and pretend it didn't drive him crazy to watch her be courted by someone else, that he didn't get stabbed in the chest at the thought of letting her go. He hoped they'd remain good friends, but her life would be taken over by being a wife and mother, and he'd see less and less of her as time went on. He'd have to be satisfied with seeing her at social events and gatherings. He could hardly wrap his head around the fact that she wouldn't be there when he went to see Aidan, there would be no more afternoon teas on a regular basis, no more comfortable evenings listening to her read aloud or play the piano.

Life was changing, and Gavin wasn't entirely sure he liked the direction it was taking. He was, of course, happy Aidan had found a love match after years of being afraid to take a chance, but at the same time, Gavin couldn't help but feel as though he was being left behind. Aidan was consumed by his new wife—and rightly so—but now rather than leaving the office and heading to White's for a drink, Aidan was rushing out the door to go home to Elizabeth. And now, Lainey would be disappearing into her own family as well.

Gavin sighed and dug his toe into the gravel like the little boy Lainey had accused him of being. This glimpse of his lonely future settled like a heavy weight on his chest, and he questioned if he'd ever be able to remove it.

CHAPTER 7

*D*inner that evening was a lavish affair. There were twenty guests in total, one of whom was Aidan's good friend Donovan Mackavoy, who had absolutely no interest (so he claimed) in seeking a match but wanted to do some hunting of a different sort, and the women were Lainey's friends from town, there for moral support and perhaps to make a match of their own. The arrival of an unexpected male had thrown off the numbers, and Lainey simply couldn't have a lone dinner guest, so she had pressed Kate, Gavin's stepmother, into service this evening to round out the numbers until another eligible lady could be found.

Lainey recognized a few of the male faces at the table, but most were unfamiliar to her. The butterflies in her stomach felt more like a bird trapped in a box as Aidan stood to welcome his guests, raising his glass in a toast.

"To friends new and old. Thank you for arranging your schedules to join us this week. My wife and I are happy to have you, and I hope you will take advantage of the fine weather and enjoy yourselves fully while you are here."

"Hear, hear!" was the joyful answer. Lainey glanced surreptitiously around the table as everyone drank. She'd met each guest as they'd arrived, and a few had sparked her interest. Gavin and Aidan had done well for her. There was Anthony Fox, the furrier, who had won Lainey over immediately by poking fun at his own name and trade, Samuel Chapman, who worked for the esteemed Frederick Worth, Philip Smith, a bank manager, and Eric Prince, head of a shipping company, all of whom seemed amiable enough on first impression. The addition of Viscount Kingston had been a surprising choice, but a welcome one. Though not in his youth, he had a delightful demeanor that had piqued Lainey's interest right away, and though they had crossed paths on and off over the years, she didn't really know him well. She looked forward to speaking with all of them at length and discovering their true personalities, and most importantly, how they felt about her work. She also took note of the ladies around the table, and who seemed to fancy whom. This was, after all, a matchmaking event. Why should Lainey be the only one to come away with an engagement?

She glanced across the table at Gavin, who was seated between Emily Hastings and Lydia Blousson. Emily was the younger sister of Anne, Lainey's best friend. She was a little young yet at nineteen, but Lainey didn't have the heart to not invite her since Anne was coming. She was delightful company, and was currently making cow eyes at the long-suffering Gavin, which amused Lainey to no end. Lydia was bubbling away about some topic or other, as was her usual state. He caught Lainey's eye with a look that clearly said, "Help me," but she just grinned and turned to the gentleman on her right.

Which just so happened to be one Charles Devereaux. Lainey didn't quite know what to make of him just yet. He was impossibly charming, but on occasion, she found that charm was a way of hiding character flaws. He certainly did make her heart race, however. The man was too good-looking for words.

"Tell me about your estate, Mr. Devereaux. Will you live there year-round or do you have a townhouse in London?"

"No townhouse just yet, though I will need one. I was hoping to choose that once I've chosen a bride. Bachelor rooms wouldn't do, I'm afraid," he said with a chuckle. "The estate is in Sheffield—Ranmoor, more precisely. My family bought property in east Sheffield in the late 1700s, and the discovery of coal there some years later changed everything. They were later able to purchase a steel mill, and with the industrial boom of the railways, life altered quite quickly for them."

"I've heard terrible things about the working conditions of those mills," Lainey noted.

"Sadly, they are mostly true. However, my family believed healthy, happy workers would be more productive, so they were given fair working hours and safer working conditions, I'm told. The mill prospered while others were rife with disease and unrest. It certainly wasn't ideal, but it was the best we could do. My family built a beautiful estate just outside of Ranmoor called Thistledown, and it is that which I have just inherited. Now, I'm tasked with learning how to run it after having been away for years. It is daunting, to say the least, but I will do my best."

"That is all we can do in life, is it not?"

Devereaux chuckled. "You are a welcome surprise, Lady Elaine. Do tell me about your plans for your future. I hear you are an enterprising woman."

Lainey stared at him. Had he actually just asked her what her own plans were for her future? Unbelievable. "Actually,

I'd like to open a help center for women who want to better their circumstances. Recent events have taught me that there are a lot of people out there who needlessly suffer because they lack education and training. I want to change that." She waited for the snort of derision, or the patronizing smile, but he just studied her, an enigmatic smile playing about his lips.

"An admirable cause indeed," Devereaux murmured, his eyes lighting over the rim of his wineglass. "Tell me more."

Lainey hesitated, but he appeared sincere, so she let the floodgates open.

GAVIN DIDN'T HEAR what Devereaux had just said to Lainey to make her face light up in delight, but he couldn't take his eyes off of her. She was absolutely glowing, animatedly gushing about something. Devereaux had put that glow there. Gavin's fingers tightened on his wine glass. The sudden urge to throw it at Devereaux's head came out of nowhere, and Gavin tamped it down immediately. *Violence is never the answer.* He grimaced and tossed back some more wine. He was looking forward to the brandy that would come later.

Dinner was interminable as he watched Lainey flirt with both Devereaux and the fellow from the House of Worth. He practically shot out of his chair as the ladies rose to retire to the drawing room. What in blazes was wrong with him? The whole point of this week was to find Lainey a husband, so why was he so on edge every time she smiled at someone else? He supposed he was just used to having her to himself. A lot had changed over the past six months, and Gavin had to admit that he was having some trouble adjusting.

The men stayed behind and enjoyed a glass of port, during which Gavin pointedly asked too many questions of

Devereaux, but ultimately found nothing he could discredit. He had money, ambition, and common sense, and he seemed a likable fellow. Gavin was rather disappointed he had come up short on skeletons.

They joined the ladies for cards and parlor games, and Gavin barely restrained his eye roll as Devereaux instantly moved toward Lainey. Really, the man was going to be a problem if no one else could get near her. Fortunately, he was intercepted by Miss Hastings. Gavin smiled to himself. Anne seemed to have noticed Devereaux's obsession as well. He made a mental note to thank her later.

Conversation flowed freely as the guests mingled and got to know one another. The liquor also flowed freely, and everyone was in a happy, relaxed state when Laincy announced it was time for a parlor game.

"Oooh!" Anne Hastings squealed, clapping her hands and bouncing in excitement. "I love parlor games!"

"I think, since we are all getting to know one another, a game of Forfeits shall be an excellent choice," Lainey said. "Ashby, will you be our judge?"

"I'd be delighted," Aidan said, rising. He left the room, and Lainey placed a tray in the center of the circle as everyone gathered round. Each guest left a small personal item in the tray, and Aidan was asked to come in again. He entered the circle with a dramatic sweeping gesture, which made everyone laugh, and set the tone for the game. He selected a ring from the tray. "Ah. Here we have a lady's ring, gold with flowers engraved on it. To whom might this belong?" he asked, rubbing his chin in a dramatic fashion.

"It is mine, Ashby, as you well know," Elizabeth teased. "What is my forfeit?"

"Ah, from you, my lady, I must demand a kiss."

"That's not a forfeit!" Lainey admonished. "You kiss her all the time!"

"Shh. You are not the judge," Aidan replied, taking his wife in his arms. Everyone laughed as he gave her a comical kiss, and then a real one for good measure, and Elizabeth's ring was returned to her. Aidan chose another item. "A money clip, with the initials CD. Hmm, who could that be?"

Devereaux stood to claim his forfeit. Aidan grinned. "I'm afraid I must make you bark like a dog."

The ladies tittered as Devereaux made a sweeping bow. "As you wish, my lord." He surprised everyone by getting on his hands and knees, and proceeded to bark like a terrier at the guests. He crawled up to Emily Hastings and suddenly changed his yip to a deep, loud bark, startling her and making her squeal with glee, which made everyone cheer and clap. He stood up to receive his money clip from Aidan.

"Good show!" Aidan said, handing it to him. Devereaux nodded and winked at Emily, causing the girl to blush to the roots of her hair. The next item happened to be Gavin's, and he groaned.

"What are you going to make me do?" he asked warily.

"I think you should entertain us with a song."

"Come now, you know that will only serve to punish everyone."

"What good is being your best friend if I can't embarrass you once in a while? Sing if you'd like your pocket watch back!"

Gavin glared at Aidan in the way only close friends could, and launched into the worst rendition of 'Twinkle, Twinkle, Little Star" anyone present had ever heard. Gavin sang louder as ladies covered their ears and men pretended to double over in pain. He looked at Lainey. She was pressing her lips tightly together in a valiant effort to hold her laughter in, and her eyes shone with mirth. He was never going to hear the end of this.

Blessedly, it was a short song, and he reached out a hand

for his watch, but Aidan held it back. "I think I should keep it just for suffering through that performance!"

Gavin gave him a good-natured shove and retrieved his watch. "You knew exactly what you were getting into."

"I may never hear the same way again," Anne supplied.

Gavin shook his head and sat down with a chuckle. Lainey was summoned next, and was challenged to walk around the circle backwards, blindfolded. She gathered up her skirts, got her bearings, and waited while the blindfold was tied. She made it almost all the way around the circle before a ruffled petticoat slipped her hold and she stepped on it, losing her balance. Down she went—straight into Gavin's lap.

"Oh!" His arms tightened around her, preventing her from sliding to the floor. "I'm sorry, who have I—"

"It's just me," he said in her ear as she struggled with the blindfold. She pulled it free and found herself inches from Gavin's face.

"Oh," she repeated softly.

There was a brief moment of charged silence, and every nerve in Gavin's body prickled with awareness. Was it his imagination, or had her gaze flicked to his lips? "Sorry to disappoint," he teased. She grinned and scrambled off of his lap.

"My apologies, Mr. Mayfield," she said, smoothing out her skirts. "Brother, I do hope I still get my trinket back. I'm rather fond of those earrings and I would look silly with just one."

"A valiant attempt was made. Therefore, I restore to you your ear bob," Aidan said, handing it to her. "I do hope you are not hurt."

"Mr. Mayfield gave me a soft landing. Only my pride was wounded!"

Gavin's arms were tingling. He belatedly realized that in

all his years of knowing Lainey, he'd not once held her in his arms in such an intimate way. And his body was telling him that that had been a serious oversight on his part.

The merriment continued on until all the items had been retrieved from the tray. It was a wonderful way of getting to know who took themselves too seriously and who wanted to have fun. Gavin had noted the reaction from Lainey when Viscount Kingston had recited a poem in a rich baritone voice that had captivated everyone. Aidan knew him better than Gavin did, but he seemed warm and genuine, with a gentle nature that would suit Lainey's personality well. He was glad Aidan had invited him.

Finally, the frivolity wound down and the guests began to drift toward their rooms. Gavin watched as the men bid goodnight to Lainey, studying her reactions to each man. He could easily pick out who had sparked her interest. Funny how he could read her so well, yet he had completely missed her feelings for him all those years ago. Perhaps he'd been oblivious on purpose.

"Well, that was a successful evening," Aidan said as he poured them both a brandy. "Lainey shined, and I actually enjoyed myself. I can't remember the last time I played a parlor game."

"We've been telling you for years you need to loosen up," Gavin chided, accepting the brandy.

"What do you make of our choices?"

"I think Lainey is intrigued by several of them. I look forward to watching this unfold."

Aidan clinked his glass against Gavin's. "Rest well, my friend. Sorry about the song." Aidan winked and Gavin chuckled.

"You are not."

Aidan grinned and gave a casual shrug, moving off to join his wife upstairs, leaving Gavin alone in the drawing room.

He took a swallow of his brandy and ruminated over the events of the evening. All in all, he thought Lainey just may find a suitable match.

Somehow, that knowledge didn't bring him the joy it ought.

CHAPTER 8

The next morning dawned cool and rainy, so the planned excursion into town was postponed until the afternoon with the hope that the weather would clear. After breakfast, the guests had gathered in the morning room to play cards. Lainey was seated on the settee by the window with a cup of chocolate in her hands. Anne and Lydia sat with her, with various men scattered around them. Lainey took a moment to take stock of her options in the light of day. She had to admit, Gavin had invited some nice choices. Anthony Fox was a dangerous-looking charmer, almost piratical with his longer, dark hair that curled up at the ends and chiseled features that were a contrast to his warm, mischievous eyes. Samuel Chapman was, of course, dressed impeccably, which aided in the impression of attractiveness, though he was not the type to stop women in their tracks. His light brown hair was short and straight as a pin, framing a round face that sported a trim mustache and gold wire-rimmed glasses. In the chair on her right was Eric Prince, the American who owned a shipping company. His dark waves would make any woman jealous. Paired with piercing blue eyes, he was striking in both his looks and his manner. And on her left was the banker, Philip Smith, a reserved blond who did not say much, but noticed everything.

The rest of the party was scattered about the room, playing cards or amiably chatting over cups of steaming chocolate. Aidan had sequestered himself in his study to do some work, but Lainey noticed Gavin sitting by himself in a nearby chair, pretending to read a newspaper, but keeping an eye on her and the men surrounding her. Had she known he was going to become her watch dog, she might have considered leaving him in London. Really, his attitude after meeting Mr. Devereaux yesterday was puzzling. She knew he wasn't happy about her seemingly sudden decision to marry, but she'd hoped for better from him. She glanced surreptitiously at him, and found him watching her with an inscrutable expression. Her stomach gave a little flutter and she pursed her lips in annoyance. There was a veritable feast of good-looking men in front of her, and she still reacted to Gavin's attention like a school girl with a crush. It was infuriating.

"Lady Elaine, Mayfield tells me you play a supporting role in your brother's import business," Mr. Chapman said, interrupting her thoughts. "Tell me more about that."

"Well, I wouldn't say it's a supporting role, but I have a small hand in what gets chosen for display."

"You have an eye for fine things. I am impressed every time I visit the shop."

"Thank you, sir, that's very kind. My brother is the one who is responsible for what comes into the store. I just advise on which I think will be the most popular."

"Well, my customers appreciate your choices."

"It must be exciting working for the esteemed Mr. Worth."

"I do enjoy my work." He smiled, revealing even teeth.

"Though I am finding of late that I wish to share my ideas with someone…at home."

Lainey returned his smile. "I understand completely." She sipped her chocolate, a little unnerved at his direct approach. It was, after all, the reason they were all here, it just seemed…forced.

"I, for one, would like to hear more about the plans you have for your future," Mr. Fox piped up. "It's unusual for a woman to seek more than marriage and motherhood. Alas, the world is changing. What do you hope your life to look like?"

"That's a big question to answer, Mr. Fox," Lainey chided. "But I will do my best. You all know I am devoted to helping underprivileged women. I believe everyone is entitled to an education, but women are at a specific disadvantage. I realized that when I met Betsy." She nodded her head toward the woman who had just entered the room bearing a tea tray. "She is a friend of Lady Ashby's who looked out for her when things were bleak. She played a major part in the reason my brother met his wife, and we were very grateful to her. Aidan insisted upon taking her in, and we've been training her, teaching her to read, letting her discover what she has a talent for…and I realized that if I could do that with one person, I could do it for many others. Thus, I saw my chance to make my mark on the world."

"An admirable cause," Mr. Prince put in.

"I'm glad you think so," she returned, smiling at him. "I will need a husband who will support my efforts, not thwart them. I find that many men are most interested in how I run a household, not a business."

Prince grinned. "In America, many women run their own businesses. Perhaps England has some catching up to do in that regard," he observed dryly.

"Oh, be careful, Mr. Prince," Anne scolded. "You are surrounded by English blood."

He laughed, a hearty sound that made Lainey smile inside. "I meant no offense. My mother is English, after all. Forgive me, I do like to tease."

"No offense taken," Lainey assured him.

"Personally, I find your drive and your passion very attractive," Mr. Fox said, his gaze sliding sensuously over her. Lainey flushed scarlet, her entire body suddenly several degrees warmer. Gavin cleared his throat, rustling his paper. Lainey narrowed her eyes at him, but he pretended not to notice.

"Sometimes it does get me in a spot of trouble," Lainey admitted. "It can make me impulsive. I have already been out looking for properties, and I found one I thought would be perfect. Unfortunately, it appears someone else has already bought it."

Gavin's paper bent down and he gave her a stern look. Well, that was just brilliant. Now Gavin was going to be scolding her about this, as well.

"Oh, that is a shame," Anne said, patting Lainey's knee.

"I haven't given up hope. I am awaiting a letter from the land agent. He's to send me the owner's name so that I may reach out to him and see if he will sell to me. I'm hoping to appeal to his heart, but we shall see."

"Well, I wish you much success with your plans, Lady Elaine," Mr. Smith said. "It sounds like something London sorely needs. I would like to be of service to you in any way I can."

"Thank you, Mr. Smith, I would be glad to take you up on that offer. I am sure some investment guidance would not be amiss. And once I get underway," she added, "I will be looking for teachers, so if any of you know anyone who would be interested in helping a good cause, please do send them my way."

"Excuse me, milady," Betsy said, approaching the group. "The skies are beginning to clear. I've been asked to see if you would still like to venture into town this morning."

"Yes, Betsy, I think that would be fun. I'm sure the ladies would enjoy some shopping and then we can dine at the tavern. The men will have earned a pint of ale by that point," she said with a grin.

"Very good, milady. I'll have them ready the carriages."

Betsy took her leave and Mr. Fox swiveled his head toward Lainey. "That is the same girl who was living on the street mere months ago?"

"I told you she was smart."

"Indeed. Lady Elaine, regardless of how things go this week, please contact me when you are getting set up. I would like to make a donation to your cause."

Lainey put a hand to her chest. "Thank you, Mr. Fox. I would be most grateful."

Not to be outdone, the other men also pledged their support. Lainey was fizzing inside. She had never in her life been the center of attention like this, and the fact that there was already support for her charity was making her positively giddy. She smiled behind her cup as she finished the last of her chocolate. A month ago, she was sitting at a dinner table listening to her dining partner suck his teeth. Today, she was surrounded by a gaggle of fine-looking men who all appreciated her for her mind and ambitions, not her dowry. It was a heady feeling, and it took the sting out of leaving her dreams of Gavin behind.

She looked over to where he sat, glowering at her. Apparently, he was not pleased with the conversation he'd overheard. Well, too bad. Lainey was her own woman, and she was tired of being managed. Particularly by her brother's handsome-as-sin best friend.

"My lady." Tibbs interrupted with a bow, offering a letter on a silver salver. "This just arrived for you."

"Thank you, Tibbs." Lainey took the letter from the tray and Tibbs departed. "Oh! If you will all excuse me, I would like to read this now. I'm sure Miss Hastings and Miss Blousson will be more than happy to entertain you in my absence." She grinned at Lydia who was wearing a besotted expression. Lainey made a mental note to ask her which man had caught her fancy.

The men stood and she departed, not noticing that Gavin had risen to follow her.

HE FOUND her in Aidan's study. She looked up in surprise, which quickly turned to annoyance. "I know you were listening to every word. If you've come here to chastise me you can just go back to the morning room."

"You never told us you'd found property already."

"Yes, well, I got a little ahead of myself, and I obviously couldn't mention it before I'd told Aidan about my plans. Besides, I wanted to look on my own. I knew Aidan would try to handle it for me if I let him tag along. That's what we were doing that day Elizabeth and I ran into you."

"Lainey, you shouldn't be scouting out potential locations without one of us."

Lainey arched a brow. "My case in point."

"I didn't mean you can't handle it. It's just that estate agents are used to dealing with men. They might try to take financial advantage of a woman who isn't used to brokering a deal." Lainey just stared at him. He swallowed hard. "That is—"

"Save your breath, Gavin. You are just digging yourself deeper."

"Aidan and I know what to look for is all I'm saying. We just want you to be a grand success."

"And you think I can't do that on my own?"

He heaved an exasperated sigh. "Of course you can. But men like to make business deals with men. It's just the way of the world."

"Well, the world is changing, Gavin. Women are smart enough to run a business and broker deals, and it's time men got that through their thick skulls." She clutched the letter in her hand. "Oh, you should see this place, Gavin, it's perfect! Affordable, a relatively safe area while not being inaccessible to the underprivileged, several rooms for classrooms, plenty of light, and room to expand…I had such hopes."

"Where is this wonder of the world?"

"We were standing right in front of it when we ran into you that day."

Gavin had a sinking feeling as he thought back on that day. They'd been standing… "Not…not the limestone building on the corner?"

"That's the one!" Lainey broke the seal on the letter. "Now to find out who I need to wheedle into giving me what I want."

"Ah…before you open that—"

Lainey gasped. "This must be a mistake." She dropped her arms, letting the paper hit her thighs with a slap, her eyes blazing. "You?"

There was no point in denying it, she had the proof in her hands. "I'm afraid so."

"Gavin! Why? What could you possibly need a building for?"

"We're expanding, Lainey. Aidan has given me a very large promotion and I am now going to be managing our new branch. It's what I've worked for since I partnered with Aidan years ago."

"Why didn't you tell me?"

Gavin spread his hands. "You were so excited about your new venture. I didn't want to steal any of your thunder. Besides, I didn't think it would have any effect on you."

"Well, it does!" she snapped. "Gavin, there isn't anywhere else that fits my dream as well as this place. Can't you find somewhere else to put a stupid factory?"

Gavin straightened. "That was unkind."

"Well, I'm sorry, but this isn't fair. You have your pick of anywhere."

"Unfortunately, this location suits us perfectly as well. It was ultimately Aidan's decision. He's the one who put up the money for it."

"Well, then he'll just have to sell it back to me. That should be easy enough."

"He's not going to sell it to you, Lainey. We both want this location. He bought it and deeded it to me as my first year's salary. This is an enormous opportunity for me, can't you understand that? A true partnership where I get to be in charge of my own half. I have a chance to finally make something of myself, not just be second in command. At long last, Aidan is trusting me to manage our new division on my own. You are not the only one with dreams, Lainey."

"But I *am* the one at a disadvantage here. As you pointed out, a woman in business is up against challenges that men don't face, not to mention I am a peer, which makes this all the more distasteful to some."

"I quite admire you for it."

"Do not try to distract me with platitudes, Gavin. I only have so much money at my disposal. I don't know if I will be able to find something else."

"You know Aidan—"

"I don't *want* his money! I don't know what I have to say to get through to the two of you! I want to make something of my life, too, and I want to do it completely on my own. My big brother cannot just step in and fix things for me my whole life."

"Then you are going to have to talk to him about this. Just try to remember that you are not the only one who is trying to make a business happen here. Others have a right to want this, too."

"Are you calling me *selfish?*" Gavin leveled a stony stare on her and said not a word, just folded his arms over his chest. She huffed out an indignant breath. "Fine. I will get Aidan to change his mind. Then we'll see which one of us is the selfish one." She stomped out of the library in a huff.

Gavin scrubbed a hand over his face. He'd waited to tell her because he wanted her to be able to share in his excitement. He thought perhaps they'd be celebrating new ventures together. Instead, she was madder than an alley cat who'd had a chamber pot emptied on him. Just bloody wonderful.

CHAPTER 9

Gavin's mood remained black as they trundled into town. The last thing he wanted to do right now was play chaperone. He detested having Lainey cross with him, and he only grew more annoyed when he noticed that Devereaux had managed to seat himself in the carriage next to Lainey, and was now tucking her hand in the crook of his arm after they had descended. He was being a little proprietary, and Gavin thought it was inappropriate. Devereaux had not been on Gavin's invitee list, after all. He knew nothing about this man, and it irked Gavin to watch him manage to separate Lainey from the other suitors so easily. He would have to have a talk with Aidan, who had miraculously escaped this little excursion by claiming he had some estate business to take care of, the coward.

Elizabeth sidled up to Gavin and slid her arm through his. "My dear Mr. Mayfield, what are you scowling so ferociously about?"

"I'm scowling?"

"Quite severely, I'm afraid." Elizabeth smiled up at him.

"Could it have something to do with the gentleman hanging off my sister-in-law's arm?"

Gavin's face heated under Elizabeth's assessing gaze. "What do you make of him, Elizabeth?"

"Aside from his astonishing good looks and charming manner?"

Gavin twisted his mouth into a grimace. "Yes," he said flatly. "Aside from those."

He thought he heard Elizabeth snicker. "I think he is quite eager to make an impression on Lainey."

"That much is obvious. But doesn't he seem a little… young…for her?"

"He is only a year younger than she. But I do understand what you mean, and I agree. He does have a school boy air about him."

"I fear he is only wanting to win the prize, not the person."

"We have only just met him. Perhaps we should wait to judge him?" Elizabeth hinted. Gavin remained silent, grinding his teeth when Devereaux leaned his head toward Lainey to say something in her ear. "He may be rushing into thoughts of marriage as quickly as she seems to be, or perhaps he's given it quite a bit of thought and Lainey happened to cross his path at the right time. We must wait and see, and trust Lainey to know what her heart wants."

"That's the thing. I think she's giving up what her heart wants."

Elizabeth gave him a sideways glance. "Interesting you should say that."

He was spared from responding, because up ahead Lainey let out a shriek. Gavin was instantly at attention. "What the devil?"

They caught up to Lainey and Devereaux and several others in their party who were gathered around something on the ground. Lainey looked up, glancing about until her eyes fell on Gavin.

"Gavin, come look! Kittens!" she squealed. She bent down and scooped up a tiny bit of black and white fluff and held it up for him to see. Gavin chuckled. He'd never met anyone who went crazy over animals like Lainey.

"Oh, Elizabeth, look how sweet!" She cradled the little ball of fur in her arms. "What do you think my brother would say if we brought home a house cat?"

Elizabeth laughed. "I have no idea, but I know I wouldn't mind!" She tickled the cat under its chin.

"Oh dear," Lainey said, shifting the kitten so that they were nose to nose. "I suppose I shall have to ask before I make a hasty decision. Do you like cats, Mr. Devereaux?" She held the kitten out to him, and Gavin was inexplicably pleased to see Devereaux recoil slightly.

"I'm afraid my affinity for animals doesn't extend beyond horses," he said honestly. Gavin had to concede a point to him for being truthful.

"Well, we shall have to work on that," Lainey replied merrily, kissing the kitten and returning it to its basket of siblings. She sighed wistfully as she took one last look at the basket of mewling creatures and its owner. "Perhaps I can come back tomorrow. I hope you find them wonderful homes," she said, subtly slipping the young boy some coins. She took Devereaux's offered arm and they moved off down the street. Companionable chatter resumed, but Gavin couldn't resist glancing back at the noisy basket. The kittens *were* rather adorable.

SOMETIME LATER, the party retired to the local tavern for luncheon. Gavin found himself at a table with Lord Kingston, one of the few peers invited to the house party. He was a recent widower, recommended by Lainey's best friend, Anne Hastings. He seemed a nice enough fellow, though he was quite a bit older than Lainey. Apparently, he was a friend of Anne's parents, and though Gavin had met him several times, they often didn't travel in the same social circle. Kingston eased his lean frame onto a chair across from Gavin and slid a pint across the wood.

"You look like you could use this."

Gavin's brows raised in surprise. "You are the second person today who has told me I seem out of sorts. Perhaps I should take more care with my facial expressions."

Kingston took a sip of his ale. "I daresay these house parties are trying on anyone of the male sex."

"I'll drink to that," Gavin grumbled. Curse Lainey for dragging him into this ridiculous affair. Finding her a husband should be Aidan's responsibility, yet who was here with a gaggle of giddy women, playing chaperone? If he wasn't leg shackled to some scheming debutante by the end of this thing, it would be a bloody miracle.

"So, Miss Hastings tells me you've known Lady Elaine most of your life, since before they inherited the earldom."

"That's true. My family's land borders Rosecroft, and Lord Ashby and I would have great fun playing knights and dragons in the woods for hours. When Lady Elaine grew old enough, she began to follow us around, so being the boys that we were, we allowed her to be the damsel in distress and tied her to a tree." Kingston made a choking noise and he huffed into his glass of ale. Gavin laughed. "It was all well and good until one day, she was being particularly bratty, so... we left her there."

Kingston leaned forward in disbelief. "You left a little girl tied to a tree in the woods?"

"Well, when you put it that way, it sounds bad," Gavin

replied defensively. "Come on, Kingston, don't you remember what it was like to be a boy?"

"All too well. I have two older brothers who made it their life's work to torture me."

"Exactly!" Gavin grinned. "We only left her there for a few minutes, just to teach her a lesson."

"And let me guess. You wound up being the lesson learner?"

"I wound up wet."

Kingston's head cocked to the side. "I beg your pardon?"

"We went back after a few minutes to untie her, and needless to say, she was rather cross with us. But, we were boys, we had important boy things to do and discuss, and didn't want Aidan's pesky little sister hanging around all afternoon so we told her to go home. She planted her hands on her hips and refused, continuing to berate us for the unfair treatment of little sisters everywhere. I couldn't take it anymore, so in my infinite ten-year-old wisdom, I turned around and told her girls were stupid."

Kingston let out a bark of laughter. "And?"

"And she promptly shoved me into the pond and stomped off."

Kingston slapped his hand on the table and threw his head back in laughter. "You were bested by a little girl, Mr. Mayfield?"

"In my defense, she was remarkably strong for a six-year-old."

Kingston wiped his eyes, still laughing, and Gavin found himself chuckling right along with him. Gavin was suddenly enjoying the outing after all. Kingston was not a bad sort. Indeed, he was rather refreshing.

"So, you are telling me to never cross Lady Elaine, or it may be detrimental to my health?"

"Or your wardrobe, if there is water nearby." Gavin smiled down into his mug of ale, then glanced around the room, automatically seeking Lainey out. She was seated at a table in the corner, having an animated conversation with Anne and Elizabeth. Lainey laughed at something Anne said, and Gavin's heart squeezed. He turned his attention back to his companion. "Lady Elaine is a special woman, Kingston. She will cut you off at the knees if she thinks you are being unjust, she is fiercely independent, and she will not tolerate being left out just because she is a woman. But if you are lucky enough to win her heart…" He glanced over at her once more, guilt washing over him yet again. "Well, if you are that lucky and you don't do anything stupid, she'll be yours forever."

He sipped his beer and met Kingston's eyes across the table, the other man studying Gavin for a long, uncomfortable moment. "She sounds like a remarkable young woman, and I look forward to getting to know her. Although, one has to wonder why you aren't on the list of suitors as well."

Gavin nearly choked on his ale. "Me? No, no. Lainey—er, Lady Elaine and I are just friends. Practically siblings, really. Besides, she's my best friend's little sister. She's off limits even if I were interested. Which I'm not." Gavin gulped the last of his drink in the effort to stop his babbling.

Kingston nodded. "I see," he said slowly, giving Gavin the impression he wanted to say more, but didn't.

Lainey and the other two ladies suddenly appeared at his side, and the chair shrieked in his haste to stand. "I think we are ready to move on, Mr. Mayfield," she said brightly. "This was a fun excursion, but the ladies and I are ready to return home to a nice cup of tea and to look over what we bought— that is always the fun part," she said, her eyes full of sparkle.

Gavin smiled warmly at her, then caught blasted Devereaux out of the corner of his eye heading toward them, no doubt ready to whisk Lainey away again. That was not happening on Gavin's watch. "Whatever you wish, my lady. Lord Kingston, perhaps you'd like to be Lady Elaine's escort on the return home?"

"I'd be delighted," he replied, offering her his arm. Gavin shot a triumphant glance Devereaux's way. The other man definitely did not look pleased. *Well, isn't that just a shame?*

He offered his arm to Anne. "Shall we, ladies?"

They left the tavern and walked back in the direction they had come, passing by the little boy with the basket of kittens once again. Lainey looked longingly at the furry creatures, but resisted temptation and walked on with the viscount. Gavin slowed his pace as he approached the bushel of cats, wondering if Aidan just might kill him for what he was about to do. He stopped and stared down at the little black and white kitten Lainey had held as the rest of the party moved ahead. Beside him, Anne smiled.

"I won't tell if you do."

Gavin snapped his gaze to hers. "I shouldn't."

"I rather think you *should*."

"Miss Hastings, has anyone ever told you that you are a bad influence?"

"Only my dearest friends." She laughed. "You will make her happy for years to come. You know she'd be delighted."

"I do." Gavin sighed. "Promise me you won't tell her who it was? I don't want it to appear as though I'm trying to buy her affections. She is here to find a husband, after all."

"I will keep your secret. Both of them," she added.

Gavin's eyes narrowed. "What do you mean by that?"

"Oh, nothing," she replied breezily. "It's just that men who don't have certain feelings for women don't usually gift them a cat."

"Men who've made an egregious error might."

"Why, Mr. Mayfield, what *have* you done?"

"Nothing you need to worry about, Miss Hastings. And

I'll thank you to get those matchmaking thoughts out of your head. There is nothing untoward between Lainey and I. We are dear friends, that is all."

"Mm hmm." Anne's expression said she clearly didn't believe him. She gestured toward the basket. "Well then, shall we give one of these little loves a home?"

She bent over the basket to play with the kittens while Gavin ground his teeth. Why on earth was everyone trying to shove him and Lainey together all of a sudden? It was downright frustrating. The kitten was an apology, nothing more. Though no one else knew he was trying to earn back Lainey's good opinion, he supposed. Still. He needed to distance himself more; he was getting too involved if people were starting to notice his attention.

He selected the black and white kitten for Lainey, and paid the boy handsomely to have it delivered to the house the following morning, promising there would be some tarts waiting for him upon delivery. The boy's face lit up, both at the amount of money he held in his grasp and the prospect of a sweet treat on the morrow. Gavin tucked Anne's hand in the crook of his elbow drawing her away from the fuzzy things so they could catch up with the rest of their party. After a few moments of silence, Anne patted his bicep with her other hand.

"Don't think I didn't notice that you gave the boy enough money to buy every kitten in that basket," she said with a smile.

After they had returned home, Lainey slipped away for a stroll while everyone went to rest. She trudged glumly through the gardens in the waning light, kicking at stones, still bothered by her argument with Gavin. Had he really called her selfish? That accusation smarted. She may be a lot of things, but she'd never been accused of being selfish. After her terrible row with Gavin, she'd gone and had one with Aidan as well. Gavin was right, Aidan would not change his mind. He explained the pressing need for space, and while he understood her ire, it would take months for her to gather everything she would need to start a new business. He was established and could start up right away, and he needed the time to prep for next year's season, which was only six months away. She plopped down unceremoniously on a bench, slumping over as far as one could while wearing a corset. She stared dejectedly down at the stone path, digging a small trench with her boot. The hem of a skirt appeared in her view.

"There you are." Elizabeth sat down beside her. "I've been looking for you."

"I don't feel like entertaining at the moment."

Elizabeth put an arm around her friend. "Aidan told me what happened. I'm sorry you fought."

Lainey sighed. "I don't like quarreling with my brother. It makes me feel like a shrew after all he's given me."

"We can't be angels all the time, Lainey. Sometimes disappointment gets the best of us."

"So, he told you?"

"Yes. Gavin is also looking quite out of sorts."

"I'm not surprised. I wasn't very nice to him, either."

"Dearest, you do realize what a momentous thing this is for him right? He's worked hard all of his life toward this goal. Becoming a full partner is a huge success for him."

Lainey choked back her bitterness. "I know. I was just so angry. You're right, I did not handle the disappointment well at all."

"I'm sure the three of you will smooth things over. I know your brother feels badly, but you know he will help you find the perfect place to start your help center. And who knows, perhaps another spot will open very near our original location? You still have a wedding to plan, papers to file, employees to hire and train. There is much to do that can occupy your time while you are waiting."

Lainey pulled a face. "Hmph. That's almost exactly what Aidan said."

Elizabeth shrugged and pressed her lips together, an indication that perhaps Aidan had a point. "He is incredibly proud of you, you know."

"Blast, Eliza! Don't make me feel worse!"

Elizabeth stood, pulling Lainey with her. "Come, it's nearly time for dinner. Perhaps that will fortify you."

"To apologize for being ridiculous?"

Elizabeth slipped an arm about Lainey's waist and squeezed. "Something like that."

DINNER HAD BEEN INTERMINABLE. Gavin had shot furtive glances at Lainey all evening, trying to asses if she was still angry with him. He'd deserted the party that afternoon after they returned and gone out for a long, punishing ride instead. Once he'd calmed down, he'd been able to see things from her point of view. It didn't change his mind, but it did help him understand. She had a right to be upset, but hopefully that would fade. Surely, she would come around.

But first, he needed to apologize for implying she was being selfish. Lainey was quite possibly the least selfish person he knew, and her anger had caught him off guard. He'd lashed out without thinking.

"Gavin? May I have a word with you?"

He looked up from his brandy snifter to find the woman he'd just been thinking about standing in front of him. He glanced around the drawing room. Everyone seemed to be occupied in their own pursuits, so no one would be paying attention to their conversation. Gavin moved to stand, but Lainey stayed him with her hand and sat down next to him on the settee.

"I owe you an apology," she said quietly.

"Lainey—"

"Hear me out. Please. I don't handle disappointment well. You know this about me. I have big dreams, and sometimes I get overly excited and I don't think things through. I should not have gone looking for a property before I even knew if any of this was possible. The estate agent said as much when I was crestfallen that the property had sold. I just…I want this so badly. I'm anxious to make my mark on the world, so to speak."

"And you will, Lainey…but I don't understand. Why are you in such a rush? I know once you get an idea in your head, you run with it, but it's unlike you to charge into a project without a solid plan. What's driving you?"

Lainey fell silent, absently twisting a piece of skirt in her fingers. She glanced across the room at Aidan and Elizabeth, and Gavin followed her gaze. She continued to work the innocent fabric into a molehill of hopeless creases. Without thinking, he reached out and covered her hand with his. Her hand stilled, and the jolt of electricity that shot up his arm at the contact robbed him of his breath. She turned her warm brown eyes to him, surprise lighting the tiny gold flecks so that they reminded him of slivers of mica catching the sunlight in a shallow stream.

"What is it?" he asked softly.

Lainey shrugged her shoulders. "I suppose I've been restless for a while." She glanced at her brother once again. "And I am anxious to start a family."

Gavin pressed his lips together and withdrew his hand.

The stark reminder of why he could never have Lainey for his own was a blow to the gut. "All the more reason to take your time and choose wisely. You want a good father for your children."

"You would not have invited anyone who would not make a good father. You are aware of my goals."

"True," Gavin conceded.

"Forgive me for being selfish?"

"Lainey, you are one of the most selfless people I know. I'm sorry I lashed out like that. It was not well done of me." Gavin had the sudden urge to pull her into his arms and hold her till their world was right again. Instead, he slapped his thighs. "Well. We've apologized to each other, enough of this dreary conversation. You have some mingling to do, and I have a game of billiards to begin." He stood, holding his hand out to Lainey to assist her from the settee. He pressed a brief kiss to the back of her hand. "Let's not quarrel like this again, all right? It doesn't sit well with me."

"Nor I," Lainey agreed. "Thank you, Gavin. I'm glad we talked." She moved off toward the gentlemen seated at the card table, and he watched as their faces lit up at her approach.

Bloody lucky bastards.

Gavin shook off the sliver of jealousy as he headed for the billiard table.

CHAPTER 10

Gavin strode into the drawing room later the next morning to find a gaggle of women clustered together, huddled over and squealing about something.

Ah, the kitten had arrived.

As if on cue, the black and white fuzzball darted out from under Miss Hasting's skirt and bounded toward Gavin. He scooped it up easily and brought it to eye level. "Well, hello there. And who might this be?"

Lainey bounced over to him and the ladies followed. "Someone has gifted me a kitten!" she announced with delight. "Isn't he darling?"

"Rather handsome little fellow, yes," he said, handing it to her. "Someone must be trying to make a good impression on you." He glanced around at the other men in the room, eyeing Devereaux, who feigned innocence and looked away. One of the ladies tittered and Gavin had a terrible thought. Was Devereaux going to try to take credit for this in order to win Lainey over? He wouldn't put it past him. He returned his attention to Lainey, who was busy snuggling the squirming kitten. "I can see we are going to have some competition for your attention, my lady."

Lainey gave him a bright smile. "Perhaps the kitten will help me decide who among you is *worthy* of my attention!" The ladies all giggled.

"What are you going to name him?" Emily asked.

"I'm not sure yet. Maybe we should have a naming competition!"

"Oh, that sounds like fun!" Emily clapped her hands.

Lainey addressed the room. "Put your thinking caps on, everyone! After dinner tonight I wish to hear your best cat names. We'll make a game of it!"

"Oh, the pressure," Devereaux drawled.

"Ah, Mr. Devereaux, I bet you will have some viable suggestions," Lainey teased.

"Indeed, my lady." He winked.

Gavin barely refrained from rolling his eyes. "I can hardly wait," he said dryly. He stroked the kitten's soft, furry head. He was curling against Lainey's bosom, purring, and struggling to keep his eyes open. He looked incredibly content.

Gavin was suddenly insanely jealous of a stupid cat.

"What pleasurable activities do you have planned for us today, my lady?" he asked, taking his hand away before he accidentally stroked Lainey instead of the kitten.

"Well, I thought we would have a game of croquet."

Gavin grinned. "Is this to be a competitive game of croquet?"

Lainey sauntered away, handing the sleeping kitten to Emily, who was clearly head over heels in love. "What fun is croquet if it isn't competitive?" Lainey asked innocently.

Gavin barked out a laugh at her guileless expression. Devereaux perked up his ears.

"Croquet a competitive sport?" he said, surprised.

"It is when Lady Elaine plays," Anne replied, a smile tugging at her lips.

"You will get to know that about her, Devereaux. Lady Elaine here cannot resist a competition of any kind. And she's not a very good loser, either," Gavin added with a grin.

"I will thank you not to malign me to my guests, Mr. Mayfield. I do like a little friendly competition, but I can be a gracious loser."

Gavin coughed into his hand, turning away. Viscount Kingston watched the exchange with interest. Lainey stuck her tongue out at Gavin's turned back.

"Don't listen to a word he says, Mr. Devereaux. He's just trying to scare you."

"It might be working," Devereaux replied with a grin.

Lainey giggled, the sound tickling Gavin's insides. "I am going to draw names for teams, and one person from each team will advance to the final round. There will be plenty to eat and drink to keep us occupied if we aren't on the field. The tables and chairs are being set up as we speak."

"Who is going to watch the kitten?" Emily asked.

"We'll bring his basket and take turns."

"Perhaps you'd like to go first, Devereaux," Gavin suggested. Devereaux gave him a look that said he didn't appreciate Gavin's suggestion at all, and Gavin chuckled inside. It was just too much fun to bait this man.

Emily laid the tuckered-out kitten in his basket and rose to her feet. She lifted the basket carefully so as not to disturb the cat, who looked as though a pack of wild, barking dogs would not wake him. Gavin glanced at Anne and gave an apologetic shrug. He guessed the Hastings household was going to be getting a cat of its own sometime soon.

"Very well, ladies and gentlemen. Croquet starts in one hour. I will see you on the field!" Lainey said brightly, exiting the room with the ladies following her like a herd of ducklings.

Kingston chuckled. "What an interesting party this is turning out to be!"

GAVIN TRIED NOT to ponder all the ways in which he could inflict harm on Charles Devereaux with his croquet mallet. Really, he did, but it was just so...tempting...to picture jabbing the man in the stomach or clocking him in the noggin every time he ogled Lainey. She didn't seem to mind, but then again, she was rather diverted by Kingston, who was finally having the chance to speak with her at length. She laughed about something he said, the musical sound floating over to Gavin on the breeze. His chest tightened.

Damn. This party had turned out to be far more difficult to endure than he'd imagined. He hadn't expected the fierceness of his desire to protect Lainey, and certainly not the violent urges that took over him every time someone dare lay a hand on her person. The fact that he was even considering smashing another man over the head with a croquet mallet spoke volumes about what kind of person that made Gavin. He was right to avoid marriage. He obviously couldn't keep his impulses in check. The only thing that was stopping him was the fact that the Lockwoods would be horrified by his behavior.

Because it would feel really, really good to jab Devereaux in the breadbasket right about now. The man couldn't keep his eyes off of Lainey. If he touched her, Gavin couldn't be sure he wouldn't give in to the urge. And that thought terrified him.

"I believe it's your turn, Mr. Mayfield."

Gavin snapped to attention, his face growing warm at

having been caught staring at Lainey. "Er—sorry, Miss Hastings."

He'd initially been paired with Emily, but Anne had seen his panic and claimed he'd gotten the wrong Hastings girl. Emily was smitten with Gavin and had been mooning over him since her first night here. Gavin's relief that Anne had stepped in and saved him from an afternoon of hero worship was palpable.

"You know, if we hadn't been friends for so long, I might take offense that you are paying more attention to someone's else's partner than to your own."

Gavin nearly missed his swing, and his ball went rolling off to the side, passing the wicket completely.

"I also thought you were a better croquet player," she observed wryly.

"I'm a bit off my game today," Gavin answered lightly.

"A bit," Anne replied, knocking her ball clean through the wicket. "I daresay, keep playing like that and you won't make it to the next round."

"More's the pity," Gavin said, frowning at his ball. He was usually quite competitive, but today he simply couldn't muster concentration or interest. He fought not to glance in Lainey's direction when she laughed again.

Anne eyed him shrewdly. "I think you've outdone yourself with Lainey's prospects. There are quite a few agreeable gentlemen here. She should be able to find a happy match if she insists on going through with this."

"Yes, well. That was the idea." He finally whacked his ball through the wicket and they moved forward to allow the next team to play.

"I do hope she's not rushing this," Anne mused. "She's waited so long for the right man, and now she's throwing it all out the window because of her stubborn independence. I worry that she's being reckless with her heart." *Thwack!*

"That makes two of us," Gavin muttered as he lined up his shot.

"I do have to note though, perhaps you and Ashby were outdone by Mr. Pritchard. It seems that she's taken quite a shine to Mr. Devereaux. And he most certainly looks at her as though she were a treacle pudding served up just for him."

Gavin swung so hard he nearly lost his balance when he completely missed his ball. Damn, he needed to get a hold of his temper before he lashed out.

"Oh dear, Mr. Mayfield! That was quite an impressive shot!"

Gavin glared at her as she pressed her lips together, trying to keep a straight face. "And what about you, Miss Hastings? Are you like me, determined to remain single for the rest of your days, or has some gentleman caught your eye?" He attempted his shot again, this time the mallet connecting with the ball in a satisfying crack.

Anne regarded him with merriment as a smile crept to her lips. "A lady never tells, Mr. Mayfield."

LAINEY COULD FEEL Gavin's eyes on her all the way across the field. It was disconcerting, to say the least. Every time she glanced at him, he was glowering in her direction. She forced her attention once again to her delightful partner.

"Tell me more about your daughter, my lord."

Kingston beamed. "Ah, she's a good girl, my Rose. She is six years old, and a sweet-tempered child. My mother insists that I dote on her too much, but I can't help myself. It's hard not to indulge her when she looks at me with those big blue eyes."

Lainey nodded and sent her ball through the wicket with a loud *crack!* "I have always had a weakness for children myself. They are just so guileless and open, and they don't give a fig about improper behavior. One can really let go around them and they won't judge you for it."

"This is true," Kingston agreed. "If anyone had ever told me I'd be sitting at a child-sized table and having a tea party while wearing a daisy crown I would have told them they were full of—oh! Pardon me, Lady Elaine. I don't mean to be vulgar."

Lainey smiled. "I know my reputation is a sterling one, but even I swear every now and again. I'm not offended by it."

Kingston studied his partner. "You are an unusual woman, my lady. I regret that I haven't come to know you better over the years."

"There is no time like the present. Getting to know each other is why we are here, is it not?"

Kingston lined up his shot and took it. "Right you are. You had just come out when we first met, and I still remember you as the wide-eyed debutante taking everything in at the ball. Ashby has spoken highly of your charitable endeavors since then, as well as your keen business sense." He turned to her, interest lighting his eyes. "Tell me about the help center you plan to open."

"Well…how much do you know about Lady Ashby's background?"

"I've heard she has had…a rough time of it."

"That would be an understatement." They meandered to the next wicket. "She came from a good family, but when she was a young girl, her home was broken into and she was separated from her parents."

"Ah yes, I remember hearing about the fire not long after it happened. Such a tragedy.""Yes, well. She was lost to her parents that night and then wound up spending eight years on the streets before she fell into our lives. When I saw firsthand what sort of conditions she'd been living in, it really struck me how this could happen to any woman. We are so vulnerable because men are in control of everything. They may spend our money and gamble away our possessions as they see fit, getting far into debt, and then what happens when they cock up their toes? Many women have no means to support themselves in that situation. What happened to Lady Ashby could happen to anyone, and she was fortunate enough to have come from a family that educated her. What of those who are kept from that? What of the women who are treated as though they are merely property, not worthy of education?" Lainey thumped her mallet on the ground in frustration. "Women have too long been seen as lesser citizens of society. When I met Lady Ashby, I realized the charity work I was doing wasn't enough. We can hand out food and clothing all we want, but if we aren't teaching these women useful skills, they will never have the chance to better their lives. I would like to help them do exactly that."

Kingston studied her silently, and Lainey worried she'd said too much. Men did not like women with strong opinions, after all. But she was here to meet someone who would support her endeavors, so she might as well be her true self. It was rather refreshing.

Kingston leaned on his mallet. "Bravo, Lady Elaine."

"I beg your pardon?"

"I admire you greatly for what you are trying to do."

"You do?"

"Yes," Kingston smiled. "I do. I hear a lot of talk in Parliament about our poorest class. All sorts of laws bandied about that will supposedly protect them, yet never do...and from our loftier members, ideas on how to suppress them even further. No one can seem to agree what's to be done. But I think you have the right of it. Education is key."

"Exactly! Every human being should have the right to

learn how to read and write. But we want to teach them life skills as well, so that they may have a way to earn a living."

"We?"

"Yes. Lady Ashby and I are joining forces to get this underway. She is going to teach sewing, as she made her living as a seamstress. I'll take the literacy facet, and then we are going to be searching for candidates to provide training for shop girls, bakeries, tea shops…any skill from which a woman with little education can earn a living, we will find a way to teach."

Kingston smiled at Lainey as they strolled to the next wicket. "You know, my lady, it's a pity you and my Annabelle didn't know each other better. I think you would have gotten along famously."

"I was so sorry to learn of her death. That must have been very difficult for you."

Kingston nodded. "I miss her every day."

"Tell me about her," Lainey said, looping her arm through his.

"Oh, you don't want to listen to me talk about my wife," he chided.

"Actually, I do." She disengaged her arm so she could line up her final shot. She sent her ball sailing through the last wicket. Kingston was quiet as he prepared to take his shot.

"She was an incredible woman," he said to the ground, so softly Lainey almost didn't hear him. He swung, finishing their round. He looked up at her, a sad smile on his face. "She was all that was good and light in my life, a gift that I never expected to receive."

They regarded each other for a moment, Lainey watching as the memory of his beloved wife spread across Kingston's face. She smiled. "Lemonade while we talk?"

He offered his arm, and they wandered off in search of refreshments while they waited for everyone's games to be finished. Kingston was quiet for a while, and Lainey thought he might not say more.

"Annabelle had a bright spirit," he said suddenly. "She was like you in some ways, warm and generous, and she wanted to help however she could. She also would fight fiercely if she felt she had the right of things, and if you asked her, she'd say that was her most fatal flaw. She claimed her feisty temper would turn men away, but I enjoyed that about her. Perhaps that's because we had little to argue about so I wasn't often the one on the receiving end of a tongue lashing," he quipped. "But I like a woman who will stand up for herself. I think we genuinely appreciated each other for exactly who we were, flaws and all, and that made our connection easy. I fell in love with her right away." He shrugged. "I'd never intended to marry, but I couldn't help myself."

Lainey smiled warmly at him. "It must be something to love someone so much that you will change your life's plan for them." She couldn't prevent her eyes from straying in Gavin's direction, a pang of regret twisting her heart.

"Indeed," Kingston replied, following her gaze. "It is an extraordinary thing to be loved so well, and love strongly in return. We had our differences, but we embraced them. She was not just my wife, she was my partner in life. That fierceness with which she would defend her position? Well, that extended to those she loved as well. She was a force to be reckoned with if anyone dared hurt her family. She was unapologetically bold, yet she was the gentlest of souls. She was a brilliant mother. Rose misses her terribly."

"I can imagine how she feels. I was only eleven when Mother died."

"Yes, it's difficult to lose a parent when one is so young. I hadn't planned to remarry but…" He trailed off, taking a sip of lemonade, seemingly strengthening his resolve. "Rose needs a mother. And I need to know that Rose will be loved and cared for should anything happen to me. Annabelle will always have my heart. But I am hoping to find a companion. If I can find a wife who will be a good friend to me and a good mother to Rose, I will be happy. I've had my true love. I don't expect to find that sort of magic again. But I can certainly be happy." He turned to Lainey. "Lady Elaine, I hope you do not find it presumptuous of me to attend this party. I realize I am a good deal older than you, and I am standing here telling you I may not love my next wife fiercely, as I did the first. But I needed to be honest with you. I have a great respect for both you and your brother, and I know you understand what it is like to grow up without a mother. I only recently decided to take a wife again, and when your brother spoke of your intentions, I wrangled myself an invitation. I do hope you can forgive me, but I can't tolerate the whirlwind that is the season, and I am too old for young debutantes anyway. I had hoped I could quietly find someone before the next season swings round again. I know the sort of company you and Ashby keep, and thought perhaps my chances of meeting someone of good moral character here were high. I beg your pardon if I am being too blunt."

Lainey shook her head. "I appreciate your candor, my lord. Your honesty is refreshing. People marry for a lot less than love, there is no shame in that. I do hope you will find someone to your liking."

"It is a big step for someone like me to marry again. It is… frightening almost. Fear of betrayal of your first love, fear of unintentionally comparing your first marriage to your second and having it not measure up…I can't quite explain it. I know it probably does not make any sense to you and you will probably warn all of your friends away from me after this conversation—"

"It makes perfect sense to me. You loved Annabelle

deeply, and she will be part of any marriage you make going forward. If any woman ever asks you to forget Annabelle or never speak of her, I beg you, do not marry that person. Annabelle should not cease to exist simply because she is no longer physically here."

Kingston pressed his lips together and looked away, but not before Lainey caught the shimmer of tears in his eyes. She laid her hand on his arm.

"I am very glad you came, Lord Kingston."

He blew out a breath and laid his hand over hers. "So am I, my lady. So am I."

CHAPTER 11

That evening after dinner, they were gathered in the parlor when Lainey made an announcement.

"All right, then. You've had all day. It's time to propose names for the new kitten."

Gavin was torn between wanting to stick a fork in his eye and hearing what ridiculous suggestion would come from Devereaux. Thank God he and Aidan were escaping within the hour for a game of cards at a friend's nearby home. If Gavin had to sit here and watch these men fawn over Lainey again tonight, he might hurt someone.

He'd always been fairly good at keeping his temper in check, but this house party was testing his control, and it was frightening to discover how easy it would be to lose it. No, he was here to make sure Lainey got what she wanted, and if she was happy, then he would be content.

Several cat names were bandied about, but nothing seemed to catch Lainey's attention. Devereaux grinned at her.

"Scout. Muffin. Crumbcake! Edward?" Everyone laughed

as Devereaux got more and more animated with each name he called out. Gavin rolled his eyes when Lainey giggled.

"Mr. Devereaux, you are just shouting out random names, you aren't even trying!" she admonished with a smile.

He shrugged. "Truly, it's a cat. It's going to ignore you when you call it anyway, so what difference does it make what you name it?"

Everyone laughed again, then lapsed into a thoughtful pause.

"Bingley," Gavin muttered into the silence. Lainey slowly swung her gaze toward him, pinning him with wide eyes.

"I beg your pardon?"

Blast. He hadn't thought he'd said it loud enough for anyone to hear. He sighed. "Mr. Bingley. You know, from *Pride and Prejudice.*"

"Yes, I know who Mr. Bingley is. I am surprised that you do."

Gavin shrugged. "It's your favorite."

Lainey stared at him, drawing her eyebrows together. "So, you read it?"

Oh, hell. There was a moment of uncomfortable silence as all eyes turned to him. He shifted in his chair. "Well. You were so obsessed with it. I just wanted to see what all the swooning was about." He cleared his throat. "Actually, it was, ah…it was quite good."

Someone snickered, and Lainey's mouth fell open slightly. Everyone was staring, the men waiting to pounce on the fact that Gavin has read what was widely viewed as a romantic novel, and the women's eyes had all gone soft. Gavin thought perhaps he'd tied his tie a little too tight because suddenly air was having trouble getting into his throat.

"So, you wouldn't name him Darcy, then? He is the romantic hero of the story, after all."

She was testing him. Gavin scoffed. "That cat is no Darcy.

I've never seen a less stand-offish creature in my life. He just wants to please you and be loved in return. That cat is a Bingley, through and through."

Oh, for Pete's sake, next he was going to be joining the ladies tea and discussing the latest fashion. Where the hell was Aidan? He needed to escape before he lost what remained of his dignity.

"I do believe you are correct, Mr. Mayfield," Lainey said softly, picking up the little ball of fluff and looking him in the eye. "What do you think? Would you like to be called Bingley?" The kitten let out a tiny meow, and everyone cheered. "Well then, Bingley it is! Thank you, Mr. Mayfield, for your excellent suggestion." She kissed the kitten and put him down to scamper over to play with the tassel on the draperies.

At last, Aidan arrived to collect Gavin, and he nearly bolted from his chair. "You are very welcome, my lady. I bid you all a good evening."

He made a hasty exit, but not before he heard Devereaux mutter, "Nancy." Oh, he would never live this down.

It was very late, and she really should go to bed, but Lainey couldn't stop reliving the moment Gavin admitted he had read her favorite book simply because she liked it so. It seemed such a romantic gesture, but she knew better than to assign any meaning to it. Well, her mind knew better. Her heart was still tripping foolishly. She told it to stop, she was clearly of no interest to Gavin, and yet...

"Desist, Lainey." She smacked her palm on her dressing table. "It means nothing, he was just curious. You are letting those romances you read go to your head." She stood up, intending to go get a book from Aidan's library, preferably something dull that would send her right to sleep. She didn't want to dream about kisses or romantic gestures or how it had felt to have Gavin's arms around her the other night, even accidentally and for just a moment—

"Gah!" She stomped toward the door, pulling on a wrapper as she went, muttering under her breath. She crept down the stairs and made her way to the library, halting just outside the drawing room door when she heard men's voices. Bother. She couldn't pass the open door without being seen, and those voices didn't belong to either Gavin or Aidan, who were both still out for the evening. She was about to turn around, abandoning her plans for reading, when Charles Devereaux's question caught her attention.

"Do you think she's *too* proper, though?"

Lainey froze. *Were they discussing her?* She knew she should leave, but her legs refused to agree.

"I like a proper lady, Devereaux," Pritchard responded. "Nothing wrong with that. Lady Elaine is a fine woman."

That answered that, and thank you, Pritchard. Glass clinked and the sound of a drink being poured reached her ears.

"Yes, of course. But I mean, I need a little adventure. I don't want a cold or distant wife, one who never likes to let loose and have a little fun. I don't know her like some of you do. She seems charming enough, but also reserved. The last thing I want is to be bored with my marriage. That's not enjoyable for either one of us."

Lainey's face flushed warm. Devereaux was effortlessly reinforcing her insecurities. Maybe she *was* boring. Too stiff. Too proper. She'd spent her life being above reproach, and then had to double her efforts when her engagement was broken. Had that made her unattractive to men as a wife? She'd thought that was the kind of person they wanted, so she'd tamped down her adventurous spirit and been the perfect example of propriety. All it had gotten her was rejection. Twice. And it appeared it may be happening again.

"I say, if you don't think she's for you, Devereaux, then back off and give the rest of us a chance," someone grumbled. It sounded like Mr. Fox.

"Right," Pritchard agreed. "I've known Lady Elaine and her family for years. She would make anyone an excellent wife."

"All right, all right, no need to get testy. I'm just looking for some insight. Marriage is a permanent situation. I want to know what I might be getting into. I'm not the type to have extramarital affairs, so I'd like a woman who enjoys bedsport as much as I do…and I'm not sure she would. I'd bet you twenty pounds she's never so much as been kissed."

"Well now you are just being boorish, Devereaux," the American scolded.

A tiny dagger of pain lanced Lainey's chest, bringing a sting to her eyes. How mortifying to be discussed in such a way.

Even more so because Devereaux was entirely correct.

Not one man had ever attempted to steal a kiss from her.

If that didn't prove she was unattractive and dull, she didn't know what did. Unable to listen to any more, she turned and fled toward her brother's study instead, all thoughts of reading forgotten.

She had a better plan. She was going to get good and drunk.

GAVIN AND AIDAN nearly stumbled into the front hall when Tibbs opened the door for them. Aidan shot him a lopsided smile as he regained his balance and handed over his hat.

"Well, that was a bloody fun evening," Aidan said, his speech slightly slurred from just one drink too many.

"It was. Talbot is a good chap. Excellent brandy." Gavin grinned.

"I'll second that." Aidan slapped his friend on the back. "You going up?"

"No, I think I need to see what I can filch from the kitchen. I'll see you in the morning."

"Goodnight, then." Aidan trudged up the stairs, whistling a little ditty as he went. Gavin shook his head, smiling. It wasn't often his friend imbibed too much, but it always amused Gavin when he did. Gavin had had his share as well this evening, but he felt oddly restless. A stolen treat was just what he needed.

On his way to the kitchen, he noticed a flicker of light under the door to Aidan's study. Curious, he peeked in and found Lainey sprawled in one of the chairs, an empty snifter dangling from her hand.

"Lainey! What are you still doing up?" *And wearing only a nightgown and wrapper?*

She turned surprised eyes to him. "Oh! Gavin. You st… startled me."

"Is everything all right?" She sounded…off.

"I s'pose so." Lainey tipped her head back against the chair. "Would you refill this for me, please? I don't think I can pour without spilling anymore."

He peered at her in the dim light. "Have you been *drinking*?" he asked, eyebrows raised in question. While Lainey enjoyed spirits, she was not one to overindulge. "Lainey, what's wrong?" He nudged the door to behind him and poured them both a small brandy. He certainly didn't need to drink any more tonight, but it seemed impolite to let her drink alone.

"Nothing, really. I'm just…I think I'm lost."

"Tell me." He sat in the chair across from her, placing an ankle on his knee and loosening his tie. He really shouldn't be in here alone with her, but she was clearly in distress. And really, no one was around to discover them together. He wasn't about to leave without finding out if he could help.

She sighed. "Gavin, am I...boring?"

His eyebrows shot up. "Boring? Certainly not! Why would you think that?"

She grimaced. "I overheard Devereaux make a comment about how proper I am and that he thought maybe I wouldn't be able to keep a marriage bed...exciting," she said bitterly.

"Devereaux is an ass." Gavin made a mental note to seek him out tomorrow and kick him in it.

"I don't know that he's wrong, Gavin. I mean, I have heard some rather eye-opening things from the women I help, so I'm not completely without knowledge about what to do, but I have no actual *experience* with anything. What if... what if I *am* a disappointment?" She stared down at her brandy then took a large swallow.

Gavin set his own glass on the table and moved to squat down before her. "Lainey," he said, taking her hands. "You could never be a disappointment to anyone."

"I was to you."

That brought Gavin up short. "Why on earth would you say that?"

"Why else would you reject me? I must have been lacking somehow."

She may as well have put an ice pick through his heart at that moment. "You...you think I won't marry you because there is something *wrong* with you?"

"Well, what else am I supposed to think? We know we'll get on well together, so that's not it. And no man would come near me after my broken engagement that year, but

I've not had any decent offers since then, either, so it must be me, so what am I—"

"Lainey, stop." He squeezed her hand. "You've had too much to drink and are spewing utter nonsense. I think it's time to—"

The unexpected brush of her lips against his sent the words in his throat to a quick death. Surprise bolted through him and he rocked back on his heels, his lips tingling from the brief contact.

"What…why did you do that?"

"Do you know that I have never, not once, been kissed? No one has ever even so much as tried." Lainey plunked her snifter on the table. "I would like to be kissed, Gavin, and I would like you to do it."

That sobered him instantly and he shot to his feet. "No."

Lainey followed him. "But I think you are the perfect person to give me my first kiss! We have no expectations of each other, and I hear you are legendary in the seduction department, so that makes you a good choice." She giggled.

"Legendary?" This was news to Gavin. "How many women do you think I—no," he said, holding up a hand. "Don't answer that. This discussion is entirely inappropriate."

"But interesting." Lainey hiccupped, swaying a tiny bit on her feet.

"Exactly how much have you had to drink?"

"Enough to ask you to kiss me." Lainey grinned, and his stomach tightened in response.

"You're serious, aren't you?" Gavin shoved a hand through his hair, not quite believing what he was hearing. Perhaps he was a little more in his cups than he thought.

"It's perfect, you see. You are not attracted to me, therefore a simple kiss should be something I daresay you'll forget about as soon as you walk out the door, and I will have at least some knowledge of what to do should the occasion arise."

Gavin stared at Lainey for a long moment, noting the slight flush in her cheeks and the glimmer of mischief in her eyes. She was utterly bewitching. He ached to touch her, if only for a moment.

"What…makes you think I'm not attracted to you?" *Walk away now,* his mind screamed through the brandy haze. *Better yet, run.* His tie was choking him, and he was surprised when he reached up to find that he'd already loosened it. He clawed frantically at the top button on his shirt when Lainey turned away and sauntered toward the fire. Air. He needed air.

"Oh, Gavin, let's be honest. I practically threw myself at you two years ago and you rejected me with some ridiculous excuse. Why else would you turn me down? You were just trying to spare an awkward girl her feelings. I understand now, but at the time I still thought I was desirable."

Gavin was rooted to the floor. The gut-twisting guilt that descended upon him took his breath away. "My God." The fire in the grate crackled in his stunned silence. His cowardice had hurt her far more deeply than he had ever realized. "Is that really what you think? That you are undesirable?" He could barely even repeat the words that cut him to the quick. He crept toward her, almost as if he were afraid of frightening her away. "Lainey," he said softly, turning her to face him, the nerve endings in his palms crying out in relief at the contact. "You…are a treasure, in so many ways. I am sorry that I hurt you badly enough to make you think—" He couldn't say it again. He squeezed her shoulders. "You must know that the problem lies with me, not you. I do not wish to marry."

"You don't wish to marry, or you don't wish to marry *me?*"

Gavin sighed, cupping her face. "Lainey…"

If you only knew.

"You are a beautiful, loving, brilliant woman, and you are worthy of so much more than I could ever give you. But do not think for one moment that I am not attracted to you."

Her eyes widened, her mouth parting slightly in surprise. Her chest rose and fell in short, quick breaths, and Gavin knew if he laid his hand over her heart, it would be thundering just as his was. Her eyes searched his in wonder.

"Gavin..." she whispered.

"We can't." But he swiped his thumb over her bottom lip, noting her sharp intake of breath. "You are my best friend's baby sister," he pointed out, more for his own benefit than hers. "You, my intoxicated little minx, are off limits to me."

"Then why are you still holding me?"

Gavin went still, suddenly aware of her soft skin under his hands. "Why, indeed?" he murmured. He gazed down at her, the firelight flickering over her heated face, beckoning him with its seductive dance.

No one will know, the devil in him said. This may be the only chance he would ever have to taste her, to hold her in his arms. This would lead to disaster, but damn if he cared right now. Before he could change his mind, he leaned down and pressed his lips gently to hers in the most chaste kiss he could muster. But even that sent blood roaring through his ears, and his body responded to her in a way that shot panic screaming through his veins. He pulled away abruptly. Kissing her even for a moment had been a mistake. He cleared his throat. "There. You've had your first kiss. Goodnight, Lainey."

He turned for the door, trying not to bolt like a frightened pony, but her quiet words stopped him short.

"That was hardly legendary," she muttered behind him.

"Pardon?" he asked over his shoulder.

Lainey chuffed a sigh. "That wasn't the toe-curling kiss I was expecting," she admitted.

He turned back to her. "Toe-curling? Lainey, who have you been talking to?" Gavin couldn't believe what he was hearing. "I'm quite sure I've never kissed any of your friends."

"Do you honestly think women only discuss fashion and society? We gossip about men too, you know. There are rumors, and we explore them. And I may have read that particular phrase in a novel," she added in a low voice, staring at the floor.

Gavin couldn't hold back a snort. "Lainey, if you are basing your expectations on gothic novels, we men are in serious trouble. I don't believe I've ever had such a kiss."

"Then what is the problem?" She tossed her hands in the air in exasperation. "It's just a simple kiss."

He closed the distance between them. "The problem is," he warned, "With you, it won't *be* a simple kiss." He searched her eyes, giving her ample time to change her mind, but all he could see was need. Words failed him. Logic failed him. Worst of all, his conscience failed him. "Ah, Christ, Lainey."

He yanked her against him, sealing his mouth over hers. She squeaked in surprise, but in the space of a heartbeat, she relaxed into his arms, and Gavin's world fell into place.

Lainey slid her hand up his chest and around his neck to tangle her fingers in the hair at his nape, and Gavin came unglued. A tidal wave of passion swamped him and he tightened his hold. She moaned against his mouth, the noise shooting straight to his groin, and all of a sudden, merely pressing his lips to hers was no longer enough. He teased her mouth open, slipping his tongue inside when she acquiesced. She stiffened at this new sensation, but boldly matched him once she realized what he wanted her to do. She tasted like the rich brandy she'd been drinking, and Gavin couldn't get enough. Sense completely deserted him as he backed her to the wall, pressing his body against hers, reveling in her soft-ness and heat. He rocked his hips into hers, her sounds of pleasure suffusing every fiber of his being. He dragged his palm over her hip, sliding higher, grazing the side of her breast on his way to caressing her neck. She groaned deep in her throat, and for one wild moment, Gavin thought about lifting her skirts and taking her right there in Aidan's study.

What in blazes was he doing? He was practically mauling Lainey. *Lainey!* Aidan's *sister*. He broke the kiss with a gasp, leaning his forehead against hers, his breath, like hers, coming in hard gulps. He slowly pulled himself away from her body, hoping she'd been distracted enough not to notice that he was hard as stone. His chest was heaving, his pulse galloping off into the sunset. He hadn't meant to kiss her quite so thoroughly—really, he hadn't meant to kiss her at all —but the moment their lips had met, all logical thought had deserted him.

The realization that he had wanted to kiss Lainey for years shook him…all the way down to his curled toes.

He slipped his hand from her neck and stepped back, needing to break this spell between them. A candlestick lay on the floor, knocked from the nearby table during his groping session. What the hell was wrong with him? "For…" He cleared the huskiness out of his throat. "Forgive me, that was…" *Divine? Earth-shattering? The most powerful moment of my life?* "Utterly inappropriate," he finished. *Brilliant, Gav.* "I'm sorry, I should not have lost control like that."

Lainey just stared up at him with a dazed expression on her face, her swollen lips slightly parted. *Yes,* he thought. *Me, too.*

"I hope that was…er…more…er, to your liking. Good-night, Lainey." He turned to go, but then thought better of it. Instead, he moved toward her, leaning forward to murmur into her ear. "Don't ever let me hear you call yourself undesirable again, Elaine Lockwood. I pity those men and their missed opportunities."

With that, he spun on his heel, trying desperately to not trip over his own feet as he practically fled the study. He made it as far as the stairs before his legs gave out beneath him, and he collapsed on the steps, heart still pounding. He slumped against the banister, trying to make sense of what just happened.

Holy hell.

What a bloody hash of things he'd made. Aidan was going to kill him.

If spending the remainder of the week under the same roof as Lainey without touching her again didn't kill him first.

CHAPTER 12

*L*ainey had barely slept all night after her encounter with Gavin, and it was a challenge to stay in the saddle. It was a spectacular day, the sky a deep cerulean blue, the sun shining brightly overhead as the party made its way to the meadow for a picnic. But inside, Lainey was a storm of emotions, all thanks to her drunken request for a kiss.

Lord in heaven, that kiss!

She'd dreamed of it for years, and it did not disappoint. She'd had no idea a kiss could be like *that*. No wonder women spoke of swooning and toe curls. However, she'd not been prepared for what kissing Gavin would awaken in her. She'd naively believed she'd be content with the one kiss, but now she could think of nothing else. Her skin prickled with the memory. Mercy, the way his arms had felt around her body, so powerful and safe, his lips warm on hers, his tongue tangling with—

"Yow!" Lainey jumped so high she nearly fell off her horse. She glared at Elizabeth. "Why are you poking me in the ribs with a stick?"

"Because you weren't paying the least bit of attention to me. Where is your head today?"

"On my shoulders, where it always is." Mmmm…how good it had felt to run her hands over Gavin's muscular shoulders.

"Pfft." Elizabeth eyed her friend. "Something has happened. Out with it."

"I don't know what you could possibly mean."

"Do not feign innocence with me, Lainey. You are a terrible liar. What happened last night? Oh! Did someone take liberties with you in a shadowy corner?" She squealed.

"For heaven's sake, keep your voice down, someone will hear," Lainey hissed. "No. No one took liberties." The man in question had been begged, after all. He was merely responding to an invitation.

"Balderdash. You are blushing."

Lainey groaned. Could it really be that obvious? Was she wearing a sign that said *"I kissed Gavin Mayfield"*? She would have to be better about hiding her emotions. And anyway, she was still processing the whole thing, she wasn't ready to share details, even with Eliza. "I'm blushing because you are embarrassing me. If you must know, I may have gotten a little drunk last night."

"Drunk?" Elizabeth studied her with momentary concern, then her face lit up. "Did *you* take liberties with someone in a shadowy corner?"

"Oh, for the love of—stop it! I just wanted to ease the stress of this party and the decision looming over me and I got a little carried away, that is all." That part was true, at least. Perhaps more than a little, she would admit.

The horses plodded along, their hooves rustling in the tall grass as Lainey returned to her wicked thoughts…which she didn't get to enjoy for long.

"It's not too late to change your mind, you know," Elizabeth said, eyeing her shrewdly.

Lainey closed her eyes on a sigh. "We've hashed this out to death, Eliza. It is what I want." She straightened in her saddle. "Oh look, we are here."

"Lucky for you," Elizabeth grumbled as she tossed her reins to a waiting groom.

GAVIN DID his best to studiously avoid Lainey, but his gaze kept wandering over to her. She was fetching in a floral sprigged ensemble and jaunty bonnet with yellow flowers perched upon her head. She was sitting on a blanket with Devereaux the Octopus. Honestly, the man invented more reasons to "accidentally" touch her than Gavin thought possible. Each graze made Gavin's blood notch another degree toward the boiling point. Each time Lainey avoided the man's grasp, Gavin wanted to pummel him for trying again. Good God, Gavin was more like his violent brother than he wanted to admit. He tamped down that urge as quickly as he could.

After a torturous hour had passed, he noticed some couples had wandered off to explore, and Lainey was nowhere in sight. Devereaux, at least, was still here and setting his sights on Anne Hastings. He moved over to where Aidan sat with his wife, adoringly playing with the stands of hair that has escaped her coiffure. He coughed to announce his presence when Aidan ignored him.

"Sorry to interrupt…have you seen where Lainey has gone off to?"

"She said she wanted a little time to herself to sort things out," Elizabeth replied. "She seems very distracted today." She pinned him with a hard stare. "Do you know anything about that?"

"Er…no. I've barely spoken to her all morning."

"Hm. I'm sure something happened last night but she won't confess."

"Is she well?"

"Physically, yes, she's fine. Perhaps a bit of a headache. She said she imbibed a little too much last night."

"Lainey?" His eyebrows shot to his hairline. He hoped he wasn't overdoing the fake surprise. "That's unlike her."

"So it is," Aidan agreed. "Perhaps you should go talk to her. I'd go but I'm very busy at the moment," he said, bopping his finger on his wife's nose. Gavin just stared in disbelief at the man his formerly serious best friend had become. A little pang of jealously zinged his heart. "She'll confess to you, not me," Aidan continued. "I would hazard a guess she's at her favorite spot." He grinned.

"Ah yes, The Pond." The infamous pond. It had been years since he'd been there. "Perhaps I will go find her. She probably shouldn't be out there alone and all."

"Mmmm," was all Aidan managed as he trailed his finger along Elizabeth's arm. Gavin practically sprinted toward his horse.

HE FOUND her on the bank of the pond, her bonnet dangling from her hand as she languidly strolled along the water's edge. He watched, riveted as she moved through the dappled sunlight, her hair a golden chestnut one minute and warm brown the next. He tied his horse with hers and set out to catch up with her.

"Penny for your thoughts?"

"Oh!" She whirled on him. "Gavin, you scared the life out of me! Don't sneak up on people like that!"

"I wasn't exactly quiet. You were just woolgathering. Elizabeth said you are out of sorts today. What's on your mind?"

Her chocolate brown eyes bored into his. He could see the moment she decided not to confide in him. "I just needed some time away from everyone to think."

"So, it's nothing to do with that kiss we shared last night?"

A flush stained her cheeks and she turned away. "No," she lied.

"Come off it, Lainey, it's me. This is exactly why I didn't want to kiss you. Now you've gone all balmy on me."

"I haven't gone—hey!"

He snatched the bonnet out of her hand and dangled it just out of her reach. "I'll give it back if you admit that kiss rattled you." God knew it had rattled *him*.

"Gavin, you nod cock, hand it over."

"You haven't called me a nod cock in years. I miss that."

"You are ridiculous." The corner of her mouth tried to tick up in a smile but she wouldn't let it.

"True. But if it makes you laugh, I'd be the village idiot." He'd taken the light out of her eyes two years ago. He wanted to put it back. He sighed. "Here, take your bonnet." He held it out for her and she glared at him. "Go on, take it."

She hesitated, then her hand shot out to make a grab for the hat, but Gavin was too fast for her and he yanked it back. "Gavin Mayfield, stop behaving like a child and give me my bonnet!"

"Oh, come now, Lainey. When was the last time I was able to tease you like this?" He waved the bonnet in front of her and she folded her arms across her chest, trying in vain to keep a straight face, but her mirth got the best of her.

"Quite some time, I should think," she said wryly. He danced the bonnet a little too close and she snatched at it. She got hold of it and the tug of war began. "Gavin," she said, using the tone of voice one uses on a child that is precariously close to being sent to bed without supper. Gavin just grinned and tugged a little harder. "Stop it," Lainey demanded, tugging back. He pretended to give, then just pulled back again. "Gavin!"

She finally laughed, which is what Gavin had been waiting for. "Oh, all right," he said, releasing the bonnet just as she gave a good yank. The sudden freedom caused Lainey's arm to fly backwards, and with it, the bonnet… which then flew from her hand, landing with a soft *plop* in the pond. They both froze, mouths open in a silent gasp. Lainey slowly turned murderous eyes on Gavin. He spread his hands.

"Oops," was all he could offer.

"That is my very favorite bonnet, Gavin."

"I'll buy you another."

"My. Favorite," she ground out. She stood looking like an Amazon warrior, arms akimbo, eyes blazing. She didn't really expect him to go in and get it, did she?

"It's probably ruined now anyway," he started.

"Gavin."

He sighed. "You want me to fetch it, I suppose?"

Her silence spoke volumes. Apparently, he was getting wet. Resigned to his fate, he mumbled, "If you insist, my lady," and bent to remove his shoes and roll up his pants to his knees. If he was lucky the pond was shallow at the edge. He waded in, careful to disturb the water as little as possible. He couldn't quite lean forward enough to where the bonnet floated just out of reach without losing his balance. He was already up to his knees and he desperately didn't want to get his pants soaked. "A little help here, Lainey?"

"And what do you expect *me* to do?"

"I need a counter weight. Hold my hand, please."

"This does not sound like a good idea."

"Would you just hold my hand? I can reach it if I have

something to hold on to." She huffed out a breath and grudgingly moved to the edge of the bank after removing her shoes and stockings so as not to ruin them on the spongy ground. She gathered up her skirts to keep them out of the mud, tucked them up in one hand, and reached the other out to Gavin. He grasped it and leaned forward. "Lean back toward the bank, Lainey. That's it. Almost got it…" He barely managed to get his fingers around the bonnet, but he seized it triumphantly. "Ha!"

But in his excitement, he moved a little too fast, tugging Lainey off balance, and he tipped backwards. He pivoted and threw the bonnet toward the shore before he plunged into the water. The last thing he heard before he went under was a feminine shriek. He got his feet under him and surfaced to find Lainey on her hands and knees, feet still on the bank, chest deep in water, her face splattered with mud. She was coughing, and Gavin lunged to get her out of the water. Her sodden skirts and the fact that her hands were stuck in the mud made the rescue a struggle, but he finally got her out and they both collapsed on the bank, gasping for breath. He didn't dare look at her. Feeling the anger rolling of off her was enough. They lay on their backs in silence for a minute or two, catching their breath. Lainey finally spoke, low and ominous.

"Give me one reason I shouldn't drown you in that pond right now."

Truly, Gavin didn't have one, but he spied her bonnet laying safely on dry land. "I saved your favorite bonnet?" he said hopefully.

She closed her eyes, as if gathering the strength to continue. Or perhaps she was plotting the various ways in which to murder him. He rolled up on his elbow and looked down into her face. It was covered in freckles of mud. "Ah, you have a little…" Gavin made an ineffectual gesture that encompassed her face, and she glared at him. She reached up to swipe at her face, but only succeeded in smearing more mud. Gavin stared at her, caught between remorse at her current state, and laughter at…well, her current state. The bubble of laughter won.

"Gavin Mayfield, you horse's ass, are you *laughing* at me?"

"I'm sorry, it's just that…oh God, Lainey, I'm so sorry. Really, I am. But you are rather a mess. Here, let me," he said, reaching into his pocket for his wet handkerchief. A tendril of hair was plastered to the side of her face, and he tenderly removed it. His fingertips tingled where they brushed her skin, and he thought he saw her suck in a breath. He slowly began to wipe the mud from her face, and she watched him as he dabbed the cloth over her skin, her gaze unwavering.

Gavin's heart was ready to pound out of his chest, and his skin felt too tight for his body. The gentle swipes became more and more sensual with each pass. Was he mad? He should never have kissed her last night. Then maybe he wouldn't be wanting to feel her soft lips on his again, or be so desperate to run his hands up her bare legs. Both were things he couldn't want.

"There," he said softly, smiling at her. "Perfection." He noticed one small speck left by the corner of her mouth, and without even thinking, ran his thumb over the spot to brush it away. She did gasp then, and Gavin froze. He could see the pulse jumping at the base of her throat, her pupils dilating with desire. He stared down at her, his honor at war with his need to kiss her again. His fingers traced her jaw, dancing over her rose petal skin. He leaned toward her, then stopped, knowing he was playing a dangerous game.

"Gavin," she whispered. Her fingers curled into his lapel.

He shook his head. "There are a hundred reasons we shouldn't do this," he said softly.

"Name one."

He was silent, studying her face, his hand still hovering at the corner of her mouth. And he realized that he wanted to kiss her more than he wanted to breathe. "I can't." And he leaned down and sealed his mouth over hers.

Bliss.

He palmed her jaw, sending his fingers sliding across the skin under her ear. She made a little noise in her throat that melted any resolve he had left, and he kissed her deeply, tasting her offered mouth, delighting in her tongue caressing his. He groaned, savoring the way she responded to him, passionate and sweet, as though she were made only for him. He caressed her neck, tangling his fingers in her damp hair, and just kept on kissing her like it was what he was born to do.

Lainey brought her hands up and pressed them against his chest, exploring the muscles there, sliding her hands under his sodden coat. She slipped them around his back and pulled him closer, and he let some of his weight fall against her, pinning her to the ground.

"Mmmmm," was all she said. Gavin knew exactly how she felt. Having Lainey in his arms just seemed so…right.

The cut of her gown left an enticing triangle of bare skin at her throat, and he couldn't help himself. He trailed kisses down her neck, following the line of her bodice until his lips reached the hollow of her breasts. She gave a languid sigh and threaded her fingers through his dripping hair. Gavin dipped his tongue into that little valley and she gasped, arching toward him. Good God, she was going to be his undoing.

He tore himself away from her creamy skin and rested his head against her chest, knowing in his heart that he must put a stop to this, but wanting to find a way forward anyhow. Impossible.

"Gavin?"

The soft question in her voice tore at his heart. Shame on him. He knew better than to treat her like this. He needed to be in better control of his urges...but Lord help him, his control just evaporated around her. He dropped one last kiss at the base of her throat and sat up. "Lainey, we can't do this. You know we can't."

"But why? What is wrong with enjoying a kiss or two?"

"Because it leads to other things."

"It doesn't have to."

"Lainey." Gavin chuckled. "I'm afraid that with you, I lack the power to remain a gentleman. Kissing you like this will most definitely lead to other things." He helped her to a sitting position. "Come. We should get out of these wet clothes." Which was precisely what he wanted to do at this very moment, but alas. He retrieved her stockings and shoes for her and deposited them in the grass beside her before settling down to don his own. He froze when she raised her skirts to her knee.

"Would you help me put them on?" She indicated the stockings that lay next to her.

Panic gripped his lungs like a vise. "Er...what?"

"It's one thing to remove them, but I can't bend over far enough in this corset to get anything on my feet. Plus, my hands are dirty and I would like to spare at least one piece of my outfit from total destruction. I'm afraid I rather made a mess of your shirt."

He glanced down to see that she had, indeed, smeared mud all over his shirt. He hastily rubbed at anything that resembled a handprint. That wouldn't do at all.

"Gavin?" She held a gossamer stocking in between her thumb and forefinger, eyebrows raised.

Bloody hell.

He could do this. He'd survived a bullet wound inflicted

by his own brother. He could put stockings on Lainey's legs. Her shapely, alabaster—

Damn it, man, get a hold of yourself.

"Ah…"

"Gavin, you have seen my legs before."

"Yes, but you were a child then."

"They are just legs, Gavin."

How could he explain to her that the mere sight of her calves was causing an uncomfortable tightening in his trousers without sounding like a lecher? Better to just be methodical and quick in his assistance. He shrugged his paralyzation off and reached for the stocking, picturing every unattractive thing he could think of before he slipped it on her foot.

Gangrene.

Hairy warts.

Kicking puppies.

It didn't help. Putting a silk stocking on Lainey had to be the most erotic thing he'd ever done. His fingers brushed her leg as he slid the stocking up to her knee, and goosebumps broke out across her skin, proof that his touch affected her. He knew he shouldn't, but he curled his fingers around the back of her knee, just to revel in the softness for a moment. What would it be like to press a kiss there? He ached to find out. His thumb brushed the inside of her thigh as he settled the stocking over her knee, and she closed her eyes and let her head fall back. He traced small circles with his thumb, mimicking the motion he desperately wanted to employ somewhere else. He'd never been so glad that women wore so many layers, because if her heavy petticoats and drawers weren't halting his progress up her thighs, who knows where his hands would have landed.

As it was, Gavin reluctantly withdrew his hand and helped her with her other stocking. When she'd replaced the garters, he slipped on her shoes, put his own on, and helped her to stand. He stepped back, eyeing her from head to toe. Mud stained her dress up to her knees, and up to her elbows, the front of her dress was soaked through, and her hair was in disarray.

"Lainey, you are a right disaster." He sheepishly plunked her bonnet on her ruined coiffure, and she rolled her eyes. "Sorry about all this." He tied the bow beneath her chin.

"Someday, Gavin Mayfield, I will get you back. Mark my words."

"I have no doubt." They walked back to the horses, his wet clothes chafing him the entire way. The ride back was not going to be pleasant. He put his hands on her waist, intending to lift her onto the horse, but they stood immobile instead, her hands on his shoulders, gazing into each other's eyes. Her mouth parted slightly, and Gavin's gaze dropped to her lips. He cleared his throat. "Just…just a minute."

He crushed her to him in a searing embrace, wrapping his arms around her like a drowning man. She melted against him, matching his tongue thrust for thrust, and white-hot sparks exploded behind his eyelids. He'd kissed plenty of women before, but this…*she*…was extraordinary. He didn't know how he was going to live without ever kissing her again.

He set her away from him, both of them panting. "I'm sorry, I shouldn't have done that."

"I'm not."

"Lainey, don't say that."

"Why not? I like kissing you. And I rather think you like kissing me."

There was an understatement if he ever heard one. "That is not the point. You are here to find a husband, and since I am not a potential one, I shouldn't be pawing at you."

"Pawing?" Her eyes danced.

"You know what I mean. We have to go back to being just friends, Lainey."

"And why is that? Why are you so against marriage?"

"I'm not against marriage. Not for other people," he grinned, tipping his head toward the horse. She jumped, and he lifted her easily into the saddle.

"This conversation is not over, Gavin," she said from atop the horse. "If you and I are such good friends, you should be able to tell me the truth."

He nodded. "I should. But I can't."

"No, you just won't." She spurred her horse into action and took off at a canter, leaving him to scramble in her wake. She was angry, and rightly so. But telling her would serve no purpose other than to embarrass him and his family. It wouldn't change things between them, and he preferred to just let it be.

They reluctantly returned to the picnic, where there would be hell to pay because honestly, it really did appear as though they had been indulging in completely inappropriate behavior. Which they had been, but no one need know that. Gavin did not want to destroy Lainey's chances of finding a decent husband.

Sure enough, when they entered the clearing, several ladies gasped, and all eyes turned to them as the party fell silent.

Until Aidan thundered, "What in blazes have you done to my sister?"

CHAPTER 13

"*A*hhh…"

Gavin's power of speech apparently deserted him, so Lainey explained. "The wind took my bonnet into the pond and Mr. Mayfield tried to rescue it for me. Only the rescue mission didn't quite go as planned, as you can see."

"I would say not," the viscount observed dryly.

"Looks more like Mayfield should have been rescuing you instead," Donovan said with a chuckle.

"Well, he did. Sort of. This is all rather embarrassing…"

"Indeed," Aidan said, narrowing his eyes at his sister. "It is time to return to the house anyway. I suspect you'll want to change?"

Lainey rolled her eyes at the earl the way only a sister could. "How very astute."

"I'll help you, Lainey," Elizabeth said, rising from the blanket and giving her husband a speaking look. "We'll ride on ahead. I trust you can gather the guests?"

Aidan nodded, moving his eyes from Lainey to Gavin and back again. Elizabeth retrieved her horse and the ladies moved off in the direction of the house. Gavin lifted a hand and indicated the ladies.

"I'll just go with—"

"You will stay and help gather everyone into the carriages," Aidan commanded. "I would like a word with you."

Gavin's throat constricted. This wasn't going to be good.

ONCE IN LAINEY'S ROOM, Elizabeth rang for Meg and helped Lainey out of her wet clothes while they waited. The horrified maid pulled a fresh outfit out of the closet and gathered up the muddy things before they could dirty anything in the room, leaving Elizabeth to help Lainey dress.

"All right, out with it," she demanded as she tightened Lainey's dry corset. "What were you two up to at the pond?"

"I told you. It was a rescue mission gone awry."

"Balderdash," Elizabeth stated. "There is something happening between the two of you, I can see it." She hooked Lainey's skirt. "He kissed you, didn't he?"

Lainey froze. Was it that obvious?

"I'll take your silence as an affirmative answer."

Lainey spun toward Elizabeth. "You mustn't tell anyone!"

"I knew it!" Elizabeth clapped her hands together. "Lainey, that's wonderful!"

Lainey snorted as she stuffed her arms into her sleeves. "Not as wonderful as you may think."

"He's a bad kisser?"

Lainey laughed out loud. "Heavens no! He's...accomplished in that department." She bent her head to do up the hooks and eyes, and to hide her furious blush.

"Then what is the issue?"

"He doesn't want to marry. Ever."

"Well, we will just have to change his mind."

Lainey regarded her friend for a moment, the awful truth of the matter on her tongue. She turned with a sigh and sank down at the vanity, removing the pins from her disheveled hair.

"Oh my," Elizabeth breathed. "You are in love with him." She came up behind Lainey and rested her hands on her shoulders when she didn't reply. She caught Lainey's gaze in the mirror. "It was him, wasn't it? He's the one who broke your heart, and you are falling for him all over again."

Tears pricked Lainey's eyes. She hated herself for being such a silly goose over someone who clearly did not return her feelings. Desire was different from love.

"I've spent two years trying to get over him," Lainey admitted. "I thought I had. I thought I was finally successful in walling off that part of my heart. I was ready to move on and make a marriage with someone else and be my own person, and then he came here—because I demanded it—and…and then he kissed me, once again because I demanded it, and all those stupid old feelings came roaring back to the surface and I don't know what to do with them because obviously nothing has changed in his mind. And he thinks he's so clever, but I know that blasted man bought me a blasted kitten and he did it just because it made me smile. Honestly, who *does* that?"" She ran out of breath and fell silent, swiping viciously at a tear that escaped down her cheek. "Oh, I am so stupid! He didn't want me then, and he doesn't want me now. Why can I not get that through my head?"

"Love makes fools of us all, Lainey. But…why did he kiss you if he doesn't have an interest in you?"

"Because I asked him to." Lainey buried her face in her hands, groaning. "Oh, my humiliation is complete, Eliza. I am so undesirable that I actually had to beg a man to kiss me!"

"Elaine Lockwood, that is simply not true!" She dragged a chair over and sat facing Lainey. "You are not telling me everything. Start talking fast before Meg comes back to fix your hair."

Lainey sighed. "I overheard Mr. Devereaux talking to some of the other gentlemen about me the other night. He complained that I might be too prim and proper for him… was worried I might not be adventurous enough for the type of bedsport he enjoys, whatever that means. He even bet them twenty pounds that I had never been kissed!"

"The cad!"

"It was mortifying to hear myself discussed in such a manner, but I don't blame him. Such things are important to men, and I have no wish to make an unhappy match, either."

"Such things are important to women too, you know," Elizabeth grumbled. "I used to think like you, too. As long as the man was happy, what did it matter if I enjoyed myself? Well, that's just rubbish! And how arrogant of him! Who's to say he knows what he's doing enough to satisfy *you*?"

Heat infused Lainey's face. "Well anyway, I was so humiliated I went to Aidan's study and got drunk."

"Lainey!"

"If you wish to hear the rest of the story you will not judge me, Eliza."

"Sorry, do go on."

"Well, Gavin came home from his evening of cards and found me there, and I thought, why not? A girl my age should have indulged in a harmless kiss or two long ago. Gavin is a lifelong friend who I trust…and I've heard rumors that he does, in fact, know what he's doing as far as that's concerned." She giggled. "So, I asked him to kiss me." She paused.

"And?"

"And he did, after I practically begged him."

"And?"

"Well, for heaven's sake, you don't need to know all the details, do you?"

"Yes!"

Lainey huffed out a breath. "It shook me to my core. And I knew then that I was not over him in the least. And then today—"

She broke off and Elizabeth's eyes grew round. "What happened today? Because it honestly looked as though the two of you were rolling around in the mud."

Lainey sheepishly pulled the last pin from her hair and Elizabeth began to detangle it for her. "You're not far off, though I told the truth about my bonnet...except that Gavin was the one who caused it to fly into the pond because he was teasing me. I tried to help him retrieve it and we both fell in. But when we were lying there on the grass after...I don't know what happened, we just wound up in each other's arms. Now that we've touched each other once, it's as though we can't stop."

"But that's wonderful!"

"No, it's not!" Lainey wailed. "I am in hell! What good is desiring a man who does not want you?"

"Oh, he wants you," Elizabeth said sagely.

"I don't mean physically. I mean for good. He just keeps telling me he can't marry me but he won't say why."

"Well...we will have to figure out what he's hiding and make him see the light."

"No," Lainey said firmly. "No, we will not. If he hasn't changed his mind in two years, he's not going to change it. I am not going to beg or force him. I need to stick with my plan and that's all there is to it. I can make a happy life with someone else."

Elizabeth eyed her dubiously. "If you say so. But I really think—"

"I mean it, Elizabeth. I can't torture myself any longer. I have to move on with my life and forget all this business with Gavin ever even happened."

"And how do you plan to do that?"

"I have absolutely no idea." The door opened and Meg returned. In a matter of minutes, she had Lainey's hair done in a simple knot, not at all fashionable but Lainey didn't want to fuss. Once she was presentable, they made their way downstairs.

"What do you think of the viscount, Eliza? I rather like him," Lainey noted.

"He seems a lovely man indeed. But he's quite a bit older than you."

"That doesn't really matter to me. As long as his character is sound and he treats me well, that is all I require. He's very easy to talk to. I like that."

"And what of Mr. Devereaux? He is obviously quite taken with you. Are you giving him any further consideration after what he said about you?"

"Ah, Mr. Devereaux. It was in rather poor taste to discuss me the way he did…but I can't really blame him for stating the obvious, can I? I *am* prim and proper. Perhaps too much so."

"Do not judge yourself on one person's perception."

"The trouble is, I don't think it is one person's perception. I've spent my life trying to be a paragon of good character. Perhaps I've taken that a little too much to heart."

"A paragon of good character wouldn't get drunk and ask a man to kiss her," Elizabeth teased.

"Oh, hush!" Lainey admonished. "My one slip and you have to give me grief about it." But she laughed in spite of herself.

"Perhaps you ought to do things like that more often. Have a little fun! Show Mr. Devereaux your adventurous side. Besides, I think Mr. Devereaux makes Gavin insanely jealous."

"Now, Eliza, none of your matchmaking interference, please. We agreed, I have to stick to my plan."

"I agreed to nothing," Elizabeth pointed out. "Regardless, I think it is time to let loose and show off your true personality, the one you show me every day. You sparkle, Lainey. A pox on anyone who makes you feel like you don't."

"I don't know, Eliza. It's one thing to say I need to l liven up, but to actually do it? I've shown one face to the world for so long...won't people judge me?"

"Do you want to find a husband who makes your heart sing?"

Lainey was quiet. The organs that sang when Gavin touched her had little to do with her heart. "Truthfully, I just want someone who cares for me as much as I do him, and accepts me for who I am."

"Then you'd better start showing your true self, or you are going to be stuck with someone who expects you to be prim and proper for the rest of your life."

"But Gavin knows that side of me and look how well that turned out."

Elizabeth pulled her to a stop. "Lainey. Trust me when I say that I don't believe the problem lies with you. There is a reason Gavin is not offering for you, but it's not because you are flawed in any way."

Easy for her to say. Lainey was so pathetic, her friend felt sorry for her after Gavin tore her heart out and offered to marry her. And then even *he* couldn't go through with it.

Then again, perhaps she'd gotten it wrong all this time. She'd seen how giggling girls attracted attention during social events...she'd always thought them insipid and silly. But she was willing to bet those girls had their first kiss before the age of twenty-four.

"All right. I will try." They resumed their path. "I do not want a husband who is distant and staid."

"That would never do for you. So, let's see if we can open our gentleman's eyes to the wonder that is Lainey Lockwood, shall we?"

"I rather think you are laying it on a bit thick, Eliza."

"And *I* rather think I am telling the truth. Come along, they will be back soon. I hope you are ready to be peppered with questions!"

WITH EVERY SHIFT of the horse's gait, Gavin chafed. He absolutely deserved any discomfort he was feeling. God, he'd had his hands all over Lainey like she was a common trollop. What the hell was wrong with him? They'd been friends for most of his life and he'd always managed to keep his hands to himself. It was that damn kiss in Aidan's study. He never should have allowed it. One ill-advised kiss had brought everything he'd suppressed for all those years roaring to life.

God help him, he wanted Lainey. If only he—

"Gav, may I ask you something?"

Gavin started. He hadn't even heard Aidan pull up beside him. "Of course," he replied, eyeing Aidan warily.

"Is there something going on between you and my sister?"

Bollocks. "What makes you say that?"

"The two of you just seem...at odds with one another. Have you been quarreling about something? She didn't push you in the pond again, did she?"

Gavin laughed. "Thank you for bringing that up. No, it happened as she said."

"Then what is going on? Is it this whole sudden marriage thing? Are you upset because she's going to marry someone else?"

Gavin snapped his head toward Aidan. "Someone *else*?"

Aidan shrugged. "I just thought…look, I know I was loaded up on laudanum last June when I suggested you marry her, but there may have been some truth in that request. The three of us have been inseparable for most of our lives. I suppose I'd always thought you'd offer for her."

Gavin groaned. "Not you, too!"

Aidan tossed him a cocky grin. "Not the first person to suggest this?"

"Not by far."

"Sorry. It's just that when Lainey got engaged you seemed so…withdrawn. Don't think I didn't notice that you two stopped speaking to each other for a while. I thought maybe it was because you were disappointed and hoping to win her for yourself. But when her engagement was broken and you didn't offer for her then, I pushed that thought aside. Now another engagement looms and I see you behaving oddly again, and I have to wonder if I may have been right? And if so, what is holding you back?"

"Absolutely nothing." *Liar.*

"Because if our friendship is preventing you from offering for her, I just wanted to make sure you know that I would be happy to have you as a brother-in-law. I know you would take care of her."

No, no, no! Do NOT give me your blessing! Gavin turned toward Aidan and held his gaze. "Aidan. I love Lainey, I do. I love you both. But Lainey and I are just friends. I don't think of her in that way." *How many times did he need to say that in order to convince himself it was true?* "I do not wish to marry anyone, let alone your lovely sister. You know my family history, Aidan. How could I subject anyone to that?"

Aidan allowed the horse to plod along in silence for a few moments. "I know that is a heavy burden for you to bear, Gav. But don't let it rule your life."

"Easier said than done."

"I know. But you deserve happiness, too."

Gavin grunted. "Marriage has made you soft, Ashby," he tossed over his shoulder.

Aidan laughed, the rich baritone getting under Gavin's skin and forcing a smile. "Trotting out the title, eh?" Aidan replied. "You only do that when you are actually trying to insult me. I do believe I'm hurt." He put his hand to his heart in mock offense.

Gavin chuckled, his discomfort momentarily forgotten. "Sod off, my lord," he said with a grin. Aidan barked a laugh and the two fell into companionable silence.

Gavin's thoughts soon turned to Lainey. Aidan had unknowingly just stripped away one excuse to not marry her. If only the other were so easily resolved. He couldn't help but wonder what it would be like to call his best friend his brother in truth and be swallowed into a family with only love to share instead of secrets.

CHAPTER 14

Lainey had awoken to yet another sunny day, perfect for the afternoon tea that she'd planned for where the archery targets had been set up outside. Her choice had been twofold: the men needed some entertainment, and archery was the perfect opportunity for the ladies to get close to the man of her choice by learning—or pretending to learn—archery from the men.

Lainey needed no instruction, but Devereaux was her target. HIs comment from the other night still stung. He'd only let his mouth run because he'd been drinking, but it was mortifying all the same. Today, she was going to show him a different side of her.

If she could stop thinking about kissing Gavin. Really, it was most inconvenient. Her body responded to him the moment he walked into the room, despite her telling it to behave itself. Even now, she couldn't stop stealing glances at him, seated with Aidan and Elizabeth…and glowering at Devereaux. Well. This should be an interesting afternoon.

"Lainey, this has been a splendid house party," Anne said

from beside her, pouring another cup of tea. "I daresay you will have a proposal by week's end."

"You may be right," Lainey acknowledged, a note of resignation in her voice. "That was the point, wasn't it?"

"Are you having second thoughts?" Anne eyed her skeptically.

Lainey glanced at Gavin, who had gotten up and was heading in their direction. "No, not at all."

"So, who is your top choice?" Lydia asked. "Swoon-worthy Mr. Devereaux? He is a dream!"

"Oh, every man is dreamy to you, Lydia!" Anne laughed.

"Well…she's not wrong, Anne!"

"Ha! See? She agrees. It would not be a hardship waking up next to *that* face every morning!" Lydia exclaimed.

"Even after you've been flat on your back staring up into it all night!"

"Anne!" Lainey gasped. The three of them dissolved into giggles.

Lainey wiped her eyes. "I suppose you do have a point."

"Think of the beautiful children you would have with him," Lydia said wistfully. "His blue eyes and those curls with your honeyed hair…positively angelic."

"They would be gorgeous children," Anne agreed. "Oh Lainey, I cannot wait to become an honorary auntie!"

"And I cannot wait to hold a babe in my arms! Oh, how I have longed to be a mother. It would be wonderful if Aidan and Elizabeth have children at the same time. It's been just Aidan and I for so long, it would be lovely to fill the house with a passel of cousins!"

"Then I think Devereaux would be your best choice. He looks like just the man for the job." Anne winked at her and they broke into laughter once again.

Lainey let her gaze wander to the man in question. Decision made, she rose. "I do believe it's time to get an archery lesson from Mr. Devereaux."

"A lesson? But you—"

"He doesn't need to know that. I promised Eliza I would be bold today, and so I shall. I think he is just the man to test my wiles on." She set off in the direction of the winsome bachelor, leaving Anne and Lydia to stare after her.

Anne grinned. "Bravo, my dear. Bravo."

LAINEY'S WORDS carried to Gavin on the breeze. *I cannot wait to hold a babe in my arms.* He froze in mid reach for a lemonade. *Oh, how I have longed to be a mother.* Gavin's heart sank. It was one thing to know that was her fondest desire, but to hear the words expressed so wistfully was a punch in the gut.

Gavin did not want children. How could he ever consider taking that away from her? He would be the world's most selfish man to even ask it of her. Just yesterday he'd thought there might be a way…

But no. Even if she agreed, it would always be a wedge between them, an invisible wall that would be built ever higher, year after year, until the resentment became a festering wound. He couldn't stomach the possibility.

He sighed, taking a sip of his lemonade and turning resolutely away, the seeds of hope scattering to the wind.

GAVIN WAS SYSTEMATICALLY REDUCING his scone to crumbs as he watched Devereux slip his arms around Lainey under the pretense of showing her how to properly hold a bow. "Idiot," he grumbled.

"What's that, Gav?" Aidan said, tearing his eyes from his

wife. He regarded the decimated snack on Gavin's plate. "I say, haven't you tortured that scone enough? Now you are just being cruel."

"Devereaux." He dusted his hands. "Lainey is the county champion. She could probably show *him* a trick or two. How can you just sit here while he paws your sister like that?"

"Because something tells me she's enjoying it." He grinned. "Relax, Gav. I'm watching her carefully. Anyone behaving inappropriately with my sister will get their arse kicked all the way back to London."

"Oh hush," Elizabeth scolded her husband as he kissed her hand. "Lainey is having a good time being fawned over like that."

Just then, the lilting sound of Lainey's laughter drifted over on the breeze. Gavin couldn't take it anymore. He left his pile of crumbs and stalked over to the flock of men surrounding Lainey. No one even noticed him approach.

"I see," Lainey was saying. "So, if I grip it like this, I can hold it steadier?"

Gavin nearly choked at the erotic image that flashed through his mind.

Devereaux closed his hand over hers, helping her aim. "Precisely. Now just let the arrow fly." She did, and hit a bullseye.

"Well! Would you look at that?" She gave Devereaux a brilliant smile.

"See? Just a few refinements and your game will improve."

Gavin couldn't hold back a snort. Lainey turned toward him, eyes narrowed in warning. He grimaced and looked away. Lainey picked up another arrow, nocked it, and let it fly. It whizzed through the air and landed with a thunk in the target—barely.

"Oh, poo! I must not have held it right that time. Could you show me again, Mr. Devereaux?"

"With pleasure," he replied, wrapping his arms about Lainey once again.

"Oh, for the love of Pete," Gavin ground out. "Devereaux, she can outshoot you with her eyes closed."

"Gavin!" Lainey admonished him, thrusting her hands on her hips.

"Sorry, Lainey, but I think there's been enough fondling for today."

"*Mr. Mayfield!*" Lainey was horrified, and Gavin knew he'd pay for it later. He didn't care. If Devereaux put his hands on Lainey one more time, Gavin was going to pummel him and then she would *really* be cross.

"I do believe someone is jealous," Devereaux drawled, winking at Lainey. He turned to Gavin. "I'm a crack shot with a bow, Mayfield. I haven't been outshot in years. And certainly never by a woman."

Lainey's head swung slowly in Devereaux's direction and Gavin nearly chortled with glee. Oh, Devereaux was going to get it now. Lainey's indignation was palpable.

"I beg your pardon, Mr. Devereaux. Do you think you can't be bested by a woman?"

His confident smile faltered as he took in the fury snapping in her eyes. "Er…that is…well, I suppose it's possible, but…"

"But what, Mr. Devereaux?" Lainey folded her arms across her chest and raised an eyebrow in challenge. "Would you care to make a bet?"

"Oh, I don't think that's necessary," he said quickly.

"Come now, Devereaux," Gavin chimed in. "The lady is issuing a challenge. Surely a gentleman would not turn her down. Unless you are afraid she's going to beat you."

A chuckle ran through the crowd of men surrounding them. Gavin smirked, resisting the temptation to rub his hands together in glee. Devereaux was trapped, and Lainey was going to positively trounce him.

"Surely, we don't need a contest, Lady Elaine. We were having so much fun just shooting." He glared at Gavin, who blithely smiled in return.

"Oh, I think a contest will be great fun! What say you all?" She glanced around at the men surrounding her, who nodded, clapped, and cheered in agreement. They could smell blood in the water. Taking a fellow suitor down a peg was always great fun. Lainey yanked three arrows out of the quiver and thrust them toward Devereaux. "Three bullseyes in a row."

Devereaux paused, seeming to weigh his odds. He grudgingly relieved Lainey of the arrows. "Very well, my lady. I must warn you, however, that is not much of a challenge."

The corner of Lainey's mouth quirked up in a sardonic smile. "With your eyes closed."

A chorus of "oos," "ohs," and laughter rose up around them, the men nudging each other in the ribs. Gavin watched as Devereaux puffed up his chest. Stupid bastard actually thought he was going to win.

"Well now, that is certainly a bit more of a challenge. But I think I am up to the task. The question is, my lady, are you? I wouldn't want to embarrass you in front of potential suitors."

"Oh, I wouldn't want that either, Mr. Devereaux." She took up three arrows from her quiver. "But I am a fast learner, and you gave me some good tips today. I will accept the risk."

"Well, then. Since this is to be a contest, there must be a forfeit, must there not?"

"I agree. Hmmm…if I win, you must include me on your morning ride tomorrow, or whichever time the weather cooperates. I haven't enjoyed a good gallop across the fields since we arrived."

"Lainey," Gavin started. "That's not—"

Lainey smacked her arrows across Gavin's chest, silencing him.

"And if I win…" Devereaux paused dramatically. "I get to claim the first dance with you at the ball."

Lainey nodded. "Done." She picked up her bow. "You'll also get bragging rights for defeating the county champion."

"The what now?"

She saluted him with her bow. "Six years running. Good luck!" she said breezily, assuming her spot on the field. Devereaux just stood there with his mouth hanging open, the men guffawing around him. He shook his head and grinned. Elaine Lockwood was a force to be reckoned with. The crowd elbowed and jostled their way over to the staging area.

"Rules are," Lainey said when Devereaux took his spot. "Take aim, close your eyes, and count to three before you shoot. Anywhere in the center circle counts. Simple. But it's harder than it sounds."

"I shall endeavor not to disappoint."

She smiled at him—a genuine smile. She was enjoying this. "Since I issued the challenge, you may go first."

"If you insist." He nocked an arrow, took careful aim, closed his eyes, and counted to three. He let the arrow fly, and it whizzed through the air, landing in the yellow center of the target. The crowd cheered and he laughed. The commotion drew the rest of the partiers over to see what was going on.

Next it was Lainey's turn. She followed the same procedure, only her arrow barely made it into the yellow circle. The crowd sucked in a collective breath and there were rumblings of disappointment. When she turned in Gavin's direction to pick up her next arrow, he caught the tiny smile on her lips. She'd done it on purpose, little minx. She was completely toying with Devereaux. God, he loved her.

Gavin froze.

Did he? Well, of course he did. Like a sister. He'd known her forever; she was a permanent fixture in his life. Of course he loved her. He'd said as much to Aidan yesterday.

But...he wouldn't kiss a sister the way he'd kissed her the other night.

Or maul her on the bank of a pond.

He mentally shook himself. Love her or not, it didn't matter. He couldn't have her. HIs blood absolutely boiled whenever someone put their hands on her, particularly Devereaux. He'd envisioned planting him a facer more than once this week, barely able to hold back, for no other reason than that he was touching her. If something so small made Gavin so angry, he couldn't imagine how he'd react if someone actually hurt her. Up until this week, he'd been able to keep a leash on his temper, but here he seemed to be struggling, and that only reinforced his fears he was going to follow in the footsteps of other men in his family. He would not put her through that. So, it didn't matter if he loved her or not.

Which was a good thing, because he was rather certain he *did*.

A roar from the crowd pulled him from his reverie, and he realized he'd missed half the contest. Devereaux had just landed his third arrow dead center in the target, having missed the second shot, and the crowd was whipped into a frenzy. He was grinning from ear to ear, shaking hands with a nearby spectator. Lainey was laughing, her eyes bright, cheeks tinged with pink. Her enjoyment was written all over her face. How long had it been since Lainey had been the center of attention? As long as he'd known her, she'd been the proper, respectable lady whom everyone adored for her kindness. But had she ever really had *fun*? Gavin suddenly wasn't so sure. Perhaps he didn't know her as well as he thought he did. He'd certainly never seen her quite like this. It was something to behold.

Devereaux quieted the crowd down as Lainey nocked her last arrow. Gavin held his breath along with everyone else. Lainey seemed to be taking an inordinate amount of time aiming. A slight breeze ruffled a curl by her face, making it dance. She waited for the breeze to pass, then closed her eyes and began to count. At the last moment, she shifted her arm and let the arrow fly. It was so quiet the whisper of the sailing arrow could be heard...until it landed with a loud *thunk!* in the center of the target.

Of Devereaux's target, that is. The crowd erupted with cheers and applause. The women hugged each other and bounced up and down, the men slapped each other on their backs, and Devereaux let his head drop in defeat. Gavin raced toward Lainey and picked her up and spun her around, laughing. She squealed gleefully as she held onto his shoulders for dear life. He stopped and let her down, and she smiled up at him with a face that positively shone with pride.

"That was magnificent, Lainey," Gavin said, a little out of breath from his exuberance.

"It was rather, wasn't it?" She giggled.

"*You* are magnificent," he said softly. She looked up at him, and her grin faded a little as her eyes dropped to his mouth. She fluttered her lashes back up and locked her gaze with his. Damn if he didn't want to kiss her, right here in front of everyone. And he knew she would welcome it, too.

He was dimly aware that he still had his hands on her waist, and hers were still on his shoulders. He stepped back quickly as Devereaux approached.

"My lady." Devereaux executed a grand, sweeping bow. "I concede the contest to you," he said, loud enough for all to hear. "I have indeed been bested by a woman. And I must say, *that—*" He pointed to the target. "Was a bloody *brilliant* shot."

He kissed her hand and the crowd went wild. Laughter bubbled out of her.

"Mr. Devereaux, so happy am I to hear those words from you that I will ignore your use of profanity!" She grinned. "Even if it *was* bloody brilliant!"

Devereaux gave a bark a laughter. "Lady Elaine, I thank you for the most fun I've had in quite some time, even if it was at my expense. May I get you a glass of lemonade?"

"That would be lovely, thank you."

Devereaux wandered off in search of the beverage, and suddenly Lainey was surrounded by well-wishers. Gavin winked at her and withdrew to let her have her moment with her friends.

"She is quite something, isn't she?" Elizabeth had appeared at his side, and she looped her arm through his.

"I would have to agree," Gavin replied, watching the woman in question accept congratulations from her admirers.

"It's going to be hard to let her go when she chooses someone to marry," Elizabeth mused. "I shall miss her."

"Mm."

"Then again, perhaps she doesn't have to go too far."

Gavin belatedly heard her comment, and turned to Elizabeth with a question in his eyes. She smiled benignly up at him, but he hadn't missed the hint.

"Perhaps."

CHAPTER 15

Gavin hadn't slept well. The week was fast drawing to a close and Lainey would be choosing a husband soon. Her decision weighed heavily on his mind. True to her word, she'd gone out riding with Devereaux this morning, and returned looking flushed and happy. It was time to see where Devereaux stood.

It was a fine day for shooting, though Gavin didn't really have any stomach for it.

The September air filled his lungs with the promise of autumn as the horses trod along. The grasses were beginning to brown, waving in the breeze in an elegant dance, first left, then right, then back again. The leaves on the trees had their first touches of color, as though a painter had dropped his palette on the ground and splashed them. By next month, they would be awash with buttery yellow, fiery orange, and rich reds. It was Gavin's favorite time of year. The heat of summer left, replaced by crisp evenings and the pungent smell of earth preparing for winter. Sitting by the fire with a brandy and a book was one of his favorite pastimes.

Thoughts of sitting by that fire with Lainey curled next to

him drifted across his mind. He smiled to himself as he pictured her barefoot, with her hair loose and spilling over his hands as he held her. He could almost feel the sense of completeness fill his soul as he bent to kiss her temple—

"Eh, Mayfield?"

Gavin snapped to attention. "Er—sorry, what was that?"

"I was saying what a fine woman Lady Elaine is turning out to be. She surprised me yesterday. I'd thought she was rather tightly wound, but yesterday was a delight!" Devereaux grinned.

"So I'd heard," Gavin muttered.

"What now?"

"Tell me about yourself, Devereaux," Gavin replied, steering the conversation away from Lainey. "What sort of things occupy your time?"

"Well, my new estate, for one. Don't know a thing about how to run it, but I'm going to learn. I expect that will take up most of my time for the immediate future."

"You do know Lainey wants to stay in London to open her help center?"

"Yes, yes. May have to make a concession there, but I think she'd be willing."

Not bloody likely, Gavin thought.

"I'll just have to keep her so satisfied she'll never want to leave my bed, ho!" Devereaux chuckled while a sliver of distaste slid down Gavin's spine. Perhaps it was just Devereaux's youth, but Gavin couldn't remember ever being so crude when talking about a woman. And Devereaux hadn't been paying attention at all if he thought Lainey would spend the foreseeable future in northern England while he figured out how to run an estate.

Gavin's horse let him know he'd unconsciously tightened the reins. He loosened his grip and slid his gaze to Devereaux. "You are going to have to learn to like cats, too."

"How do you know I don't like cats?"

"I saw the way you reacted to them the other day. And you were the only one who didn't ooh and ahh over him when he arrived."

They reached the clearing where the shoot was taking place. Devereaux's eyes narrowed as they stopped. "How do you know I'm not pretending just to throw Lady Elaine off track as to who bought her the kitten?"

Gavin leveled a stare at him. "Just a feeling."

Devereaux paused, then shrugged. "Eh. The cat will be happy in the barn catching mice. How much bother could he be?"

"Highly unlikely he's going to be living in the barn," Kingston offered, reining his horse in next to them. "In case you haven't noticed, Lainey has hardly put the thing down since it arrived. If you marry Lady Elaine, that cat is going to rule your household."

Devereaux dismounted and tipped his hat jauntily. "We shall see. Happy shooting, gentlemen." He strode off to join the others.

"Young pup," Kingston scoffed, dismounting.

"Couldn't agree more. How old is he, anyway?" Gavin tied his horse's reins to a branch.

"Just turned twenty-three. I hope for my sake Lady Elaine prefers older men."

Gavin chuckled, pausing to watch the men gather in the field. Kingston eyed him askance.

"You're not anxious to shoot?"

Gavin shook his head. "I'm only along for the ride out, I leave the shooting to those who enjoy it. Never found it sporting to shoot a defenseless animal for fun."

In truth, Gavin had never fired a gun because he was terrified he was going to like it. The one time it had mattered, he couldn't bring himself to do it. His fugitive brother had been on the other end of the barrel, and had dared Gavin to take his life.

"Go on, Gavin. Do it."

The gun wavered in Gavin's hand, his sweaty palm nearly causing him to lose his grip, his chest heaving as his heart threatened to burst through it. Garrett sneered at him.

"You won't do it. You won't do it because you're afraid. You are terrified that firing that gun and taking my life is going to make you just like me." Garrett scoffed and turned away. "We share the same blood, brother," he taunted as he walked away. "No matter how hard you try to control it, the evil is in you. The difference between you and me is I'm not afraid to embrace it."

He whirled around, pulling a pistol from a hidden pocket in his coat. Gavin dove to the side, but not before the bullet tore through his arm. He hit the ground with a painful thud and watched helplessly as Garrett disappeared into the woods on a stolen horse.

He'd had the opportunity to stop Garrett, to put an end to the violence and senseless murders. But his twin's words had struck terror in his heart. *The evil is in you.* If Gavin had pulled that trigger, the door would be open, so to speak. He had spent his entire life learning how to control his temper, but once that first step was made, who knew what would follow? Would it feel satisfying? Would he want to do it again? Would he follow in the footsteps of all the violent men in his family if he let go just this once? The fear had paralyzed him, and Garrett had gotten away. Gavin's failure to pull the trigger when he'd had the chance had led to more people suffering at the hands of his brother, and ultimately, had nearly cost Aidan his life. The guilt was suffocating. What kind of man can't protect the people he loves?

"I'm a peaceful man myself," Kingston agreed, oblivious to Gavin's inner turmoil. "At least we'll be eating what they bag today. Perhaps you'll join me for a spell in those chairs over there? I'd like to get to know the man outside the business."

Gavin chuckled. "And perhaps fish for some information about Lady Elaine?"

Kingston responded with a grin. "Something like that."

Gavin slapped Kingston on the back as they moved toward the chairs. "I like you, Kingston."

"I'll consider that a point in my favor."

They sat in the shade of a giant oak, safely out of range of any stray bullets, and watched as the beaters went to work flushing out the birds. Ordinarily, a shoot lasted three days, but since that wasn't the purpose of this house party, Aidan had arranged for the single day of entertainment for his male guests. A man needed to escape the torture of endless teas and marriage-minded females, after all.

Kingston settled back in his chair. "You and Ashby have been working together a long time. Seems as though you've found an ideal partnership."

"We've been very lucky. We bonded the moment we met and that hasn't changed in all these years. We work well together and trust each other implicitly. It's been us against the world for as long as I can remember."

"Well, and Lady Elaine, of course."

Gavin chuckled. "Yes, and Lady Elaine. As I told you at the tavern, we tried to shake her loose but she just wouldn't be left out."

They both laughed, then jumped as a shot rang out. A bird came tumbling out of the sky and landed unceremoniously in the field. Shooting was paused while the bird was retrieved. Kingston reached over, plucked a long strand of grass, and studied it while he rolled it between his fingers. "I imagine it must be hard to have the balance upset by Ashby's taking a wife."

Gavin thought before answering. Kingston had somehow voiced exactly what Gavin had been feeling, but couldn't confess out loud. "I love Lady Ashby dearly, but it has been an adjustment, if I'm being truthful."

Kingston nodded. "Change always comes with growing pains." He continued to twirl the strand of grass. "Do you suppose," he began, not looking at Gavin, "that that may be the reason for Lady Elaine's change of heart where a husband is concerned? Ashby has always talked of her settling for nothing less than true love."

Gavin slowly turned his head toward Kingston, suddenly at a loss for words. He'd been so wrapped up in his own feelings that he hadn't really thought how Aidan's marriage would affect her. Hadn't Gavin just said she'd always refused to be left out? But now she was being forced out…unintentionally, of course, but the addition of a bride in the house had to be distressing, regardless of how much she loved Elizabeth. Lainey was no longer mistress of the house, and Aidan rightly focused on his new wife, so she must be feeling left behind. And being left behind had never sat well with Lainey.

"Do you know, Kingston, you are a very astute man? I'm ashamed to admit I didn't think about how all the upheaval must be affecting her." Gavin huffed out a breath. "She tried to tell us, in not so many words, and I took them at face value. She said she was tired of waiting for love, she wanted a family now, and she needed to have purpose in her life."

"Because her purpose is now married," Kingston agreed. "Her brother has spent all these years thinking he's been taking care of her, when I suspect it has been the other way around, he just never knew it."

Gavin pinched the bridge of his nose. "It all makes sense now. I couldn't understand why she was suddenly so willing to forego what she's been waiting for all of her life, but now that Aidan is settled, she is probably feeling in the way and needs a new project, so to speak. She's always been busy with one thing or another, it just makes sense that she would fill the void with something else."

"And don't we all want to feel needed, whether we can admit that to ourselves or not?"

Gavin nodded. "I suppose you are right."

Kingston was silent for a moment, watching the shooters prepare for another startled bird. "I have not spoken to Ashby yet, but I know you and Lady Elaine are quite close, so I am going to be blunt." Kingston turned, leveling an intent gaze at Gavin. Gavin suddenly felt as though Kingston had just seen right through him. "I wanted to talk to you first, to get your honest opinion. Sometimes our friends know us better than our family," he said ruefully. "I want a mother for my daughter, and would like more children. Being without a mother has been hard on Rose, and I think she is desperately lonely and would appreciate a sibling or two. I've always thought Lady Elaine a remarkable woman, even though we've only known each other in passing. I see how she treats others, and I think she will be an excellent mother. I know she has big aspirations with her help center, which I admire, and I will support that so long as it doesn't interfere with raising our children. I know I am a good deal older than Lady Elaine, but I do think we would get on well together."

Kingston paused, a faraway look coming into his eyes. He averted his gaze, looking out over the field. "But I loved my wife deeply. Even now, I am not quite ready to let her go. I believe Lady Elaine understands that, and there will be room for the both of them in my heart, but I may never love her as I loved my wife. I want to know if you think Lady Elaine is being honest when she claims she no longer wants a love match, because I do not want to be the one who takes that chance away from her if she is not sincere in her choice."

Gavin's gut tightened while yet another shot rang out. For a brief moment, he wished the shot had missed the bird and hit him instead. Kingston was going to offer for Lainey, she would accept, and then she would be lost to Gavin forever.

This was, after all, the entire point of this house party. So why did it feel like he'd been run through with a broadsword? But God help him, he wasn't about to sabotage her chances by lying, no matter how he felt about it. He nodded slowly.

"I do believe she is sincere, yes. Her decision does feel rushed, I will admit, and I wish she would reconsider, but she will not. Once she gets an idea in her head, she follows through with it. This help center means everything to her, and she will do what it takes to bring it to fruition."

Kingston tied his piece of grass in a knot. "Do you think she and I would be a good match, despite my advanced age?" He grinned.

"You are not quite a doddering old man, Kingston. I think you've a few good years in you yet." He sobered, the weight in his chest trying to suffocate him. He forced the words out anyway. "Yes, I think you and Lady Elaine would do well together. You have a good heart, will treat her well, and most importantly, I think you understand her in a way the others don't. Ashby should have no qualms about giving you his blessing."

"And what about you?" Kingston asked casually, casting the knotted grass aside. "Do you also give your blessing?"

Gavin wanted to say no. "I have no say in the matter."

"Ah, but I think you do." His shrewd gaze landed on Gavin once again.

"What are you getting at, Kingston?"

He shrugged in answer. Gavin wanted to tell Kingston to bugger off, that Lainey was his and no one else's, but he couldn't. He had to get this desire for her under control before things got out of hand. And from the sound of this conversation, she'd be affianced soon. For her own happiness and safety, he had to let her go.

"For whatever it's worth, Kingston, you have my blessing."

BOOM! Another crack rent the air. Gavin needed to get out of here before he yanked a rifle out of someone's hand and laid waste to all of Lainey's suitors.

"I do believe I am going to go for a ride," Gavin announced. "I enjoyed our talk. I'll see you back at the house." He practically ran to his horse, suddenly angry. Jealousy did not look well on him.

BOOM!

He took off at a gallop.

CHAPTER 16

Gavin tossed the covers off with a groan. The full moon lit his bedchamber up enough for him to see his pocket watch. Half past one. He heaved a sigh and went to the open window. It was an unusually warm night, and the faint breeze that stirred the curtains did little to cool him.

Gavin felt his time with Lainey slipping through his grasp like so many grains of sand. The ball was in three days, and he expected she'd announce an engagement…and that would be it. He'd be left alone with the choices he'd made.

It was for the best, really. Every time he allowed himself to dream of a life with Lainey, Garrett's sniggering voice echoed in his head, dredging up horrifying memories of his childhood, things he'd never told anyone. He absolutely would not—could not—take the chance that he might create a son like Garrett.

And therein was the crux of the problem. Even if he could overcome his fears of what darkness lay inside him, which thus far had been impossible, he could not take away Lainey's dream of motherhood. It was a position she was meant to have, and by God, Gavin was going to make sure she had it, even if it meant he would be miserable.

Damn it all, he shouldn't have kissed her. He'd been doing just fine ignoring his feelings until that night. Now he was being forced to deal with them. Why couldn't he have just gone upstairs with Aidan and called it a night? But no, he'd gone and not only kissed her, but held her soft curves pressed against him as he wrapped his arms about her. That had ignited an inferno of desire for her that he had kept so carefully banked for years, and now he could think of nothing but having her in his arms again. It was killing him to pretend he didn't want her.

Because he'd come to the realization that he very much *did* want her. Terror snaked through him as both his arm and shoulder began to throb, a stark reminder of what a violent act could do to a person long after the act had been committed. He'd kept those demons at bay for so long, but here, at this blasted house party, they were coming out in droves to haunt him. A sheen of sweat pricked his skin at the thought of losing control of his temper, which he'd nearly done countless times this week. He was fit to be no one's husband, let alone a father.

He sat a hip on the window ledge, sighing his frustration. If only he were a better man, a stronger one, he could—

He sat up straight as a ghostly figure passed below his window in the garden. He'd rarely seen her with her hair down, but he'd recognize Lainey anywhere. His body knew hers even from this distance. What was she doing walking in the garden so late? And alone? He watched her meander along, lost in thought, the white of her wrapper a beacon in the moonlight. She seemed as restless as he.

Gavin rose to pull on his trousers and shirt, stuffing his feet into leather slippers as he went, telling himself he was only going so he could protect her. A woman shouldn't be out alone at night. One never knew what dangers awaited.

HE FOUND her in the summer house, draped across an upholstered bench and gazing up at the stars that shone through the domed glass ceiling, a beam of moonlight washing her in a soft glow. His pace slowed as he took in the scene. Lainey seemed oblivious to his presence as she tilted her face to the sky, studying the pinpoints of light overhead, her legs stretched out before her, crossed at the ankles. He hadn't been out here in quite some time, and marveled at the proliferation of roses that now climbed the graceful columns, though they were mostly past their bloom. Welcoming cushions adorned various seats and oversized benches like the one upon which Lainey reclined. Gavin could imagine sleeping out here on a warm summer's night, listening to the crickets play their evening songs, a soft breeze drifting through the columns. The thought of having Lainey in his arms while he did so brought him back to the present as he climbed the three stone steps.

Lainey bolted upright at the sound of her name.

"I'm sorry, I didn't mean to frighten you," Gavin said, holding up a staying hand.

"Gavin! What are you doing out here?"

"Funny, I came out here to ask you that exact thing. It's nearly two in the morning. You shouldn't be out here alone."

"I'm perfectly safe in my own garden, Gavin." She leaned back on her hands and resumed her perusal of the sky. "I couldn't sleep."

Gavin desperately tried not to notice how her position offered her breasts up to him like a delectable feast. Images of baring them and taking one in his mouth flooded his imagination. He tore his gaze upward and fought to concentrate. "Me neither." He indicated the bench. "May I?"

She wordlessly shifted her legs over to make room for him, and he sat so his right hip touched her left one. "What's on your mind?" he asked, trying not to think about what happened the last time he'd encouraged her to confide in him, or how easy it would be to crawl over her, covering her body with his while he—

"What isn't on my mind might be a better question," she replied, blissfully unaware of that fact that Gavin was removing every stitch of her clothing in his head. "This week has not gone quite as I'd planned."

It hadn't gone the way Gavin had planned, either. Quite the opposite, in fact. "Are you changing your mind? You do not need to accept any offers, you know. Aidan would probably be ecstatic."

Lainey chuffed a laugh. "Probably so. But I still intend to go through with my plan, if anyone decides they want me. I just hadn't expected...I'm just...conflicted."

"Lainey, why on earth do you keep claiming that no man would want you? I don't like hearing you talk about yourself that way. You are a very desirable woman."

"Am I?" Lainey sat up, folding her legs beneath her so that they were sitting incredibly intimately, thighs pressed against each other. Gavin made no effort to move away. "I'm so desirable that I had to beg you to kiss me?"

"You didn't have to beg."

"Would you have kissed me otherwise?"

"You know I would not."

"Well then, there we are."

"Lainey, I would not have kissed you because you are my best friend's sister, not because you are not desirable."

"You're just saying that."

Gavin stared hard at her. "Do you not feel my desire

when I kiss you? Did I not voluntarily kiss you by the pond? Do you honestly have no idea how much I want you?" The moment the words were out, he wished them back. Lainey looked stricken. "I'm sorry, that was inappropriate."

"Actually, Gavin, this is a most refreshing conversation." She shrugged. "Two rejections and no offers later does something to a girl's self-esteem. But this week…things have been different."

Gavin ignored the stab of guilt in his gut. "How so?"

"I feel…" Lainey waggled her fingers around in a helpless gesture. "Everyone is focused on me. I've never had so much attention. It's almost as if I'm on constant display, and I'm desperately trying to measure up."

"Lainey, you have nothing to prove. You don't have to be anything other than yourself."

"I'm only starting to see who that really is."

An odd pang rippled through his chest. This marvelous woman hid such insecurities in her heart. He leaned toward her, placing one hand on the bench beside her hip, and the other covered the hand in her lap, giving it a reassuring squeeze. "Lainey, if it took this house party for you to learn to let your true self show, then I am thrilled that you suggested it. I've always known what an extraordinary woman you are."

She stared at him, but said nothing. The air seemed to grow thick between them, buzzing with a current he could feel in his fingers. His heart sped up. "You are intelligent and kind. You have drive and ambition, and you are fiercely loyal. You are elegant, gracious, and refined…and yet you harbor a passion beneath the surface that you never let anyone see. But I see it, and it's beautiful. *You* are beautiful."

Lainey's eyes shone bright with unshed tears. "You are the only one who sees that."

"That's because you choose to portray a paragon of

society rather than let your passionate side show. But you've never been able to hide from me." He rubbed his thumb over the back of her hand. His head was screaming at him to get up and go back to the house, but an invisible force kept him glued to the bench.

"And you don't think those things make me unattractive?"

Gavin blinked. "Unattractive? God, no! But to some men, those things may make you intimidating."

"Intimidating? Me?" Lainey scoffed.

"I have news for you, dearest. Men don't like rejection, either. In fact, some are true cowards. It is hard to lay your heart at a woman's feet, and sometimes a man will offer for the woman he thinks will have the least reasons to object to his suit. You are smart, attractive, and strong. Those qualities are very intimidating to many."

Lainey frowned as she digested this information. Her brows knit together. "Do *you* find me intimidating?"

Gavin paused, his pulse a deafening roar in his ears. He stared at her for a long, fraught moment before he gave up the fight. "No," he said quietly, "No, you do not intimidate me." He reached up to trace a finger along her jaw. "You…set me on fire."

LAINEY'S HEART STOPPED. Gavin's finger stroked her skin, leaving a trail of goosebumps in its wake. His heavy-lidded gaze dropped to her mouth, then back up again. He wanted to kiss her, of that she was sure. She'd never wanted anything more. Her breath stuttered in her chest as he placed his finger under her chin, drawing her imperceptibly closer. She closed her eyes.

"Lainey," he whispered in warning.

"Shh. Just kiss me."

He did not disappoint her. He touched his lips to hers softly, a butterfly kiss, gentle and loving, speaking words he would never say. Gavin moved to cup her jaw with his palm, and she sighed into the pleasure of it. His other hand came up from the bench to rest on her hip, the warmth of it seeping through her night clothes. It was oddly both comforting and thrilling, but Lainey wanted more. She rose up on her knees, wrapping her arms around his neck and pressing her body against his.

Gavin welcomed the shift in control. He moaned, urging her lips apart, his hands moving possessively to the small of her back, clutching her to him. The kiss rapidly went from tender to demanding as he claimed her mouth, tightening his arms about her waist. Everything around her melted away, and the only thing that existed for her was Gavin. Lust roared to life inside her, burning from the inside out, threatening to reduce her to ashes. Heaven help her, but the man could kiss!

Just as she was pondering how he would react if she crawled into his lap, Gavin pulled away from her reluctantly. "We should…" He gasped for air. "We should really—"

"Kiss some more?" Lainey said breathlessly.

Gavin chuckled. "Stop. We should stop."

"No. No, we should definitely not stop."

"Lainey—"

"Argh!" Lainey rolled off the bench, needing to put some distance between them. She knew she was being rash. She knew she shouldn't ask this night of him. She knew it would be best if she just went back to her room. But God help her, as she looked at Gavin sitting on that bench, washed in moonlight, his shirt gaping open at the neck, leaving his bare chest on display like a dessert that had been partially unwrapped from its fine paper, all she could think of was how she yearned to feel his skin against hers. To know what it's like to be worshipped and connected in the most intimate way, with someone she loved.

She gave him a hard stare, coming to a decision. She was done with being proper. She was done with doing what was expected of her. And she was absolutely done with putting aside her own wants and needs. Tonight, she would take what she wanted.

Gavin, blast him, read her mind. "Absolutely not."

She sauntered toward him, loosening the belt on her wrapper. She nearly laughed out loud at the combination of excitement and terror on his face, as though he couldn't decide if he should bolt or attack her.

"Lainey, this is not—"

She put her fingers on his lips to shush him. "Gavin, listen to me. I…have wanted you ever since I was old enough to understand what desire is. I did not plan to have you follow me out here, nor did I have any hope that I would ever find myself in this situation. Yet here we are, with an opportunity I don't want to waste staring us in the face. You do not wish to marry; I will place no expectations on you in that regard, but Gavin, I am so tired of being perfect. I'm tired of what everyone thinks I should be or say or do. Tonight, I choose what I want. And *you* are what I want."

"Lainey, we cannot possibly—"

"Oh, but we can. We are alone. No one knows we are here. It is just you and me and the moonlight." She reached out and laid a hand on his cheek. He closed his eyes briefly, covering her hand with his.

"It's not that I don't want you. I do. I've been nearly out of my head with desire every moment I've been near you this week. But you are about to marry another man. I should think he would expect you to be a—"

"If you are referring to the archaic notion of that little piece of tissue you men value so highly being intact, then let me enlighten you. I'm an avid horsewoman, Gavin. That tore a long time ago. It happens. It doesn't mean I've been with anyone. And I highly doubt that Kingston cares if I am a virginal bride or not. In fact, he might appreciate my not being completely ignorant on my wedding night."

"So, he's offered for you, then?" Gavin's face tightened.

"No. But I have reason to believe he will."

"Then it would be dishonorable to—"

"No more words, Gavin. I am done with words." She pulled her hand from his and shrugged out of her wrapper. She was inordinately pleased when she saw the flare of desire in his eyes as he boldly perused her body. The silk and lace negligee did not hide much. "This moment will never come again. I want to continue where we left off at the pond. I want to feel your hands caressing my skin, touching me where no one else has..." She hiked up her negligee and kneeled on the bench, straddling him. Oh, she was too wicked! Gavin tensed beneath her as she leaned forward to whisper in his ear, "Most of all, I want to feel you inside me and hear you cry out your pleasure."

"Christ, Lainey."

She moved her hands down and slipped them beneath his shirt, trailing her palms across the planes of his lower back. He jumped at her touch, but she forged on, pressing a kiss to the hollow of his throat. His pulse pounded beneath her lips. Satisfaction threaded through her, knowing that he was as aroused as she was. His skin was so soft and warm, shockingly so. She nuzzled his neck, drugging herself on the heady scent of him...woodsy, like cedar, with a hint of cinnamon perhaps? Delicious. She glided her lips to his collarbone and gave him a little nip. He drew in a sharp breath, but she instinctively knew it was born of lust and not pain. She'd never been so bold in her entire life, and it was thrilling beyond belief.

"Lainey," he said into her hair. "In about ten seconds, I am going to lose control and thoroughly ravish you." His voice was thick and heavy with need. She licked his earlobe, grazing it with her teeth, and thought she heard him whimper. "You now have about three seconds left to change your mind."

Lainey grinned, sitting back. "Time's up."

Gavin was on her in an instant, yanking her to him and searing her mouth with a kiss. His tongue plundered her mouth, and she responded eagerly, letting years of pent-up passion flow through her like molten glass, igniting every nerve ending in her body. Gavin's arms tightened about her and he groaned low in his throat, a possessive, guttural noise that told her he, too, had been keeping himself in check for far too long. Lainey grabbed fistfuls of his shirt, tugging it up toward his head. He allowed it, pulling back from her...then suddenly he was bare chested before her, and Lainey's mouth fell open. He was a wonder of sculpted muscle that she never would have suspected was hidden under his fine clothes. She skimmed her hands up his front, exploring the highs and lows, marveling at how a person could be soft and hard the same time. His chest heaved as though he'd just run up the stairs as Lainey curiously tickled her fingers over his nipple.

"Are these sensitive like mine?"

"Probably not as much, but I don't honestly know." He slid a finger beneath the strap of her gown. "I want to see you, Lainey. I think I may expire if I don't." She nodded, and he tugged the bow at the front and slipped the gown from her shoulders. The silk slipped down to pool about her hips, and Gavin's expression changed from mere desire to raw hunger. Perhaps he didn't want to marry her, but it was clear to Lainey that he desperately wanted her body, which pleased her immensely.

Gavin reached out to trace the edge of one breast, circling

the globe and cradling it in the palm of his hand. "So beauti-ful," he murmured, leaning forward to take it in his mouth. Lainey gasped at the sensation. He cupped her other breast and squeezed gently, stroking her hardening nipple with his thumb. Lainey drove her hands into his hair, finally knowing what those golden locks felt like sliding through her fingers, letting her head fall back with a sigh. She'd had no idea her breasts could be this tied into lovemaking.

His free hand skimmed along her thigh. She could feel his arousal pushing against her most private place, and she faltered for just a moment, worried about how this was all going to work, and if Gavin would enjoy it. Or if she would. She'd waited a long time for this. What if this whole making love business was a disappointment?

"Stand up, Lainey. This needs to come off," he commanded, tugging at her negligee. "I want to see all of you." Her heart thundered at the thought of being completely nude before him, but she hesitated only a moment before she complied. She stood, clutching the negligee against her. Taking a deep breath, she let go, and the gown whooshed to her feet with a whisper.

Gavin let out an incoherent noise and squeezed his eyes shut.

"God have mercy."

CHAPTER 17

*A*ll the blood in Gavin's body rushed to his groin with such speed that it was a wonder he didn't lose consciousness. Seeing Lainey standing before him, utterly naked, hair flowing about her shoulders and silk piled at her feet, was so surreal that his mind took a moment to catch up to reality. He stared at her, slack jawed, for so long that Lainey moved to cover herself.

"Don't you dare," Gavin growled.

Lainey froze. "I…I thought you might be judging and finding me lacking," she said shyly. "I'm heavier on the bottom than on the top, and—"

"You are magnificent."

She paused. "Oh."

There was a moment of awkward silence, during which Gavin questioned if he was going to be able to live without ever seeing her like this again. At the moment, it seemed unlikely.

"Lainey, you are sure about this? It will change our relationship irrevocably." She gave him a decisive nod. "Then come here." She stepped out of her gown and came toward him. He took her hand. "Sit." She did, and his hand went to the button on his trousers. "Your turn to judge," he teased. He removed them and stood before her, allowing her to look her fill. Her eyes went wide as she took in the sight of him, curiosity written on her features. He felt every bit of the shyness she had experienced only a few moments ago.

"I believe I've seen a statue of you at the museum," she finally said, giggling. She reached a hand toward his obviously enthusiastic member. "May I?"

"I am yours to explore."

She gave him a tentative stroke with her fingertips. Gavin hissed through his teeth. Lainey glanced up with a worried expression.

"No. That felt good," he said, answering her unspoken question.

She returned to her perusal. "So soft," she whispered. "But...not. I've never felt anything quite like it. It's...velvety, almost." She closed her hand around him and he groaned, so she gave him an experimental stroke. He nearly spent himself right then.

So, he was completely unprepared for when she leaned forward and slowly licked the head of his cock. "God above, Lainey!"

"I'm sorry, was that wrong to do?"

"No! I mean...ladies don't...I...are you sure you haven't done this before?" he choked out, his voice cracking.

Lainey laughed. "I work with underprivileged women. They are much more willing to discuss such matters than society ladies are. I've never had the chance to put them into action before, though, so I don't know if what I'm doing is right."

"You're doing fine," he squeaked as she stroked him again. "There is no right or wrong. You learn with your partner what brings the greatest pleasure. For example..." He closed his hand over hers, forcing her fingers a little tighter around him. "Now try." She did, and he saw stars.

"Tell me if this feels good." She looked him straight in the eye, and with a mischievous glint in her own, took him in her mouth, closing her lips about him and stroking down his length with her hand.

"Oh, *God.*" Gavin's knees nearly buckled. "*Yes,* that feels good." He fisted his hands in her glorious hair. "So good," he groaned. He enjoyed her ministrations for a minute, but then he had to interrupt her before he embarrassed himself. "Remind me to personally thank these women for their honesty." He pushed her back on the bench. "Now it's time to show you what *I* know."

Lainey looked a little apprehensive, but she lay back against the cushions willingly. Gavin crawled up her body like a tiger stalking prey. She shivered and he grinned before he kissed her soundly. He covered her body with his and at last, they were skin to skin. She moaned aloud.

"I wasn't expecting it to feel like this," she admitted. "It's wonderful."

He nibbled on her neck, purposely sliding his body against hers, and she moaned again. "It's divine," he agreed. "But there is so much more."

He came to his knees and kissed his way down her silken belly, making her giggle. Ah, so she was ticklish. He nipped her waist, eliciting another breathless laugh. He continued on his path.

"Gavin, what are you doing?"

"I want to taste you, like you did me."

"You can do that?" She sounded incredulous.

Gavin couldn't help himself, he laughed. "Quite easily, as a matter of fact."

"But that seems so…naughty."

"No more so than what you did to me…and I do so love

to be naughty," Gavin said, his voice gravelly. He gently encouraged her thighs apart. "May I?" he asked, echoing her earlier words.

"If…If you really want to."

"Oh, I want to." He dipped his head and kissed the crease of her thigh before flicking his tongue over her most sensitive flesh. She nearly arched off the bench.

"Do you like it?" He licked her again.

"Ermgh."

Gavin's shoulders shook with mirth. It wasn't often that Lainey was speechless. She struggled up on her elbows to look at him. "That is…quite amazing."

He grinned wolfishly and returned to the task at hand. Her head lolled back on her shoulders.

"Lainey, look at me," he commanded.

"Oh, I couldn't…" But she met his gaze as he gave her another stroke of his tongue, and Gavin thought he might explode with the sensualness of it. Her eyes were locked on his as he licked and sucked until she collapsed against the cushion, writhing with pleasure. Gavin tore his mouth from her, kissing his way along her thigh as he sat up.

"Oh no! Don't stop, Gavin," she pleaded.

He slipped his hand between her thighs, taking over the stroking with his thumb. Lainey gasped, and he knew she was close to reaching her climax. "I want to watch you come, Lainey. Let me see that passion I know you have inside you. Don't be afraid to show me."

He slid a finger inside of her, circling his thumb on her clit and increasing the pressure. Little incoherent noises came from Lainey as she clutched the edge of the cushion, her knuckles white. Gavin kept up his rhythm, sliding in another finger, watching the strain on her face build, until finally, she cried out, arching against his hand, her muscles convulsing tightly around him. Her breath froze in her lungs as waves of pleasure washed over her, until the tension faded and her limbs went limp. She opened her eyes and Gavin smiled at her.

"That was glorious to watch."

"It wasn't so bad on my end, either."

Gavin chuckled and stretched his body over hers, settling between her legs, nuzzling her neck. Her arms went about him, trailing her fingers lightly across his back, and he couldn't help but think how natural it was to have her here like this, naked beneath him, running her hands over him while he inhaled the scent of her. In fact, it scared Gavin to death.

Because the truth of the matter was, Lainey made him feel whole. Like he wasn't a monster living inside a friendly facade, a ticking bomb. Bedding her would change their friendship forever, but then again, so would her marriage. Tonight, she was asking him for something he was all too willing to give…with the hope that he would be able to purge this desire for her from his system. He was in for a miserable existence otherwise.

"Lainey…" he whispered, brushing the hair back from her face, kissing her reverently. He kneaded a breast in his palm, moving against her but not entering her, until she was squirming with anticipation.

"Gavin, please. I cannot wait any longer."

"Patience, my dear," he said, taking himself in hand and stroking his head against her pearl. Lainey let out a guttural sound at this new sensation, and Gavin enjoyed watching her grow more and more aroused. She was so wet and ready for him, it was hard to hold back.

"*Gavin,*" she choked out, frustration coloring her voice.

He snickered. "Yes?"

"Gah."

"I'm afraid I didn't quite get that. What is it you want?"

"You." She was panting with need now, and Gavin was fighting to maintain control.

"I'm right here." He pressed against her, but not enough to breach her entrance.

"Gavin!" She grabbed at his arms, his shoulders, whatever was in reach. "You. Inside me. *Now*."

"Open your eyes and look at me." She did, and he slid into her wet heat.

"Oh! Oh, God. *Gavin*."

"Is this what you want?" He pulled back and then thrust in a little farther. Her eyes drifted closed again, her lips parted.

"God, yes. *Yes*."

There were no more words after that. Gavin gave her body time to adjust, then fully seated himself in her, groaning as he savored the feel of her around him. He began a steady rhythm, which she naturally picked up, whimpers of pleasure coming from both of them. He thought she might be close to a second orgasm, and he desperately wanted to feel her come around him. He was too close to his own release, so he interrupted his rhythm for a moment to sit on his knees. Lainey looked at him with desire clouded eyes.

"What are you doing?" she murmured.

"Put your leg on my shoulder." She looked doubtful, but did as she was asked. He repositioned himself and entered her again with a slow, long stroke.

"Oh. *Oh*."

Gavin couldn't keep the satisfied smile from his face. He placed his thumb on her clit and began to stroke while he thrust in and out. Lainey's body tightened almost instantly as this new assault of pleasure.

"Gavin," she breathed.

He couldn't decide which he liked better: watching the

pleasure on her face or watching his cock drive in and out of her. He was rapidly losing control.

"Come on, Lainey," he encouraged. "I want to feel you come around me. Ah, yes," he rasped as she tightened around him. "Come for me, Lainey." He thrust faster, and in moments she cried out, convulsing around him, drawing him close to his own precipice. A few seconds more, and he pulled out of her, stroking himself with a loud groan, spilling his seed on the ground. His heart hammered in his chest as he collapsed next to her, pulling her into his arms while they both recovered from their exertions. He pressed a kiss to her temple, unable to find words. They both gasped for air while they lay looking up at the stars.

As his breathing returned to normal, Gavin had to admit a few things to himself. First, it was incredibly stupid of him to think that bedding Lainey would quench this lust he'd been experiencing of late because, second, now that he had had her, all he could think about was having her again. And again. Third, watching her marry someone else was going to absolutely crush him.

Because whether he wanted to or not, he cared very deeply for her. Lainey had been "his" for most of his life, and he found he didn't like the thought of sharing her with anyone else. When he thought of Devereaux or one of the others touching Lainey the way he just had, his vision blurred. He didn't want any man's hand on her but his.

And therein lay the other part of the problem. The jealousy that rose in him made him lose control, and Gavin must always remain in control. It was dangerous for him to give in to his anger; he was frightened of what may be unleashed. He couldn't trust himself, and he would never subject Lainey to an unstable marriage or put her in an unsafe situation.

But now, lying here with her in his arms, listening to the crickets chirp around them, peace stole over him, a kind of restfulness he had never before felt in his life. He took these moments with her and wrapped them safely in his heart, just like the precious gifts that they were.

"You are very quiet," Lainey observed softly.

"Woolgathering, I suppose." He raised up on his elbow to look down at her. He stroked his knuckles down her cheek. "Are you all right?"

She took a breath to say something, then seemed to decide against it. She smiled. "I am well. Indeed, that was…" she trailed off, searching for the right words. When she could find none, she hesitantly asked, "Is it always like that?"

Gavin regarded her with seriousness. "No. In fact, I've never experienced anything so incredible in my life."

"Truly?"

"Truly. But that is not to say it is not enjoyable at other times," he added at the worried look on her face. "If one's partner is willing to learn one's needs and likes, it can be quite a bit of fun. There isn't much point in being a selfish lover. Lovemaking is so much more satisfying when both parties are finding it equally enjoyable."

Lainey gazed up at him, an inscrutable expression in her eyes. She reached out a hand and rested it over his heart, fanning her fingers out against his silky flesh. She stayed like that for a few heartbeats, staring at her hand.

"Gavin," she whispered. "I-" She broke off suddenly, thinking better of whatever she had been about to say. She looked ruefully into his eyes. "I should probably get back to my room. It's late."

LAINEY SILENTLY CURSED HERSELF. She'd been about to ruin the most perfect moment of her life by telling Gavin that she loved him, which undoubtedly would have sent him fleeing.

But she could hardly keep the words from spilling from her lips. She'd thought she would get over him eventually, thought perhaps setting her cap for someone else would ease the ache in her chest, but she realized now that Gavin was always going to have her heart. She could share it, but a large piece of it would always belong to him.

She traced a finger over his skin, pressing her lips together. She wished she could stay here with him till the sun rose. "Thank you for tonight, Gavin," she said softly.

He cupped her cheek, his eyes searching hers. She thought she detected regret in them, but didn't want to examine that too closely. He leaned down to kiss her, moving his lips over hers tenderly, showing her what he couldn't say. Finally, he raised his head.

"I'm sor—"

"Don't." Lainey sat up, reaching past Gavin's hip for her discarded robe and dragging it over him. He looked positively delectable, lying there with his hair tousled, the robe just covering him at the waist, moonlight dusting his skin with a pearly glow. It was all she could do to not throw herself on him and beg him to make love to her again. "Let's not tarnish this memory. It was a perfect night. You were... perfect." She gave him a sad smile. "I really should go."

She bent to retrieve her nightgown and slipped it over her head. She stood, reaching for her wrapper. She hesitated. "I'm afraid I'm going to need this."

Gavin waggled his brows. "Go ahead and take it."

Lainey grinned, swiping the fabric from him with a whispery swish. Her mouth went dry at the sight of him reclining, shamelessly naked, on the bench. She boldly swept her gaze up and down his sculpted body. "Hm."

"Hm?" Gavin chuckled. "Who knew you were such a minx, Lainey Lockwood?"

She slid into her wrapper, tying the belt. "I daresay you

did. Goodnight, Gavin." She turned to go, but paused at the top of the stairs. "I'm glad you found me out here. I meant what I said. This was a beautiful night."

She disappeared into the darkness.

Gavin watched her go, then rose to dress. A weight settled in his chest. As much as he had enjoyed their time together, he didn't feel entirely good about what he'd done. It was obvious Lainey still carried a torch for him, and he was selfish to encourage her. And God forbid Aidan found out; he would tear Gavin limb from limb.

But truthfully, it was the fact that he realized he had come to care for Lainey so deeply that terrified him. There were only two days left of this cursed party, and then she would belong to someone else. He shoved his hands in his pockets and looked to the stars for an answer. They blinked back down at him, but offered no advice. He sighed heavily.

He simply needed to stay away from her. That would be the best solution. If he wasn't around her, he wouldn't be tempted by her, and she would be free to focus on the reason she was here in the first place. It would be breaking his promise of support, but it was the only option he could see. He would go mad otherwise.

He heaved a sigh and headed back to the house, his body still buzzing from holding Lainey in his arms.

CHAPTER 18

Twenty-four hours later, Lainey sat fuming on the sofa, barely registering the buzz of after dinner conversation going on around her. Gavin had been conspicuously absent all day and evening. He'd pulled further away from her ever since their liaison in the summer house. She hadn't expected an offer of marriage—he'd made it pretty clear that was not going to happen—but she also hadn't expected him to distance himself so thoroughly.

Lainey tried not to slump in her seat. There was an ache in her chest that threatened to consume her. She'd hoped the one night with Gavin would get him out of her system once and for all so that she could move on and make a choice, but her plan had backfired miserably. She wanted him more than ever. Now that she had tasted such passion with him, how could she settle for something mediocre with someone else?

But at least there were others who wanted her, made her feel like she was someone special. After so many years of self-doubt, it was nice to be desired. She saw the truth now of what Gavin had told her; the men here were genuinely interested in her. She felt sure the viscount was going to make an offer, and though she hadn't intended to marry a peer, she was quite certain they would suit and that he would not meddle in her business affairs. In fact, she expected he would support her whole-heartedly. Plus, he had a daughter who needed a mother, and Lainey was definitely looking forward to filling that role. Excitement pinged her heart at the thought of adding her own children to the family.

A movement out in the darkened hall caught her eye. Gavin had returned from wherever he had been all day and was trying to make an escape up the stairs without being seen. Well. Lainey had had just about enough of that. She told Elizabeth she was going up to get her shawl and strode purposely from the room.

GAVIN KNEW HE WAS A COWARD. He'd managed to successfully avoid Lainey all day and had gone to dine with his family that night. His ill-timed return had him skulking in the hall, trying not to be seen as he snuck past the drawing room door. He'd almost gotten away with it, until he made the fatal mistake of stopping at the top of the stairs to play with the cat. A rustle of silk alerted him to Lainey's presence. He didn't need to turn around to know who it was.

"You have been difficult to find today, Gavin," she drawled softly behind him, an unspoken accusation in her voice.

He grimaced. "This is your fault," he whispered to Bingley before standing. "Hello, Lainey."

"Hello to you, too."

Silence fell awkwardly between them, during which Gavin pictured her as she was the other night, her nightgown pooled around her hips, passion clouding her eyes, her hair tumbling about her shoulders. What he wouldn't do to see that again. "Was there something you wanted?" His voice was brusque, distant.

Lainey opened her mouth, affronted by his tone, but no words come out. She worked her jaw a few times before she finally said, "No. I just...you've been avoiding me all day."

"I've been busy, that's all."

"Really? And here I thought you were just being a bounder." Lainey folded her arms across her chest. "What is the *matter* with you? Last night was—"

"A mistake."

Lainey was stunned into momentary silence. Hurt flooded her face and Gavin knew he'd gone too far. "A...mistake?"

"Yes. No. I mean—argh." He dragged his fingers through his hair. "I mean, we shouldn't have complicated things between us like that."

"I see," Lainey said slowly, her expression saying she didn't understand at all. She stared stonily at him. "Had I known it was going to mean so little to you, I would have spared myself the humiliation."

"That's not what I meant."

"Then what, exactly, did you mean?"

"We can't discuss this here." He glanced up and down the hallway to make sure it was empty, and grabbed her arm to steer her into the nearest room. He shut the door firmly behind him, facing the fiery ball of anger that was Lainey. He jammed his hands on his hips, which seemed to release a pent-up breath that went whistling through his lips. "I'm sorry. I didn't mean to make it sound like it meant nothing. I was trying to make this easy for you."

"Make what easy?"

"I wanted to stay out of the way so you didn't feel awkward."

"Awkward?" Lainey's brows shot up. "I don't feel awkward, Gavin. I feel used."

"What? No." Gavin shook his head. "That was not my intent. I was trying to be sensitive to—"

"Sensitive? You think ignoring me for a whole day after what we shared is being *sensitive*?"

"Well, when you put it that way…"

"I do not know what has gotten into you! You have been cranky and out of sorts this entire week. You glare at every man who gets near me despite the fact that you brought them here to meet me. It's almost as if you don't *want* me to find a husband."

That arrow hit its mark. He moved past her, one hand rubbing his neck as he strode over to the window, staring sightlessly out at the gardens.

"Is that it, Gavin?" Lainey asked softly. "*You* don't want to marry me, but you don't want me to marry anyone else, either?" A gossamer thread of silence stretched between them, suddenly broken by Lainey's snort. "You are unbelievable, Gavin Mayfield."

Gavin whirled around. "I think you are blowing this out of proportion."

"Oh, am I? I don't think so. I think I've just been an utter fool all these years."

"What do you mean by that?"

"I mean, I've spent years of my life pining away for you when you don't give a fig about me."

"That is not true. I care deeply for you."

"No, you care about yourself. Your best friend has gone and gotten married and left you behind, so now you want me to take his place and stay with you. Well, I deserve a life too, Gavin."

"Of course you do! I want your utter happiness! That is exactly why I can't marry you!"

"That doesn't even make sense!" Lainey shouted. "You claim our lifelong friendship whenever it is convenient for you, yet you can't bring yourself to trust me with the truth! You have been constantly alluding to some mysterious reason we can't be married, and I'm sick of it. What *is* it, Gavin? Why are you so hell bent on avoiding marriage?"

"Because I am afraid!" he roared. He covered his face with his hands at Lainey's shocked expression, muffling a groan. That was probably the last thing he'd wanted to admit out loud. Hell, he'd never even admitted it to himself. Devil take it, this woman drove him mad.

"Afraid of what?" Lainey asked, exasperated. "Of spending your life with the same woman?"

"No," he ground out. "Of carrying on the family tradition."

"What?"

Gavin sighed. It was time to open Pandora's box. "Garrett was not the only violent man in our family," he said in a rush. "It is somewhat of a family trait."

Lainey wrinkled her brow and waited for him to continue. When he didn't, she surprised him by saying, "I'd heard rumors…I didn't really think they were true."

"Unfortunately, they are. I did my best to keep you—and society— from the worst of it." He sighed. "My family tree is littered with worthless garbage. My uncle was a brute and repeatedly beat my aunt and anyone who defied him, including me on a few occasions. You may recall the summer I broke my arm? I didn't do it falling off a horse like I told you. It was broken for me because I was disobedient."

"Oh, Gavin," Lainey breathed.

"My father's grandfather abused his wife," he continued. "Several cousins followed the same path. One particular shining star of the family produced many offspring by forcing himself on the young maids who worked for him.

Fortunately. my father was one of the male line spared this loathsome affliction, so when Garrett started showing signs of this kind of behavior, we thought…well, we thought we could change him. Thought it must have to do with how he was raised, and hoped a loving home would be the answer. But as you know, it didn't make a damn bit of difference," he said bitterly. He paused, lost in the horrifying memories he'd kept buried for so long. "I still struggle with guilt. Garrett was my twin. We had a connection that I don't think other siblings have. Maybe I should have treated him better. I just thought he was misbehaving because he wanted attention. He was always sick or weak or left behind, and despite our trying to make sure he knew he was loved, he just got worse and worse. But I keep thinking that if I had just paid more attention to him, maybe tried to be a better brother—"

"Gavin. You were a child. You could not possibly know what he would grow up to be. I certainly didn't. You were busy being a young boy, enjoying what life had to offer. You *were* a good brother to him, perhaps even in times when he didn't deserve it. You and your family did everything you could for him. It is no one's fault that he made the choice to get involved with villains and thieves…but what does this have to do with avoiding marriage?"

Gavin turned back toward the window, unable to look at her. "What if I develop this violent streak that is so prevalent in my family? I would never be able to live with myself if I ever hurt you."

The air in the room went still, and a long, heavy silence enveloped them like a thick, dank fog settling in at the docks. Gavin slowly forced himself to face Lainey. She did not appear sympathetic. In fact, she looked very much like she wanted to murder him.

"Gavin Mayfield, do you mean to tell me you broke my heart because you are afraid of turning out like your brother?" she snapped. "You are twenty-eight years old. If you were going to have a violent streak, don't you think you would have developed it by now?"

He spread his hands in supplication. "I don't really know."

Lainey stared at him, incredulous. "You bloody arse!" she exploded, advancing on him. "You are nothing like your brother and you never will be. For God's sake! How could you ever think you'd inherited this awful family trait?"

"I don't want children," he ground out.

That stopped her. The color drained from her face. "What?"

"I will not have children, Lainey. I cannot risk passing this horrifying attribute on to my sons. You want nothing more than to be a mother. How could I take that away from you?"

There was an awful silence as Lainey took in this admission, slack jawed. She stared hard at him, and a pang of guilt zinged through him. He'd never seen her look so…betrayed.

"That is why you rejected me?"

Her voice sounded small, and it crushed Gavin's heart. "That is the biggest reason, yes."

"Not because you didn't want me, but because you thought you knew what *I* wanted?"

Gavin started to squirm. He'd thought Lainey would understand once she knew he refused to have children, but she didn't appear as though she was feeling charitable. "I thought I was protecting you. I still am protecting you. Marrying me would be a risk for any woman, and I'll not ask you to undertake it."

She was silent, a myriad of emotions marching across her face, none of which Gavin could accurately discern. "I see."

He hated it when she said that, because clearly it meant she didn't. "You would resent me eventually, Lainey. I see the way you look at other people's children. The longing is palpable. I would not rob you of being a mother."

"That was not your decision alone to make, Gavin," she said quietly. "If you had just been honest with me..." She shook her head and reached for the door. "I need to get back to the party."

"Lainey..."

She turned, hand on the knob, waiting.

"I...I'm sorry. I wish things could be different."

She glared at him, her lips set in an angry line. She raised a brow. "Do you?"

She stared at him a moment before yanking the door open and sailing through. The door clicked closed behind her, a fitting metaphor to the current status of their relationship.

LAINEY LEANED against the pillar at the top of the stairs, debating whether or not she should throw herself down them. All this time...all those years she had spent thinking she wasn't good enough, that she needed to be more perfect to be attractive, that it was *her* fault that Gavin didn't want her, when it was really his misguided sense of protectiveness that prevented him from offering for her. Had he never stopped to consider that he might only have girls, who didn't seem to be cursed with this violent streak? Or that she might be willing to adopt? Or that she might even be barren? Obviously, he hadn't. No, he had just made the decision without so much as an explanation, leaving her to question her self-worth.

As angry as she was, she did understand his fear, irrational though it may be. Garrett had been a terror, and it had nearly torn their family apart. Gavin had been through hell, and it must have been a constant weight on his chest trying to keep the family's secret. But how he could believe he could become a violent man was beyond Lainey. He melted every time he laid eyes on Bingley, for heaven's sake. What violent man turns into a marshmallow when a kitten enters the room? She had never seen him be anything but gentle.

But Lainey had known Gavin for most of her life, and she knew he would not be convinced. If he were ever going to change his mind, he had to come to that conclusion on his own. To force him into it would only make them both miserable, and Lainey was tired of waiting. She could love someone else. She could. She would. Gavin Mayfield was not the only attractive, single man in England. It was time to let him go.

She took a few more moments to compose herself before heading down the stairs. She didn't truly feel like returning to her guests, but remaining upstairs would cause gossip, and that was the last thing she needed right now. So, she would paste on a smile and pretend as though her world had not just been shattered.

She had just reached the bottom of the stairs when a figure loomed out of the darkness.

"Ah. Lady Elaine, might I have a word with you?"

CHAPTER 19

"Mr. Devereaux! Is something wrong?" She glided down the stairs to the foyer, taking in his slightly disheveled state, as though he'd anxiously been running his fingers through his hair.

"Lady Elaine, it is most imperative that I speak with you."

"Right now? In a darkened hallway?"

"It is of utmost urgency. You see…" He swallowed hard and swayed toward her slightly.

"Have you been overindulging, Mr. Devereaux?"

"Perhaps just a little. Forgive me, my lady, I felt I needed the courage. You see, I have developed…feelings for you, and I…I wish to beg you not to marry Mayfield. Marry me instead."

Lainey's mouth dropped open. "Marry…Mr. Devereaux—"

"Hear me out, my lady. I am fascinated by your sharp mind and your genuine soul. I see how you care for others and I believe you would be a wonderful mother to my children. We would do well together, you and I. I know a marriage to me would make running your help center less feasible, as we would have to spend part of the year at the estate, but we could find a way. I did not come here looking for a bride, but you have bewitched me."

"Even though you think I'm boring?"

Devereaux blinked. "Eh, what now?"

"I heard you in the parlor the other night. You were afraid I was too proper and wouldn't make you a good bed partner. You actually bet the others that I'd never been kissed."

Devereaux had the good grace to turn scarlet. "I beg your pardon for my crude comments, my lady. I was a bit in my cups and my thoughts flowed too freely. I did not know you at all then, but in the days since, you have proven to me that I was mistaken in my judgement. You are more adventurous in spirit than I'd first thought." He grinned. "As far as the rest is concerned, perhaps we may settle that right now."

Before Lainey could protest, Devereaux swooped in and slanted his mouth over hers. For a moment, she was too shocked to do anything but let him kiss her. After all, this was the first man who'd ever tried to take advantage of her. It was a little thrilling and she was enjoying it. But it didn't take long for her to realize that, although Charles kissed quite nicely, she wasn't quite ready to be kissed by someone other than Gavin. She made a noise of protest in her throat that he must have misinterpreted as enjoyment, because now he was trying to deepen the kiss as his arms went around her. She managed to wedge her hands between their chests and tried to shove as she leaned back, but the message was not getting through to his drink-fogged brain.

In the next second, she was free and Devereaux was being yanked backwards. It took a moment to register Gavin's furious countenance, and before she could stop it, he landed his fist into Devereaux's face with a roar, sending him sprawling. Gavin lunged forward and grabbed him by the lapels, yanking him partly off the floor and drawing back to hit him again, despite the fact that he'd already bloodied Devereaux's nose.

"Gavin! Stop it this instant!" Lainey shrieked, grabbing his arm. He tried to shrug her off, but she had a tenacious hold, and he was busy pinning a squirming Devereaux down.

"I say—" Devereaux began.

"What the devil is going on here?"

The thundered demand froze all three of them, and they turned as one to look in Aidan's direction. Lainey could only imagine the tableau that was being presented to him and the other guests as they filed out of the drawing room, stunned expressions on their faces.

"Let him go this instant, you bloody arse!" Lainey hissed in Gavin's ear. She was never going to live this down.

Gavin unceremoniously dumped Devereaux back on the floor, whirling to grab Lainey roughly by the arms. "Do you see, Lainey?" he cried. "Do you *see*? I am no better than—"

"Mayfield! In my study. Now," Aidan barked.

Gavin shot an agonized glance at Lainey and slunk off to the study, stepping over Devereaux, who was still prostrate. Lainey was furious. She didn't think it was possible to be more humiliated than she'd been the night of Gavin's rejection, but this managed to exceed the glory of that evening. She just might throttle him herself.

A groan from the floor drew her attention and she dropped to her knees beside Charles. "Mr. Devereaux, I am so very sorry. Are you all right?"

He struggled to a sitting position. "I say, that was unexpected." He fished in his pocket for a handkerchief and pressed it to his bleeding nose, wincing. "Perhaps I shouldn't have had that last brandy. It appears my judgement has been impaired."

"Oh, Mr. Devereaux, this isn't your fault. Come, let me help you up and we'll get you a cold compress."

"I'll have it sent to my study," Aidan clipped out. "I'll be along in a moment. I trust you all can behave for five minutes?"

Lainey glared at her brother, taking Devereaux's arm and aiming him toward the study. Aidan ushered the guests back into the drawing room, instructing Tibbs to open a very good bottle of brandy and encourage everyone—ladies included—to indulge. Elizabeth shot him a worried glance.

"Can I trust *you* to behave?"

"If you mean will I punch anyone, you can rest easy. I'll take it out on Gavin later when no one is around."

"Aidan—"

"I'm jesting, my love. But he can't just go around starting fist fights with the guests. I don't know what has gotten into him this week."

Elizabeth stared at him. "Isn't it obvious?" Aidan just gave her a blank look, and she threw her hands up. "Oh, my Lord in heaven, men are hopeless. Go straighten things out, and don't be bullheaded. Give them a chance to explain what happened. I will take care of our guests."

GAVIN'S HEAD was in his hands when the door to the study opened. He was mortified by his own behavior. He'd come upon Lainey struggling to break free from Devereaux's grasp and he'd seen red. Didn't even think, just flew into a rage. And he'd wanted to pummel him. Would have if Lainey hadn't stopped him. All the years he'd spent trying to control his temper, and in a flash, he'd turned into the thing he'd feared most.

Lainey and Devereaux entered. She looked as though she could chew glass as her eyes shot daggers at him. Well, fine. She could be angry at him all she wanted. This little episode just proved to him that he'd been right about being cursed with a violent temper, and that he was a stupid, besotted fool to believe he could be anything else. For Lainey's own safety, he needed to stay away from her.

The door banged open and Aidan stormed in, tossing a compress at Devereaux. He strode over to his desk and perched on the edge, folding his arms over his chest. "Now. Does someone want to explain to me exactly what just happened out there?"

For a moment, no one spoke, then all three started at once.

"Gavin misunderstood a situation—"

"That bounder was kissing your sister—"

"I was making my feelings known to Lady Elaine—"

Aidan help up a hand. "One at a time." His head swiveled toward Devereaux. "You were kissing my sister?"

"Er—come again?" He tugged at his collar.

"Why, Devereaux, were you kissing my sister?"

"Uh, well, I had just made my intentions known and—"

"Your intentions?"

"Er—yes. I impulsively asked her to marry me instead of Mr. Mayfield."

"Mr. Mayfield?" Aidan swung an incredulous gaze in Gavin's direction, who shrugged in confusion. He looked back at Devereaux. "And then what?"

"And then I kissed her. And the next thing I know I'm bleeding."

Gavin snorted. "You were forcing yourself on her. You're lucky I didn't break your neck."

"He was not forcing himself, Gavin. You don't know what you saw," Lainey snapped.

"So, you weren't trying to push him off of you, with no success? Did I misinterpret that struggle?"

"You had no business attacking him—"

"So, I'm just supposed to stand there and watch while someone mauls you?"

"Enough!" Aidan shouted. "Devereaux, I am going to assume that you know you behaved in a deplorable manner toward my sister, unless she *asked* you to kiss her?"

"She did not," he admitted. "Forgive me, Lady Elaine. I was overcome and did not stop to think that perhaps my advance was unwanted."

"Forgiven, sir. No harm was done. At least, to me," she added, grimacing.

"Devereaux," Aidan mused, "What made you think she and Mayfield are betrothed?"

"Well, I—" He stopped, sending an apologetic look to Lainey and twisting the bloodied compress in his hands. Whatever he was about to say, it was clear he didn't want to admit it. Dread formed in Gavin's gut, a cold, hard knot of trepidation.

"You what?"

"I...I saw them...together," Devereaux continued. "Late the other night, in the summer house...and I just assumed their behavior to be that of a couple who is either engaged or about to be."

Gavin's heart stopped. Literally stopped.

Bloody hell. He'd seen them? Bloody, bloody hell.

Across from him, Lainey's head fell back on her shoulders and she appeared to study the ceiling. Aidan came to attention and pushed off the desk. "What kind of behavior?" he said darkly.

Gavin pinched the bridge of his nose. Why hadn't he just stayed in his room that night?

"All right, that's enough, Aidan." This, from Lainey. "Mr. Devereaux, I trust you will want to go clean yourself up and turn in early. Gavin and I will take it from here. You and I will speak in the morning. Good night," Lainey said, effectively dismissing him. The man glanced at Aidan for approval and then bolted from the room, leaving the three of them alone. A terrible silence descended.

"What exactly happened between you and Lainey in the summer house?" Aidan growled.

"I don't think that is any of your business," Lainey responded.

"I am not asking you. I am asking Gavin. What. Happened?"

Gavin's jaw was clamped so tightly he thought he might crack a tooth. He'd known full well to stay away from Lainey, but he just couldn't keep his damn prick in his pants. And now his whole world was about to be blown to pieces. He saw it implode the moment realization dawned on Aidan's face.

"Did you…did you ruin my sister?"

The betrayal in his eyes was too much for Gavin to bear. "Aidan, I—"

"Did you *ruin* my sister?" Aidan bellowed, fury rolling off of him.

"I am still a perfectly good human being," Lainey snapped. "Don't make me sound like a bottle of spoiled cream."

Aidan silenced her with his hand, his gaze never wavering from Gavin's.

Gavin hung his head and sighed. There was no point in anything but the truth. "Yes." The silence that followed his admission was deafening. He wanted to kick himself for giving in to Lainey, for not having the strength to resist her. He'd known it would come to this.

"How could you?" Aidan asked quietly. "How *could you?*"

The agony in Aidan's soft question tore at Gavin. All of his biggest fears were coming to a head. He was going to lose the people he loved most because he couldn't control his baser instincts.

"Because I asked him to."

"Lainey—"

"No! There were two people involved in that decision."

"This is between Gavin and me."

"Actually, it's between Gavin and *me*. None of this is any of your business."

He ignored her. "You knew better!" he shouted at Gavin. "You shouldn't have gone near her!"

"Don't you think I know that?" Gavin shouted back.

"Then *why*, Gavin? Why would you do such a thing?" Aidan roared.

"Because I—" Gavin broke off. His breath came in short bursts, chest burning with anger. Realization of what he had been about to say sank into his bones the way the ground soaks up rain after a long dry spell. No matter what he told himself, he could no longer deny that he was in love with Lainey. Hell, he always had been. But once the words were out, he couldn't take them back, and Lainey needed to marry someone else.

"You have exactly ten seconds to answer me before I break your jaw."

"That is enough, Aidan Lockwood," Lainey snapped.

"Lainey, I will deal with you later."

"I beg your pardon?" Lainey drew herself up to her full height. "You will *deal* with me? Aidan, I am not a child you need to punish. I am a grown woman capable of making her own decisions about what she does and does not do with her own body."

He whirled on her. "I am sorely disappointed in you, Lainey."

"Stop right there. You have no right to chastise me for doing what you and Gavin have both done plenty of times since you were adolescents. Hell, you are practically expected to 'sow your wild oats' when you are young…you are even lauded for it at times! You men place so much value on a woman's virginity and completely forget that her actual value is what kind of person she is, not what she does with her body."

"Now see here—"

"No, *you* see here," she bit out, pointing a shaking finger at Aidan. "Gavin is not at fault for what happened. I begged him. He tried to say no but I wouldn't listen. Aidan, for once in my life I wanted to *live*. I wanted something just for the sake of wanting. I am so tired of being this proper miss who everyone likes but no one really sees. Gavin sees me. He *sees* me, Aidan. He always has. And I wanted to be seen. I didn't want to be a terrified bride on her wedding night, and I trusted him."

"So did I," Aidan replied evenly, glaring at Gavin. In that awful silence, Gavin wondered if he would ever be able to repair their friendship. "I hope it was good for you," he said, returning his attention to his sister. "Because you'll be marrying Gavin."

Gavin opened his mouth to reply, but Lainey beat him to it. "I most certainly will not. Gavin does not want to marry me and I won't let you force him over stupid honor."

"Your reputation is going to be ruined, Lainey. Do you want to endure another scandal?"

"There won't be a scandal if you keep your mouth shut," Lainey snapped.

"And how do you figure that?" Aidan asked icily. "Devereaux will probably shout it to the rafters, and everyone witnessed your behavior this evening."

"Despite what everyone seems to think, Charles Devereaux is a good man and I don't believe he would say anything that would purposely hurt me. He didn't even want to tell you, but you bullied him, as usual." Aidan opened his mouth to defend himself, but Lainey held up her hand. "And let's not forget that he knew about my indiscretion and chose to propose anyway. Apparently, *he* thinks I have value despite my supposed impurity, which is more than I can say for you."

"That's not fair."

"Isn't it?"

This conversation was making Gavin sick to his stomach. He'd never seen Lainey this furious with her brother over anything. They usually always got along, even when Aidan was being pig-headed. Gavin hated that he had a part in this argument. Aidan turned to him, pinning him with a hard stare.

"Are you going to do right by my sister, Mayfield?"

The knot of dread that had been growing in his gut since Devereaux started talking suddenly burst into what he could only believe to be the actual flames of hell licking at his soul. His eyes moved from Aidan's stony face to Lainey's hopeful one. Oh, she tried to hide it, but he could see the flicker of it in her eyes. This was his chance, his opportunity to make everything right. To have what he had come to realize he wanted.

But fear is a brutal beast.

"I can't," he said quietly. "To do so would condemn her to a life she does not want."

Aidan's disgust was palpable, his expression completely shuttered as he snorted and turned away. Gavin's betrayal was complete.

Lainey's eyes filled. "Yet you would condemn me to marrying someone I do not love."

The soul-crushing disappointment in him that skittered across Lainey's face made him despise himself.

"I just want what's bes—"

"You do not know what's best for me!" A tear slipped down her cheek. "*I* know what's best for me. Not you. Not my brother. Only I know that, and I am tired of being treated as though I don't." Lainey swiped viciously at the rogue tear and assumed her most regal bearing. "You behaved abominably tonight, Gavin, and you will apologize to Mr. Devereaux first thing tomorrow. And we are all going to pretend we are happy even if it kills us because I am not going to endure one more scandal because of you. You are going to attend the ball and be your usual charming self and dance with the ladies and play cards with the men and you are going to wish me happy no matter what happens or what I decide. What *I* decide," she added, tossing a fierce glance at her brother. "And after that, Gavin, I don't believe I want to see you anymore."

Her words stabbed him like a bayonet. More accurately, like she had cut him open, physically reached into his abdominal cavity and yanked his guts right out of his body, stomping on them for good measure. She didn't really mean that, did she? Was there no way back for them? He looked at her steadily, for some sign of weakness or regret, but there was none. Only resolve and anger looked back at him. He dropped his gaze to the floor, defeated, as she swished past him and marched out the door, and out of his life.

"Aidan—"

"I suggest that you go home with your family after the ball for an extended holiday. I will inform you when I no longer wish to kill you," Aidan bit out.

Gavin wanted to apologize. He wanted to make Aidan understand that not marrying Lainey was a better option than marrying her. He wanted, more than anything, to go back in time and listen to his instincts when they had told him to stay away from her. He wanted forgiveness that would likely never be granted. He wanted to say…

But he simply nodded once, and left.

CHAPTER 20

Gavin slammed through the stable door and ordered his horse saddled post haste. The shocked stable boy hurried to obey him, and Gavin was thundering off into the night in record time. He was so blinded by anger and despair that he didn't even know where he was headed until he'd arrived at Howarth Hall, his family's estate. He burst in the front door, startling the butler before he even reached for the handle.

"Sir! Back so soon? Is ought amiss?"

"Are my father and Kate still awake?"

"Yes, sir, they are in the drawing room. Shall I alert them you are here?"

"Thank you, I'll just go on in," he replied, shrugging out of his coat and handing over his hat and gloves. He strode down the hall and found his parents sitting cozily by the fire that was more for appearance than warmth.

"Gavin! What's wrong?" His stepmother exclaimed as he burst into the room, alarm coloring her voice. Gavin flung himself down on the settee across from them and let his head drop back, scrubbing his hands over his face. A vise of shame squeezed his lungs so hard he could barely breathe. "I've ruined everything. Everything. I am such a bloody idiot."

George and Kate exchanged worried glances, and George went to the sideboard to pour his son a brandy. He placed it down on the table in front of him and allowed Gavin some time to collect his thoughts. He settled onto the sofa and squeezed his wife's hand.

"Do you want to tell us what happened?"

Gavin just sat there, staring up at the ceiling, hands lying limply by his sides. He was drowning in anger and embarrassment, with no piece of flotsam in sight for him to grasp. The weight of his guilt pinned his arms to the cushion upon which he sat. How could he have behaved so abominably? To make such a scene in front of everyone at his best friend's party was unconscionable. If Aidan never spoke to him again, he would not blame him. He'd lost Lainey, of that he was sure. She would never forgive him for this, nor should she. He'd been a proper arse.

"Son?"

Gavin drew in a breath and raised his head to look at his father and stepmother. They wore matching, concerned expressions. He wanted so much to confide in them, but was unsure of where to start, and, quite frankly, afraid of their censure. He was absolutely disgusted with himself. The hurt in Lainey's eyes when she had left the room tonight would haunt him for the rest of his days. He'd known he was going to lose her the moment he'd taken her in his arms that fateful night, but he'd made love to her anyway. But Aidan…Aidan had looked at him with utter contempt. Aidan. The man he considered his true brother, the one who had been by his side through every awful moment Garrett had put his family through and had never once judged Gavin for a single decision he'd made, the man who had given Gavin a career and a partnership, securing his financial future. Gavin owed him everything, and had completely broken Aidan's trust. Gavin's throat tightened, his eyes burning. Good God, he was going to cry.

"I've done something terrible," he forced out.

His father shot an alarmed look at Kate. "Is everyone well, son? Has there been an accident?"

Gavin could only shake his head. He belatedly realized how those words could frighten his father, but he couldn't find his voice through the ache in his throat. A tear fell to his cheek, followed closely by a second and third. George sent a questioning glance to Kate, who moved to sit beside Gavin, draping a comforting arm around her stepson.

"What is it, darling? What has you so upset?"

Gavin wiped the tears from his face and reached for the brandy. It tasted like the Thames. He swallowed painfully and sighed.

"I've gone and fallen in love with Lainey," he admitted. How strange to say that out loud to another person. "I've fallen in love with her, and she's going to marry someone else. And tonight, I humiliated her in front of everyone by giving Devereaux a face full of my fist for kissing her. I lost my temper and beat him like a schoolboy. Bloodied his nose, for Christ's sake. And now she doesn't ever want to see me again, and honestly, I'm not sure Aidan does, either. I've broken his trust. I am a terrible friend."

Both his father and Kate blinked at him, trying to absorb the torrent of information that has just been regurgitated. Kate was the first to recover.

"Lainey doesn't ever want to see you again because you punched someone in her defense? That seems a bit extreme."

"No, it's not just that. I...it's complicated," Gavin finished, unable to admit the entire truth.

"I should think Aidan would be thanking you for protecting his sister," George observed.

"That's just it. I didn't." He stared miserably at the floor, tears threatening once again. God, he'd been blind and selfish.

The clock ticked off a few seconds in the ensuing silence, during which Kate put the puzzle pieces together.

"Gavin, has something happened between you and Lainey?" she asked quietly. He nodded mutely.

"Son, exactly how far has this thing between you and Lainey gone?"

Gavin's face flushed a deep red as he met his father's eyes. "Exactly far enough to make Aidan expect me to marry his sister."

"Oh, Gavin, you didn't!" Kate exclaimed. Her disappointment in him was palpable.

"I'm missing something here," George put in. "You love her, and you'll offer for her, so what is the problem? You are not the only man in England who anticipated his wedding vows. Surely Aidan must realize that, even if it is his sister."

"Except that I refused to marry her."

"What?" Kate gasped.

"Gavin, I didn't raise you to be that sort of man," his father snapped.

"I know. I didn't intend…that is, I never meant to…she…" Gavin gave up trying to explain and let his head fall into his hands. "I've ruined everything," he said to the carpet. "And I don't know if I can ever fix it."

"You'd better stop sniveling and tell us what this is all about, young man," his father barked. "We can't help you unless we know the whole story, and clearly, we haven't heard it yet. So start talking."

Gavin stared at the floor a moment longer, collecting his thoughts into something that would make sense. With a sigh, he raised his head and began to speak.

Words poured out of him in a tidal wave, everything he

had kept bottled inside for years. He went all the way back to the night Lainey had suggested they marry and he refused her, how their friendship had altered because of it, and how badly he had hurt her then. He admitted to agreeing to help with this asinine search for a husband because he thought it would help absolve him of guilt for breaking her heart, but instead it had backfired on him. He explained about the night in Aidan's study, and how he'd just wanted to show her that she was not undesirable, but it had only served to stir up his feelings for her that he'd kept so ruthlessly suppressed. How he had naively thought that he could walk away and turn his back while she married someone else, and how every moment of watching her with other men brought his biggest fear to the forefront because he wanted to throttle all of them, until his control had finally snapped and that's exactly what he had done. He told them of the awful scene in Aidan's study, and the damning words that had been said. And when he finally ran out of words, a long, peaceful quiet fell around them. George finally spoke.

"If you love her, and she loves you, why *don't* you want to marry Lainey?"

Gavin looked miserably at this father. "Lainey wants to be a mother more than anything in the world, and I...I don't want to have children."

There was a moment of stunned silence, during which understanding registered on George Mayfield's face. "You are concerned about our family history." Gavin glanced away. "My boy, I don't think that should preclude you from having a happy marriage."

"It wouldn't *be* happy, that's the problem. Lainey wants children more than anything. She would grow to resent me in time, and I couldn't bear that."

"You don't know that," Kate insisted. "Love can overcome a great many things."

"Or it can tear you apart. Look at what happened to Aidan's parents."

"That was grief, son. That's a very different thing. Aidan's father, God rest his soul, was not the type to bear loss easily. I barely made it through losing your mother…but Kate found me and put me back together."

"I rather think it was the other way around," she replied, lacing her hand with his. She turned to Gavin. "Sweetheart, have you told her any of this?"

Gavin shifted uncomfortably. "We quarreled about it earlier tonight. And then everything really went to hell."

"I wish that you had told me of your fears long ago, son," his father said quietly. "You must know, you are not your brother. I am sad that you could ever think you were."

"Why wouldn't I? We were twins. We share blood. Why could I not share that trait as well?"

George gave a sad shake of his head. "You never had it in you. Your memories are colored through a different lens, son. You were a child. You don't remember the early years." George sighed and took a swallow of brandy. "Garrett was different from the very beginning. Yes, his weakened condition made things worse, but even as a toddler, he was a brute. Smashed all of his toys, bit his nurse, threw violent temper tantrums. We tried everything we could think of to stem his behavior, but none of it worked. We even tried doctors, but they had nothing to offer us. It became clear as he grew older that he was going to remain a problem, but your mother and I foolishly thought that we could control him, that perhaps we could "love" him out if it." A forlorn smile touched hips lips. "No one wants to admit one's child is not like all the others. Sometimes, a parent can be blind to these things. It is difficult to come to terms with what feels like a failure on your part."

"You didn't fail with him, Father."

"I know that. But we did fail to protect others. We should have had him committed, but we couldn't bring ourselves to do it. Despite what he was, we still loved our son."

"But this is exactly what I'm talking about. I cannot bear to go through what you and Mother did, and I would sooner rot in hell than subject Lainey to a life of misery and pain. What if our children are like that? I do not want to be responsible for bringing another monster into this world."

"You don't have to. But I will tell you that your mother and I tried for more children after you, even with Garrett being the handful that he was. It just wasn't meant to be for us. Yes, we were scared, but you had turned out well, and we thought it was worth the risk. Granted, as he became a young child, we knew we were in for a rough road and it was probably for the best that we never had any more children because we had to focus so much attention on him, but that didn't stop us from wanting more children to love."

"Truly? Even with all that Garrett put you through?"

"Even then."

"But...Mother died because of him. How can you encourage me to marry *anyone*?"

"Son, your mother had a weak constitution. We hid that fact from you boys as much as we could. She was never a healthy woman; it was why she couldn't carry more children. Her heart was not strong, and as I told you, grief is suffocating, and it comes in many forms. When she heard that Garrett had killed that man in cold blood, her distress overtook her. She simply lost the will to live when she took ill that year. But we have no way of knowing if she would have survived had she been happy, either. Fact is, she was sick, and sometimes even previously healthy people don't survive."

"But I saw her crying over his picture every day. He broke her spirit."

"You are right about that. But I am still here. And so is

Lainey. She didn't desert you during any of the hardships you faced, did she?"

Gavin conceded that she hadn't. "I've kept a lot of our family history from her."

"But she knows now. What was her reaction?"

Gavin smiled ruefully. "She called me a bloody arse."

His father guffawed. "I'd have to agree with her in this case."

Gavin let his father's words sink in, little grains of sand sifting through the cracks in his soul that began to make a complete picture. "I've been so angry this week. Every time I see one of these men kiss Lainey's hand or watch her with a lustful eye, I want to pound them into the dirt. Christ, I nearly tore Devereaux's head off just for kissing her. I didn't even think about what I was seeing, I just flew into a rage."

"Sweetheart, jealousy is different than anger."

He looked at Kate. "How so? I still wanted to break something. Preferably his nose."

"It's true jealously drives us to quick-tempered reactions. I don't condone hitting another human being, but I also don't think you wanted to do him serious harm."

"Oh, but I did. I've never wanted to beat a man so badly."

"And why was that?"

"Because I thought Lainey was being assaulted."

"So, you were protecting her."

"Of course! I will always protect her."

Kate smiled at her stepson. "Did you even hear what you just said?" She gave his shoulder a squeeze. "You would never physically hurt her. You want to keep her safe. Those are not the words of a violent man."

Gavin stared at her, dumfounded. She patted his knee. "Do you remember the day we met?"

"Of course I do. It's burned into my memory forever."

"And when we met, was I afraid of you?"

Gavin thought back to the horrifying scene he'd stumbled upon nearly nine years ago now. Kate had been Garrett's captive and was near death, but she'd witnessed the scene between him and his brother. Aside from being near delirious, she'd never been afraid. He shot her a curious look, and she smiled.

"I put my trust in you immediately, didn't I." It wasn't a question, but a statement.

"Yes…you did."

"I like to think myself a pretty good judge of character. I was terrified of your brother from the moment he broke into our house, and all the days that followed. But you…I recognized the good in you right away. Gavin, you are no more like you brother than your father is. Garrett would not have let Devereaux go. Garrett would have beaten him senseless, and probably would have hurt Lainey as well when she tried to interfere. You…came here. To confess that you are in love."

"But…" Gavin swung his gaze to his father, at a loss for words.

George leaned forward. "You, my boy, have filled your life with light and love. We all get angry, and do stupid things we regret. You are a human being, after all. Don't let fear be your guide. Trust yourself."

"I don't know how to do that."

"You will learn. And Lainey will help you."

"Lainey is never going to speak to me again."

"Don't be so sure about that, sweetheart. Love is strong, and a woman's heart is full of it. Even when you behave like a bloody arse." Gavin's eyes widened in shock. He'd never heard Kate swear before. She grinned. "You have some groveling to do, but don't count her out just yet."

George stood, taking his brandy with him. "It's late, and I think you should stay here tonight while things settle down.

You have a lot to consider. Go back in the morning when you've had some time to think. Talk to them."

"I don't think they are going to want to talk to me. Aidan is ready to separate me from my head."

"You boys have always been like brothers. I was never so grateful when we moved here to escape society and you befriended the Lockwoods. They gave you the love and camaraderie you should have had with Garrett. Aidan feels betrayed, and we say things we don't mean when we are hurt. You'll work it out."

"But Lainey...I've failed her twice now. She won't forgive me."

"She will in time," Kate said, covering his hand with hers. "But you need to decide what it is you want before you talk to her. You cannot toy with her heart any longer. Either marry her, or let her go and be happy for her. Things have changed irrevocably between you, but time will help heal the wounds. Believe me, I know." She squeezed his hand before rising to join her husband. She bent to bestow a kiss upon his head. "Good night, my dear. Try to get some rest. You have a daunting task before you tomorrow."

They left him sitting alone by the fire, staring into the dying flames. He picked up his brandy snifter and reclined on the sofa, swirling the alcohol and watching the color play in his glass. Firelight turned the liquid to a rich, reddish amber hue. He continued to shift the snifter in lazy circles, his thoughts chasing the liquid around the glass.

He felt absolutely wretched. He'd treated Lainey poorly, betrayed Aidan's trust, and embarrassed himself by punching a guest in Aidan's home. His pride certainly didn't want him to go back to Rosecroft tomorrow. His pride wanted him to turn tail and run. But his friends did not deserve that, and it would solve nothing. He had a business reputation to uphold with many of the guests, and he had behaved abominably. He owed every single person an apology—starting with Devereaux.

Aidan would be a tougher sell, but Gavin believed deep in his heart that they could repair the damage. It would take time, but Aidan would learn to trust him again. There would certainly be gossip in town—he didn't for one second believe that every guest there would be circumspect and not tell of his astonishing behavior, but hopefully they would spin it so that he looked less like an idiot and more like a man who was protecting someone he loved. He'd survived scandal before, and he could do it again. With Lainey safely married, her reputation would remain intact with no one the wiser.

The question was, who was she going to marry?

Gavin's heart told him how he wanted to answer that question, but his head overruled him. Despite what his father and Kate had told him, he was still uneasy. He'd lived with this fear his entire life; he could not let it go in one evening. But the thought of walking away from a life with Lainey burned like acid in his gut. He didn't just physically desire her; he wanted the completeness he felt when he was with her. She'd given him her love so freely, even though she'd known Garrett, and he'd not believed in it.

She was right. He was a bloody arse.

He took a swallow of brandy, surprised that it no longer tasted like sewage. A plan formed as he sipped at the rest of it. It may not work, but he'd never forgive himself if he didn't at least try.

There was an express train to London early in the morning, and he had to be on it.

CHAPTER 21

The next morning, Charles Devereaux approached Lainey and asked if she would care to take a turn about the garden. They walked in silence for a bit, then Devereaux drew them to a stop.

"Lady Elaine, I have to apologize for my appalling behavior last night. I have no idea what came over me. I just had this silly notion in my head…"

"Mr. Devereaux." Lainey squeezed his forearm. "May I call you Charles? I think once you've shared a kiss, you can no longer say you are not friends."

He blushed and gave her a genuine smile. "I'd be honored if you'd consider me so."

"And you must, in return, call me Lainey. I have been Lady Elaine'd to death this week, and I truly abhor my name!"

"I think it rather pretty, but far be it from me to argue. Very well then…Lainey."

She grinned. "Much better. Now that that is settled, I hope you believe me when I say I hold no ill will toward you."

"Truly?"

"Truly. Have we not all done reckless things once in awhile?" She tugged him forward on the path. "Yes, Charles, even me."

He chuckled. "I am very grateful you are so understanding. I would hate to think I ruined your good opinion of me."

"You have not."

"However, I am deeply sorry I caused you such embarrassment. That I cannot forgive myself for."

"I believe the embarrassment was entirely caused by Mr. Mayfield. I do hope he will be apologizing to you later. I am sorry about your black eye. How is your nose feeling?"

"Tender, but doesn't appear to be broken. Lady E— Lainey. Although I made a hash of things, I was sincere in my proposal. Have you given it any thought?"

"I have." Lainey drew them over to a bench and sat, pulling him down next to her. "I am deeply honored by your offer, but I'm afraid I can't accept."

Charles nodded glumly. "Mayfield wins after all, eh?"

"Actually, no. I've accepted an offer from Viscount Kingston."

Devereaux's eyebrows shot up. "Kingston? But he's… rather older than you."

Lainey nodded. "I am well aware. But he is a good man. As are you, which is why I cannot marry you." She laid her hand on his sleeve. "Charles, you have a lot to offer a woman. You are handsome, and charming, and tender-hearted. You have financial security, an amiable nature, and I think you will be a wonderful father someday. Honestly, it rather pains me to turn you down!" Lainey laughed. "But I would be doing you a disservice by marrying you. You deserve someone who will love you with their whole heart, and sadly, I cannot."

"I see." He patted her hand. "I thank you for your honesty. But...does Kingston know your heart lies elsewhere?"

"He does, and that is acceptable to him. He's had one great love. Now he just wants someone to grow old with, who may love him in a different way."

They fell into companionable silence while Charles mulled over her answer. Finally, he asked, "And what of you, Lainey? Do you not deserve to be loved wildly as well?"

Lainey tried to ignore the stab of pain in her heart. "I do. But I've altered my life plan. I'm tired of waiting. I want to open that center and make a difference. If that means I settle for a different type of marriage, then so be it. Love comes in many forms. I'm sure Kingston and I will be quite happy together."

Charles studied her profile, then placed his finger under her chin and turned her face to meet his. "You are an amazing woman, Elaine Lockwood. I am delighted I have gotten to know you this past week."

Lainey smiled, her insides warming. "And I you, Charles Devereaux. I do hope when you return to London, you will call on me."

He returned her genuine smile. "With pleasure, my lady. With pleasure."

THE GUESTS HAD all scattered to their rooms to rest and prepare for the ball later that evening. Lainey, Elizabeth, and Anne sat in Lainey's room trying to decide how Lainey should dress her hair. They were giggling like schoolgirls as they took turns giving Lainey terrible hair-dos.

"Really, you girls aren't helping," Lainey admonished as she looked in the mirror. A giant feather hung out of the side of her head like a sad, droopy chicken.

"Oh, but it's such fun!" Anne laughed. She hugged Lainey from behind, meeting her eyes in the mirror. "Viscount Kingston? Truly?"

Lainey sighed and turned toward the two closet friends she had in the world. "I think he's perfect. He supports my endeavors, he's easy to converse with, has a lovely disposition, and is financially secure. We suit quite well."

"That's a rather dry list," Anne said wryly. "I'd always thought Mr. Mayfield—"

"I do not want to talk about Gavin Mayfield anymore. He has made his choice, and I have made mine."

"But he loves you, I am sure of it!" Elizabeth exclaimed.

"Whether he does or not makes no difference. He will not marry me, and I wish to marry."

"I don't understand why he is so dead set against marriage," Anne mused.

"Because he's terrified of turning out like his brother."

"What? But that's preposterous!"

"I know that, and you know that, but it's what he truly believes. And he doesn't want children. He fears he's going to pass on that violent streak to them. He knows how much I want to be a mother and said he couldn't take that away from me."

Elizabeth stared at her, dumbfounded. "That's his reasoning for passing on the love of his life? I may throttle him myself."

"It sounds ridiculous to us, but fear is a strong emotion. There isn't anything I can do to change his belief. He has to come to that decision himself. And I don't want to wait anymore."

"Oh, Lainey," Anne said, regret tinging her words.

"Do not pity me. I will get over him, just as I did before."

"Before?"

Lainey looked at the two women and decided it was time

to come clean. The whole humiliating story poured out of her, about her declaration and rejection, her hasty failed engagement, and how it all left her feeling unsure of herself. "All these years, I thought it was me, that I was simply undesirable. So, I redoubled my efforts to be the perfect woman, only it turns out no one can be perfect and perfection isn't all that exciting."

"I am definitely going to throttle him," Elizabeth announced.

Lainey giggled. "I appreciate your loyalty, but I'd rather we all just move forward. Mr. Devereaux has shown me the error of my ways and I am betrothed to a man who doesn't find me boring in the least."

"Speaking of Mr. Devereaux," Anne drawled, "What exactly happened last night?"

Two expectant faces waited for her reply. "Well, for heaven's sake, do I have to tell you everything?"

"Of course!"

Lainey rolled her eyes and turned back to the mirror, picking up her brush and stalling with a few strokes of her hair. "If you must know, Mr. Devereaux also proposed. He was a little overzealous in his enthusiasm when he kissed me, and Gavin came upon us when I was struggling to break free. So, Gavin punched him."

"He *kissed* you? Heavens, Lainey, your lips have seen their share of—" Elizabeth broke off at Lainey's quelling glance.

"Wait, Mr. Devereaux proposed as well? Goodness, perhaps I should have a house party!" Anne laughed.

"And you chose Kingston over Devereaux?" Elizabeth said in disbelief. "Lainey, have you lost your mind?"

"Kingston is a perfectly amiable gentleman."

"But he's forty if he's a day!"

"He is thirty-seven, Eliza. Not decrepit yet. I know you

are quite taken with Mr. Devereaux, but I thought he deserved more than I could give."

Elizabeth paused. "You mean your heart. Oh, Lainey, this is just not right."

Lainey put down her brush. "It is what I am choosing. I will be perfectly happy with Kingston. I like him rather a lot. Now, you two must go get ready for the ball. Gavin has asked me to meet him on the terrace at seven, and I agreed."

"I can't believe you are even still speaking to him at this point," Anne said dryly. "I'd rather like to bludgeon him myself."

"You will do no such thing," Lainey scolded. "There's been enough bloodshed. I can handle him myself. He can say his piece and then take himself off to wherever he is going to go, and I can be done with him."

The two women exchanged glances behind her and left. Lainey regarded her reflection, the truth of the matter showing in her eyes. She scoffed at herself. "You are a fool if you think you are ever going to be done with Gavin Mayfield." She scowled. Oh, well. After tonight, she would have a fiancé to focus her love on and a new life ahead, one that did not include a handsome, misguided soul who turned her world on its ear.

GAVIN CONSULTED his pocket watch once again. One minute later than the last time he had looked. He'd barely made it back from London in time, but everything was in place. He had not yet spoken with Aidan, but he fervently hoped he would understand. Gavin had absolutely no idea what had occurred in his absence today, but he prayed he was not too late.

A rustle sounded behind him. He turned, and his breath stole from his lungs. Lainey stood before him, hair done in soft curls about her head, twined with hot house roses. The beads on her gown reflected the torch light, the diamonds at her throat winking at him, all making her sparkle like a woodland nymph sprinkled with the stars. The silk of her gown had an iridescent quality to it that changed color from pink to blue every time she moved. He couldn't tear his eyes from her.

"God, Lainey..." he breathed. "You...you look—"

"Was there a reason you called me out here?"

Ah, so she was still cross. She had every right to be. "I...I wanted to apologize."

"Save your breath," she snapped, turning to go into the house.

"Wait! Please, wait." His heart was pounding so hard he was sure she could hear it. He held his breath, but slowly, she turned to face him, her gaze cool.

"I behaved abominably. I honestly don't know what I was thinking, and I wouldn't blame you if you never wanted to speak to me again."

"Then we are done here."

"But—" he said quickly. "Eighteen years. For eighteen years you have been part of my life. I would hope that counts for something in this situation." She continued to stare at him stonily, her jaw set. But she wasn't leaving, so Gavin plowed ahead. "Before I say anything else, I must know...are congratulations in order for you and Devereaux?"

"Does that change your apology?"

"Er—no. But it does have some bearing on what I'm about to say."

Lainey let him squirm a few moments more. "No," she finally said. "I am not engaged to Mr. Devereaux."

He nearly fainted with relief. He wasn't too late. His heart leapt with joy. "That's—that's good, because—"

"I've accepted Viscount Kingston."

"You—what?" Gavin's leaping heart crashed, splatting somewhere near his feet.

"I've accepted the Viscount's offer. It will be announced at the ball."

"But—" Gavin's vision swam before him. He'd thought Kingston was going to wait until he could introduce her to Rose. He'd thought with Devereaux out of the way—

"Gavin? Have you more to say?"

Gavin's mouth opened and closed like a fish gasping for breath. He couldn't feel his fingers, couldn't find his voice. He had known this was a possibility, but hadn't allowed himself to believe it.

He'd lost her.

All he had done today was for naught.

And it was no one's fault but his. He knew he should say something, but he could barely breathe, let alone speak. He was paralyzed by the reality of spending his life without her, watching her with someone else, building a life that would only include him on social occasions, if he was lucky. No more afternoon teas with endless discussions of politics and theater, no more late nights sitting by the fire with her and Aidan, listening to her read or chatting amiably about their day, no more consulting behind Aidan's back on which silk she thought would sell better. No more early morning gallops through the fields of Rosecroft, when the mist was just burning off and the dew was sparkling on the grass in the rising sun.

No more kisses in the study at night. Or under the stars. Or anywhere. Ever. Someone else would have that privilege now.

The reality of that came crashing down on him, practically forcing him to the ground with its weight. He knew he'd propelled her to this decision. He knew the blame for this mess lay squarely at his feet. He also knew he should be a man and offer congratulations, despite dying a slow death inside. But when he opened his mouth to wish her happy, what came out instead was, "Don't marry him."

CHAPTER 22

"I beg your pardon?"

She did not sound pleased in the least. Gavin swallowed hard. "I love you, Lainey. I always have. I know it may not seem—"

"You love me?" She spoke so softly he barely heard her.

"Y—yes." He couldn't get a read on what she was thinking, but she didn't exactly look like the news thrilled her. "I have been an utter fool, and I realize that this is a sudden declar—"

"You *love me?*" That was much louder. And definitely more shrill. Her nostrils flared and fire snapped in her eyes.

"Lainey—"

"No." She held up her hand. "Just stop talking."

"But I—"

"Stop it," she hissed. "Stop it right now. How dare you? You had two years. *Two years,* Gavin," she bit out.

"Lainey, I am so sorry. I wanted—"

"Save your apologies, they mean nothing."

Well, that stung. But he conceded he deserved it. He took in Lainey's high color and her flashing eyes. Right, then. She was good and furious with him.

"After everything you have put me through, you think you can suddenly decide you love me, and I am going to what, fall at your feet?" A bit of hysterical laughter bubbled out of her. "Oh, this is rich." She covered her eyes with a hand, still chuckling.

"Lainey, I know I've behaved abominably—"

"You are damn right you have," she snapped. "Your behavior last night was unconscionable. I was mortified. *Mortified!*"

"Perhaps if you would stop interrupting me, I can explain."

"I don't want your explanations, Gavin. You made your choice. You had plenty of opportunities to opt for another path, yet you still chose the one that didn't include me."

Pain infused every word she uttered. Gavin wasn't sure there was going to be a way back from the mess he'd created, but he had to try. "Lainey, I have been a bloody idiot, I know that. I've been selfish and callow and I probably don't deserve your forgiveness. But I'm asking for it. I am begging you to give me another chance."

"Another chance?" Lainey marched over to Gavin and glared up into his face. "How many chances do you think you should get, Gavin? How many times should I be stupid enough to fall for you? How many times do I let my heart get broken?"

He gripped her shoulders. "I was wrong to—"

She wrenched free from his grasp. "Do not touch me, Gavin. You have lost the right to touch me," she hissed. "I laid my heart at your feet, and then you rejected me out of hand for some silly notion that you might turn out like your brother. But you didn't even have the decency to tell me that. You just let me think I was undesirable, a ridiculous young girl who was infatuated with her brother's best friend."

"About that—"

"I am not done speaking!" she shouted. Her chest heaved and her eyes were feverish. Gavin wasn't entirely sure he wasn't about to be slapped. "I was so devastated that I accepted the first offer of marriage that came along simply because it made me feel wanted. Do you have any idea what it's like to entrust your heart to someone who you are so sure feels the same way as you, only to have that person utterly crush it?"

"I am beginning to understand that, yes," Gavin said softly.

"I almost married the entirely wrong person for me because of *you.*" Lainey flung her words at him, jabbing a finger into his chest. "And then that man couldn't bring himself to marry me, either! I suffered through a scandal thanks to you. I was a social outcast because of you. I felt *worthless.*" Her voice broke. "Because of *you.*"

Gavin was fervently wishing she *would* slap him. Anything was better than seeing tears sparkling on her lashes and knowing that it was his fault they were there.

"Do you know what I gave up for you? Years. Years of my life wasted, waiting for you to change your mind. Oh yes, I was that stupid to believe that you didn't really mean what you'd said, and that you'd realize that we were perfect for each other. I didn't stop loving you when you rejected me, oh, no. So, for the past two years, I have choked down my humiliation and pretended that we are just friends, when I have wanted nothing more than to be swept into your arms every time you walked into the room. And when it finally happens, what do you do? You tell me that the most beautiful experience of my life was a mistake."

Gavin cringed. "That was insensitive of me. I didn't mean it."

"And now," she continued as if he hadn't spoken, poking him again. "Now that you have frittered away the last two years, now that you have been here for a solid week, fighting this so-called attraction, *now* you have decided all of a sudden that you love me?"

"I didn't just decide—"

"Now, after you have humiliated me once again, and so publicly, you have the gall to ask me to break my engagement to another man because it is suddenly convenient for you to love me? How dare you, Gavin Mayfield?" she choked out, the tears finally spilling down her cheeks. "How *dare* you?"

That last question was barely above a whisper and so laced with agony that Gavin's gut twisted in on itself. He wanted to speak but his tongue was blocking his throat. In fact, he couldn't seem to move at all except for the shallow rise and fall of his chest.

He was such an arse.

A bloody, *bloody* arse.

How could he have been such a careless fool with her heart? How could he have not seen the pain he had caused her?

And why, *why* had he let fear guide him, instead of love?

"Forgive me, Lainey. I thought I was protecting you."

"I didn't need your protection, Gavin. Damn you!" she cried, striking his chest with both her fists in tandem. "I just needed your love." She swiped angrily at the tears on her face. "Damn you," she whispered, broken.

Her words were a sucker punch. He couldn't believe how thoroughly he had cocked things up. They stood, staring at each other, the sound of ball preparations drifting out onto the terrace…muffled voices, the clink of silver…the insects in the garden waking up to sing now that darkness had fallen around them.

"Christ, Lainey." Gavin stood helplessly, watching an invisible door slam shut in his face. "I'm so very sorry." He searched desperately for something to say that would make the world right again, but he was at a loss. "Tell me what to do. There must be some way I can fix this."

Lainey shook her head sadly. "I've lived with the pain of loving you in my heart, goading myself into believing that someday you would open your eyes and see me standing there, and you would love me back, but you never did," Lainey said quietly. "Now, it's too late. It was foolish of me to hope, but I will be a fool no longer." Lainey squared her shoulders. "I will not break my promise to Kingston, Gavin. I will marry him, as I agreed to do. But don't worry," she added. "You'll get over me soon enough. Perhaps in a couple of years. Good evening, Mr. Mayfield. I wish you well."

With a swoosh of silk, she melted into the shadows and disappeared into the house. Gavin watched her go, wretchedness enfolding him. What a hash he had made of things. Kate was wrong. Lainey would never forgive him, not this time. Their friendship, as he knew it, was over.

He put a hand on his hip, the other raking through his hair, and blew out a breath, studying the flagstone as if it was going to give him advice on what to do next. With a groan, he spun around, tearing at his hair. What had he done?

He collapsed on the balustrade, leaning heavily on his arms and staring blindly out over the now dark garden. He'd just let the best thing in his life slip through his fingers. A deep, dark pit opened up inside him, swallowing the light. Gavin had yet to speak to Aidan. He was terrified he wouldn't be able to repair that friendship, either, and then Gavin would be well and truly lost.

A flare in the darkness caught his attention. He turned to find Viscount Kingston lounging against a pillar across the terrace, standing in a pool of light spilling out from the ball-room, cigar smoke curling about him like a lover's caress. The Viscount strolled over to him and Gavin sighed. Best to get this over with.

"I hear congratulations are in order," he said with a cheerfulness he did not feel.

"I thank you," Kingston acknowledged, setting down a snifter of brandy on the balustrade beside Gavin. "I thought you might need this."

Gavin's gut tightened and he slid a suspicious gaze to Kingston. "How much of that conversation did you hear?"

Kingston took a puff on his cigar. "Enough to know we must have an honest chat." He copied Gavin's position and flicked some ashes into the garden below. "I have watched you and Lady Elaine closely this past week. There is clearly a special bond between the two of you, and I question why you have not offered for her yourself?"

Gavin watched as the man casually took a puff of his cigar and blew the smoke out. "You are nothing if not direct," he replied drily.

"I see no reason to dance, do you?"

The men fell silent and Gavin reached for the snifter, inhaling the spicy aroma. Aidan must have poured his best to celebrate his sister's engagement.

"You love her, do you not?"

Gavin let the fine brandy roll down his throat. Admitting to a man you respected that you were in love with his fiancée was rather awkward. "Yes. But I cannot marry her. At least, that is what I thought."

"And why is that?"

"My family…has a dark past."

"Ah yes." Kingsley nodded. "I've heard of your brother. Very sad indeed."

Gavin scoffed. "If it were just my brother, I wouldn't have been so worried."

"There were more like him?"

Gavin could scarcely believe he was about to say this out loud. "I think my brother was the worst of the lot, but yes, there were more." Gavin took a deep breath and gave Kingston a brief history of his family tree, the scandals that had followed the family for generations, and how hard he'd fought to be a respected member of society.

"And what does all this have to do with you not offering for Lady Elaine?"

Gavin stared out over the garden, the memory of the night in the summerhouse assaulting him. He could still feel Lainey's body beneath his, her dewy skin beckoning him to touch her. His groin tightened at the memory. He'd never shared a night like that with anyone.

Might never again.

"I will not allow my family line to continue. I cannot. There has been too much bloodshed, too much abuse. I will not be part of that. My brother was a horrible person, and given that we were twins, I feared the chance of passing those tendencies on was too great a risk."

"I see. And Lainey, of course, wants children."

"She wants to be a mother more than anything. I could not take that from her."

"And you've discussed this with her?"

Gavin shrugged. "More or less."

"Hmpf," Kingston snorted. "I suspect less."

Gavin clenched his jaw. "It's more than just that." He went on to describe everything he had confessed to his parents last night about his fears of not being able to control his own temper. The more he spoke, the more weight lifted off of his shoulders, and he realized what a burden this secret had been. "I would never forgive myself if I physically hurt Lainey."

"You wouldn't." Kingsley took another drag on his cigar.

"How can you possibly know that? Christ, did you see what I did to Devereaux last night?"

Kingston puffed out the smoke. "Well, that pup deserved it. I would have pummeled him, too."

Gavin stared in shock at Kingston. "You…you would?"

"Of course! Any man who forces a kiss on a woman should have his ears boxed. Stupid pup. He needs to stop drinking, only gets him in trouble." He chuckled at the shock on Gavin's face. "You're a good man, Mr. Mayfield. You did what any feeling human being would do, even a peaceful one such as I. And the stakes are always higher when someone you care about is involved. Actually, I'm quite sure Devereaux was lucky it was you who stumbled upon them and not her brother. I fear Ashby may have done much worse."

Gavin shook his head. "But it felt so…satisfying. I'm ashamed of feeling that way."

"Look, Mr. Mayfield—"

"Please. Call me Gavin."

"Very well then. Gavin. Humans are wired to protect. All you did was follow your instincts because Lady Elaine was being threatened. It's nothing more than any of us would have done. It's natural to feel embarrassed about losing control. We all like to show our best selves to each other."

"Funny, my father said much the same thing to me last night."

"We parents do sometimes know what we are talking about. If only our children would listen," he chided. Gavin snorted and took another sip of brandy. Kingston straightened. "I have a confession to make." He leaned a hip against the balustrade. "Madness runs in *my* family. My father was a stark raving lunatic. I shared your fears once upon a time. Just like you, I was determined not to take a wife lest I subject her to a future of misery, and I was absolutely convinced I would not have children."

"But you married."

"I did. Once I met Annabelle, I could no more walk away from her than I could topple an oak with my bare hands. She was the part of me I'd been missing my entire life. But I was bullheaded, like you, and almost lost her when I informed her that I couldn't marry her. But when she asked me why, I decided to tell her the truth rather than try to hide it. She said that decision wasn't up to me, that it was ours to make together, and so we married. It was a risk, but one she was willing to take because she loved me. Of course, we never imagined it would be she who left me, but if I hadn't let her make up her own mind, I'd still be a solitary bachelor living out a bleak existence, waiting to see if I was going to lose my mind or not, and if that was the case, I'd be doing it alone. But Annabelle...she filled my life with light and love, and left me with a beautiful daughter. I'm still terrified I'm going to subject those I love to the madness that my father had, but that is a risk I have to take in order to have a rich life. And that, my friend, far outweighs simply existing."

Gavin's throat grew suspiciously tight and he didn't trust himself to respond. He looked down at the brandy in his hands that had suddenly lost its flavor. He didn't dare meet Kingston's eyes. "Why are you telling me this?" he asked hoarsely.

Kingston remained silent for a long while, making a show of stubbing out his cigar on the stone. He sighed heavily. "Lady Elaine is a gracious, intelligent, and strong woman. When she gives her heart, she gives it completely, and she deserves happiness such as Annabelle and I had. I want what's best for her...but I am not entirely sure that is me."

Gavin turned to regard the viscount. "What are you getting at, Kingston?"

The man shrugged. "I gathered from your conversation with Lady Elaine that you have changed your mind about marriage, but there is now the impediment of her engagement to someone else in the way."

Gavin watched Kingston's face in the darkness, the torches that had been lit in the garden below dancing over his features. "I'm too late."

"It's never too late to make things right." Kingston smiled slowly. "Come walk with me in the garden a bit where no one will overhear our conversation. We have more to discuss, you and I." He moved off toward the stairs, disappearing into the night until he walked through another circle of light thrown by the torches. He paused and turned back to Gavin, raising a brow, and then vanished out of the light again, leaving Gavin to scramble after him.

An odd feeling bloomed in Gavin's chest. Something that might be akin to hope.

Gavin watched Lainey twirl gracefully about the dance floor from his spot near the potted palm. She was enchanting, her smile genuine though he knew he'd upset her terribly. He'd avoided the ballroom as long as he could without being conspicuous. There were many whispers, but thankfully, his friends were too kind to bring up the scene he'd made last night. He'd apologize to all of them later, but for the immediate moment, his focus was on the woman in Donovan's arms, laughing as though she had not a care in the world. Gavin recognized her mask.

Kingston had surprised him this evening, and now Gavin had a plan. This simply had to work. He was so enthralled watching Lainey that he didn't hear Aidan approach.

"She's a vision, isn't she?"

Gavin snapped his head toward the voice to find Aidan standing next to him, his gaze directed out to the dance floor, gazing at the graceful couples. Gavin just stared at him for a few moments, wanting to say so much, yet at a loss words, his throat thick with emotion. He turned his head back toward the dance floor, trying to decide what to say. Finally, he chose the simplest but most important place to begin.

"Aidan, I am so sorry."

Aidan nodded but didn't take his eyes off Lainey. "How long have you been in love with my sister?"

That brought Gavin up short, and he searched his heart before giving an honest answer. "I think just about as long as I've known her."

Aidan turned to face him. "Then *why*, Gavin?" he asked softly. "Why didn't you offer for her years ago? Did you think I would be angry?"

"She's your little sister, Aidan. One does not pursue the younger sister of his best friend. It's in the gentleman's code book."

"Gavin, you are practically family already. Nothing would make me happier than to see the two of you together, you must know that. So, what is it, really?"

Gavin looked back out over the dance floor. "You know my family history, Aidan. I was terrified I ran the risk of turning out like all the other rotters in my family, especially since Garrett and I were twins."

Aidan nodded. "Elizabeth said as much. I didn't believe her. How could you ever think you were that kind of man?"

Gavin sighed. "Because I am a complete and utter fool." He grimaced. "I'm assuming you've been told the whole story by now."

"Elizabeth filled me in on the most important parts. Lainey kept her distance today, but I know I owe her an apology." He turned toward Gavin. "You could have saved us all a lot of heartache and embarrassment by talking to us, you know. You have always been part of our family. You are like a brother to me. It pains me that you couldn't just be honest with me."

"I know. I'm sorry. But I was ashamed. And I truly

believed I was doing the right thing by keeping Lainey at a distance."

"What changed?"

Gavin flushed. "I kissed her. And everything fell into place."

A smile tugged at Aidan's lips. "I remember a similar feeling with Elizabeth."

The two men stood silent once again, letting the music and the din of voices swirl around them. Gavin's expression turned troubled.

"I hurt Lainey badly. I didn't mean to. I thought I was protecting her, but instead I crushed her heart. I don't know if the damage is repairable, but I would like to try."

Aidan was quiet. "My sister loves you, of that I am sure," he finally said. "It will take some time, but I think she will forgive you."

"Do you?"

Aidan studied his friend for a long, agonizing moment, then laid his hand on Gavin's shoulder and squeezed. "I do." A pause. "You know I love you, right?"

"I do."

"You are a bloody, cork-brained numbskull."

Gavin chuckled. "I know that, too, but thanks for making it clear." He sobered. "I really am sorry for my behavior and all the drama I caused. I hurt you both, and I deeply regret my actions. I hope you can forgive me."

"Just so long as you understand that if you hurt my sister again, I *will* have to kill you."

"That sounds fair."

"Then you are forgiven."

Gavin's eyes welled up, and if he wasn't mistaken, so did Aidan's. Hard to be sure in the dim light. Gavin desperately needed to defuse the emotional moment before he started blubbering again. "You know, Lainey really did ask me to—"

"Pray you, do not finish that sentence. I *know* you are not blaming my sweet, little, innocent sister for what happened in the summerhouse."

Gavin grinned. "She's not so innocent as you might think."

Aidan was scandalized. "Gav, these are things I definitely do not want to hear!"

"You said to be honest."

"Not like that!"

"All right, all right." He rocked on his heels. "Best damn night of my life," he muttered.

"Gah!" Aidan stuck his fingers in his ears. "Stop it! Stop it right now!"

They dissolved into laughter, and some of the leaden weight in Gavin's chest lifted. Things would be all right.

Aidan hesitantly removed his fingers from his ears. "Are you done?"

"I think that will suffice."

"Dunderhead."

Gavin shoved his hands in his pockets, still chuckling. He had been blessed with this man's friendship; how he had so willingly jeopardized it, he would never know. He would never risk it again.

"Well," Aidan said, clapping him on the shoulder once more. "I'm glad we've worked things out, because I would have really hated to cut you out of the business. I rather need you."

Gavin smiled, the tightness in his throat returning. "I rather need you, too."

Aidan returned his soft smile. "I spoke with Kingston. You are sure about this? There is no going back."

Gavin nodded. "I love her, Aidan. I have to fix this. She deserves no less."

Aidan regarded his life-long friend, understanding and

acceptance shining in his eyes. "Well, then. I do believe I hear a waltz."

~

AS THE EVENING WORE ON, the knot in Lainey's stomach grew. Her engagement would be announced at the end of the supper waltz, which was rapidly approaching. Once announced, her fate was sealed. Gavin was present, but had avoided her all evening, as she wished. She'd seen him shake hands with Kingston earlier, presumably offering congratulations. The nerve of that man! Did he really think he could swoop in at the last moment, turn her world upside down once again, and expect her to fall at his feet with gratitude? Hardly! She was not one to break her promises.

Still. As Lainey had danced and laughed and faked her way through conversations, her ire had faded some. Finally being able to confront Gavin and tell him just how much agony he'd caused her had been cathartic. She was still hurt and angry, yes, but did she really mean to cut Gavin out of her life so completely? She couldn't imagine a life without him in it. He'd been a blundering idiot, but she'd had some time to digest everything he had told her, and although she wished he'd just been truthful with her from the start, she could see how he thought he'd been protecting her. Men. Why did they all think women needed protecting like a delicate flower? She snorted. She'd like to see a man have a baby, then we'd see who was delicate!

She took a moment to herself as she sipped a glass of lemonade, watching Gavin surreptitiously as he made his way around the edge of the dance floor, looking as handsome as sin. Her stupid, blasted heart still fluttered at the sight of him. She rolled her eyes in disgust, annoyed with herself for wavering. Because as much as it pained her to admit, if Gavin asked her to dance, she would have to say yes, and if she spent any time at all in his arms, she wasn't entirely sure she could go through with her engagement to Lord Kingston, and she must. Women were depending on her, and she so desperately needed to build this business by herself, for herself. She had worth and a sharp mind, not just a pretty face, and it was high time she own up to it. This center was something she would accomplish all on her own, and be proud of it for the rest of her days.

She slammed her punch cup down on the table. To hell with Gavin Mayfield. He was missing out on something—someone—bloody brilliant. More fool he. *She* was going to have a wonderful life, whether he was a part of it or not.

Kingston materialized in front of her. "Are you ready, my dear?" he asked as he took her hand, kissing it.

"What?"

"They are cuing up for the supper waltz."

"Oh! Yes. Yes, of course." Lainey placed a hand on her stomach to still the butterflies and gave Kingston what she hoped was a genuine smile. "Shall we?"

He led her out onto the dance floor, and as he took her into his arms, Lainey saw Gavin watching them from the side of the dance floor. They made eye contact and she froze. Gavin stared at her for a long and excruciatingly uncomfortable moment, the stark need in his eyes making her breath hitch.

"Are you all right?" Kingston asked.

"Perfect," she replied brightly, turning back to him.

Kingston followed the direction of her gaze. "I can't help but notice that Mr. Mayfield seems to harbor some feelings for you," he said as the music began.

"Gavin? He's just a friend."

"A friend who smashed his fist into Devereaux's face?"

Lainey grimaced. "That was badly done of him, I assure

you. He was being over protective of a woman he thinks of as a sister."

"Hm." Kingston's eyes crinkled. "Or was he a man who acted out of jealousy?"

Alarm bells started going off in her head. "Richard, why are we discussing Gavin and his supposed feelings?"

"Because…because I think perhaps you return them."

Lainey's face grew hot. Had Devereaux told him about the night in the garden? She would throttle him if he had. "Don't be ridiculous. I have no particular feelings for Gavin Mayfield."

Kingston twirled her under his arm and back into his embrace, regarding her with understanding eyes. "Don't you?" he asked softly.

Lainey looked up at him, her throat tightening, strangling any reply she was trying to give. She wanted to say no, she didn't give a fig about Gavin Mayfield any longer, but the truth…she knew the truth was written on her face. Despite everything, she still loved Gavin. She always would. "Richard…"

"My dear. I loved my wife with every fiber of my being. I will always love her, and she will be a part of any marriage I make going forward."

"And I understand that. There will be room for her in my heart as well."

Richard looked over her head, his eyes suspiciously bright. "And that is one of the many reasons I offered for you. You are such a caring, selfless woman, and someone who I think understands me on a deeper level than most. I believe we could have a comfortable marriage, and that is all I want at this stage in my life. I've already known true love, and I know how absolutely magical it can be. And I could never stand in the way of that for someone else, no matter how much I would like her for myself. You deserve more than a comfortable marriage."

Panic rose in Lainey's chest. "What…what are you saying?"

Kingston pulled her inappropriately close to whisper in her ear. "I am releasing you from our engagement."

"What? No!" This could not be happening. She was so close to achieving her goal, she couldn't fail now.

"You are a remarkable woman, Lainey, and I know you are going to accomplish great things. I do hope we will remain friends so that I may share in those joys with you, but I cannot let you sacrifice yourself." He squeezed her hand. "I wish you every happiness, my lady."

"You can't mean—"

But Richard twirled a protesting Lainey away from him once more.

Right into Gavin Mayfield's arms.

She stumbled into his chest. "Oh!"

"Hello, love." Gavin pulled her into his arms and smoothly continued the waltz. She tried to distance herself, but he held her fast.

"That was a dirty trick, Mr. Mayfield," she growled. He knew full well she couldn't leave him on the dance floor without making a scene.

"Lainey, I know you are angry, and rightfully so, but please, hear me out."

"I have heard quite enough from you. I thought I made that clear."

"You did, but when have I been one to obey? Please, Lainey. We cannot end our years of friendship on this awful note. I ask for just a few minutes of your time, and then I will abide by your decision. I owe you an apology, and I pray you will listen to it.""

She glared at him, ruthlessly tamping down all the

tingling that was racing through her body at his touch. Was she doomed to spend all eternity desiring this man? She didn't say anything, so Gavin forged ahead.

"I have made an absolute mess of things, and I am desperately hoping that you will be able to forgive me for being so dim-witted. You see, eighteen years ago, my family bought an estate next door to the most wonderful family, and I was fortunate enough to become friends with their children. There was, in particular, this little girl with a sunny smile and a voracious appetite for adventure. But I was an older and smarter boy, and boys know that little girls can't keep up with boys and just get in the way of our adventures because they don't like to get dirty and they are afraid of everything. That little girl kindly pointed out how small-minded I was by pushing me into the pond."

The music ended and they drew to a stop, but Gavin didn't release her. "I fell in love with her that day. The years went by, and every day I grew to love her more. But then her family inherited a title, and suddenly she was a lady, and I was still plain old me. I wanted better for her. I convinced myself I wasn't worthy of her. She deserved every happiness in life, and I was afraid I couldn't give that to her. My family was surrounded by scandal, and as my brother's behavior spiraled out of control, I became terrified that one day I, too, would be like him. So when she came to me and confessed she loved me, I panicked and rejected her. I let my fear cloud my judgement and I believed I couldn't be what she wanted, what she deserved.

"I thought I was doing the right thing, but all I did was hurt her...hurt *you*," he whispered, the sheen of tears glinting in his eyes. "I'm so sorry, Lainey. I thought I was doing what was best for you, but instead I broke your spirit."

Lainey tried—really tried—not to cry, but a rebellious

tear slid down her cheek. Her anger with him was rapidly melting away.

She slowly became aware that not only had the music stopped, but she and Gavin were the only ones left on the dance floor, and no one had moved into supper. Well, of course not, they were waiting for her. She stepped out of Gavin's embrace.

"Gavin, I have to lead everyone to—"

"It can wait."

She glanced around the room, realizing that every pair of eyes was on them, whispers swirling about like mist on the moor. No one seemed interested in supper. Her gaze fell on Elizabeth and Aidan, who were both watching her and…grinning?

"Gavin?" she asked absently. "What on earth is going…" She turned back to him and the intensity in his expression stole her breath.

"Lainey, I love you. I have always loved you. And I'm sorry it's taken me this long to come to my senses and realize that I am nothing without you. You are the one who makes my heart skip beats, the one who makes me laugh…the one who stood by me throughout every scandal my brother brought upon our household. The one who believes that I am a better man than I think I am. And it took almost losing you to someone else for me to wake up and realize how desperately I need you in my life, always. I'm fortunate that Kingston is a very understanding man." Lainey could only watch in bewilderment as he exchanged nods with Kingston. Gavin waited for the chucking to die down before he continued. "As I was largely unprepared for this moment, I have only this to give to you." He pulled a folded piece of paper from his coat pocket and handed it to her.

"What is this?" she asked, as she took it and unfolded it with shaking hands.

"It's the deed to the property on Fenchurch Street. You are now the sole owner, free and clear. On the condition that you allow it to be a wedding gift from me."

"Gavin!" she gasped, her gaze flying to the paper in her hands. She scanned the parchment, not quite believing what she was seeing. "But I thought you and Aidan…" But no, there was her name, in bold script, listed as the owner of the property. She raised her shocked gaze, only to find Gavin on his knee at her feet.

"I should also mention that I am hoping that wedding includes me. Marry me, Lainey. Be my wife and I will try to be all you've ever wanted."

A sob tore from Lainey and she pressed a hand to her mouth. She couldn't speak past the lump in her throat, just stared at Gavin in utter bemusement. She searched out Kingston in the crowd, and he met her eyes with a smile. He bowed slightly, and Lainey suddenly understood the meaning of the earlier handshake with Gavin. They'd made a deal, and Kingston had given her up with his blessing. The selfless man had bestowed upon her a most precious gift, one for which she would be forever grateful.

"Lainey, I hate to rush you, but my knee is protesting loudly," Gavin implored.

"Oh! Gavin, please, do get up," she managed, offering her hand and helping him to a standing position. He took her face gently in his hands and wiped away her tears with his thumbs.

"What do you say, Lainey?" he said softly. "Will you marry me?"

"Oh, Gavin," she whispered. "Are you sure?"

"I've never been more sure of anything in my life. I'm sorry I was too dimwitted to see how very much you mean to me. I want it all, Lainey. I want you, I want to raise our children together no matter what challenges may come, I want to be by your side while you build your help center from the ground up and see all the women whose lives you are going to change. I want to grow old with you and love you all the days of my life, if you'll have me."

The crowd around them was tomb-silent as they collectively held their breath in anticipation of her answer. Lainey drew in her own deep breath...then spoke the words that would forever change her life.

"I will."

A great cheer went up, and Gavin swept her into his arms and kissed her deeply, encouraging hoots and hollers from their audience. Satisfaction seeped into her bones and a feeling of rightness settled over her as she sighed against his lips.

"Does this mean you forgive me?" he murmured.

"Perhaps," Lainey replied, laying her hand against his cheek. "But don't worry, you have the rest of your life to make it up to me."

Laughter rumbled in his chest as he pulled her close. "I will work all of my days to do so. I love you, Lainey. So very much."

"And I love you, Gavin. I always have, and I always will."

"I'm counting on it," he murmured, lowering his lips to hers once again.

CHAPTER 24

It was late in the afternoon the following day when the last of the guests departed. Lainey was exhausted, but happy, as the well-wishers bid fond farewells. All in all, she'd have to say the party was a success, though it certainly hadn't ended as she had initially planned. She had to admit, she preferred this outcome.

She turned away from the door and Elizabeth put her arm around her. "Looks like you could use a cup of tea. I think I'll join you."

Lainey smiled gratefully at her sister-in-law. "That sounds like an excellent idea. My head is spinning."

"I imagine so."

"Lainey," Aidan interrupted. "Before my wife steals you away, could I have a word with you in my study?"

"Of course. I'll meet you in the drawing room in a few minutes, Eliza."

She followed her brother to his study, the scene of both her first kiss and the disastrous argument the other night. It was an odd juxtaposition of memories. Aidan took his favorite position, perching a hip on the edge of his desk.

"Are you happy?"

"Of course! Why would you even ask that?"

"Because I thought I knew what you wanted…hell, I thought I knew *you* up until the other night."

"Did you bring me in here to chastise me again?"

"No. I brought you in here to apologize for being so high-handed with you. I love you, Lainey, and I've only ever wanted what I thought was best for you, but it turns out, I didn't know what that was, and that threw me."

"Oh, Aidan." Lainey came to stand beside him, slipping an arm around his waist and resting her head on his shoulder. "I know you love me, and I know you have done the best you could being father, mother, and brother to me all at once. It was a lot for you to take on at such a young age, and you have been nothing short of marvelous at it. I don't know what I would have done without you. But I think somewhere in there, you just didn't realize that I had grown up and needed to make my own choices."

He draped an arm across her shoulders and dropped a kiss on her head. "You grew up far too quickly for my liking."

She laughed, relishing the comfort of her big brother's arm about her. "I love you, even though you were a boor."

Aidan chuckled. "You cannot blame me for being shocked. You are still my little sister. I will protect you all of my life. *With* my life, if necessary."

"Oh dear, let us hope it doesn't come to that!" She pulled out of his embrace to look him in the eye. "Are *you* happy?"

"About you and Gav?"

She nodded. "It's not…awkward, is it?"

"As long as I blot the events of the other night out of my mind, not at all." He burst out laughing at the stricken look on her face. He reached for her hands, squeezing them reassuringly. "Lainey, I could not be more thrilled to welcome Gavin into this family—officially now. I had secretly hoped

the two of you would marry someday, but he was so disin-
clined toward marriage I'd given up the notion."

"You and me both. He was the reason behind the John
Danby disaster, you know." Surprise flitted across Aidan's
face. "It's true. I'd practically thrown myself at Gavin and
he'd refused me, so I accepted the first offer of marriage that
came along. Thankfully, John came to his senses before it
was too late."

"Wait. You threw yourself at Gavin?"

"I suggested the idea of marriage. He practically ran."

"When was this?"

"Two years ago. I think John proposed out of pity."

Aidan's warm, brown eyes clouded with hurt. "Lainey…
why didn't you tell me?"

"That I was in love with your best friend? Because you
would have bullied him into choosing something he didn't
want, just like you did the other night. He needed to arrive at
that conclusion himself or he would never have been happy,
and neither would I. Besides, he's your closest friend. You
must concede it would have been at least a little awkward for
me to tell you the truth about how I felt, especially given that
he didn't feel the same."

"Lainey, I had no idea…" Aidan shook his head. "Never
think that you can't talk to me about something. I am always
here for you. Promise me you will always be honest with me
from now on and tell me what's on your mind. I don't like
having secrets between us."

"Neither do I. But I was so worried I was going to ruin
your friendship…and I would have never forgiven myself for
that."

"Well, you did your best the other night, and Gav and I
are still on speaking terms, so I think we'll always be friends."

"You are never going to let that go, are you?"

"Nope. What are big brothers for? Come," he said, rising.

"I'm famished. Let us go have tea with Elizabeth and the two of you can chatter my ears off about wedding plans." He pulled Lainey into a tight embrace. "Lainey, my dear," he said softly. "My heart is so full."

"Do not make me cry on your superfine," she said into his shoulder. She drew back to look into his face. "Thank you for being such a sensational big brother."

"Ah, you make it easy, Lainey." He grinned and they headed for the drawing room.

GAVIN RETURNED FROM HIS PARENTS' home sometime later and joined them in the drawing room. The late afternoon sun was turning toward its golden hour, glinting off the mullioned windows and washing the earth with a soft glow. Lainey couldn't keep her eyes off of her fiancé, his blond locks glinting with a copper tint in the sunlight. She was still adjusting to the fact that he *was* her fiancé. Last night seemed almost a dream, and she was afraid she was going to wake up any moment. Gavin caught her eye.

"Lainey, I wonder if you would accompany me on a short ride before dark?"

"Oh, Gavin, I really am very tired—"

"Please. It won't take long."

They had barely had a moment alone since last night, and tired as she was, she was eager to have him to herself for a while. "I'd be glad to. I'll just need to change."

"We aren't going that far. What you have on will do. I'd like to be back before sundown."

"Very well, then let's be off."

They excused themselves and headed for the stables. Once Lainey's horse was saddled, they cantered off toward the pond. They rode in companionable silence for a few moments.

"How are you today?" Gavin asked her.

"A little worn out, and still in shock, I think."

Gavin smiled ruefully. "I'm sorry for the subterfuge. I was desperate to fix things and you wouldn't speak to me."

"Can you blame me?"

"No…no, I cannot. I am ashamed of how I handled this whole thing."

"I'm still rather miffed at you."

Gavin chuckled. "Miffed?"

Lainey gave him a sideways glance. "I can think of other words, but they are less polite," she said dryly.

"I deserve that," he agreed. "Lainey, I am sorry. I'm sorry I hurt you so badly as to make you feel worthless. Those words stabbed my heart last night. I had no idea I made you feel that way. I had hoped you were merely infatuated back then and would find someone decent to love. I didn't want you to live in the hell that I was in, wanting you so badly, but knowing I could never have you."

"Yet that is exactly where you consigned me."

"I know that now. It's been a miserable existence for both of us. And when you'd finally decided to move on, I thought I could let you go. I tried, for your sake. But then you kissed me—"

"Ah, *you* kissed *me*," she teased.

"—then you *asked* me to kiss you, and the moment I had you in my arms I knew it was all over. I was terrified to lose you and terrified to ask you to be part of my life. And I made the wrong choice. I know it will take time, but I hope one day you will forgive me for bungling things so badly."

They'd arrived at the pond, and Gavin reined his horse in. Lainey drew up beside him, and together, they dismounted, tethering the horses to a nearby tree. Gavin reached for her hand and kissed it, tugging her gently toward the pond. She fell into step beside him, but remained silent.

"There is something on your mind that you are not telling me, my darling." Gavin squeezed her hand gently. "What is it?"

Lainey bit her lip. This still seemed such a fragile reality, she was frightened to trust it. But she had to know for sure. They stood looking out over the still water, listening to the bees buzzing and the birds chirping while she gathered her thoughts. Finally, she took a steadying breath.

"Gavin, are you sure?" She asked in a small voice.

"Am I sure? Of what?"

"Do you really want to marry me?"

Gavin swung around in front of her to grip her shoulders. "Yes," he said fiercely. "Yes, I want to marry you. I don't ever want to be without you."

She cast her eyes downward, and Gavin moved his hands from her shoulders to the sides of her face. "Lainey," he said, tipping her head up to look at him. "I know last night was sudden and confusing…in the space of twenty-four hours, I tossed years of resistance aside, and you went from never wanting to see me again to being my fiancée. But believe me, I have never wanted anything more. I was slow to allow myself to have what I wanted, but now that it's been given to me, I can't wait to spend my life with you." He frowned in concern. "Perhaps I should be asking you the same question. We may have a potentially difficult road ahead of us. Now that you've had some time to think on it, do you still want to marry *me*?"

The corner of her mouth quirked up. "That's all I've ever wanted, Gavin. Nothing will change that."

He smiled, caressing her cheeks with his thumbs. "I love you, Lainey."

"And I love you," she whispered.

He pulled her to him for a languorous kiss, and she melted against him. It wasn't a dream; he was hers.

He pulled back, reaching into his pocket. "I know my proposal was a bit unorthodox, but I'm hoping this will dispel any lingering doubts about my intentions."

He produced a small box, opening it for her. Inside, nestled in silk, was a gleaming diamond ring in the form of a flower trailing around the wearer's finger. The afternoon sun sent sparks winking from the box.

"Oh, Gavin," she breathed. "It is stunning."

"It was my grandmother's. I think she would be happy for you to have it."

Her took her left hand in his and slid it on her finger. She fought back tears of joy.

"Gavin, it's perfect. I've never seen anything so perfect in my life."

"I'm glad you like it."

She lay her hand against his chest, admiring the fiery ring. "We are really doing this?"

"We are really doing this." He kissed her again, making her toes curl in her boots. Thank heaven she had a lifetime of this to look forward to.

"Do you have any idea how hard it was for me to keep from ravishing you on this very bank the other day?" he said against her lips.

"Oh, you mean on the day you ruined my very favorite bonnet?"

"You are never going to let me live that down, are you?"

"Oh no, I'm still plotting various ways to get back at you."

Laughter rumbled in Gavin's chest. "You know," he said, waggling his eyebrows. "We are quite alone out here," he said, dropping his voice to a husky tone and dragging a finger down her throat. "We could pick up where we left off the other day…" He let his words trail off suggestively.

"We *could...*" she agreed. "But there is something wrong here."

"What is it now?"

"You, my darling, are far too dry."

She brought her other hand up to his chest and his eyes widened with sudden understanding.

"Don't you da—Lai—!"

The resulting splash was *incredibly* satisfying. She grinned. "All right, we are even now," she called as Gavin came up to the surface. "I'm not even miffed anymore!"

Their joy-filled laughter rang out across the water, filling the shadows of the trees with light.

EPILOGUE

EPILOGUE

hree years later

LAINEY MOVED around the office with purpose. She checked to make sure everything was in order, and that the accounts were all settled, and there were enough supplies to at least guarantee no one was left in the lurch.

"You are going to wear the floorboards out, m'lady," Betsy observed wryly.

Lainey stopped her frantic bustling. "I'm sorry, I'm just nervous, I suppose. This place means a lot to me."

"And I'm going to take good care of it. You have done an incredible job here, but it's time to let someone else take the reins while you focus on your family."

Lainey sighed. "You are right, of course. I just didn't think it would be this hard to go."

"Well, for heaven's sake, you aren't going away forever. You'll be back once the babe is born, it just may be in a different capacity. You can teach whenever you want, and I would be disappointed if I didn't see you in here several times a week checking up on everyone. But you'll have a little one to contend with now, and if I know you, you aren't going to be a mother who lets the babe's nurse raise her child."

"Certainly not." Lainey rubbed her slightly rounded belly. It would be some months yet, but soon Lainey would fulfill her dream of having children.

Not that she wasn't already a mother. Through the help center, she'd met so many women with children who also needed help, and she'd fallen in love with each and every one of them. But there was one special child, one whose mother had succumbed to illness, that had captured Lainey's and Gavin's heart, and they had adopted her. Alice was six, and about to become a big sister. She couldn't be more excited.

"How is Mr. Mayfield?"

"He's doing his best, but he's still apprehensive. He is trying not to let his fears overwhelm him."

Betsy nodded sagely. In the years since the help center had been opened, Betsy and Lainey had become good friends, and they held no secrets from one another. Betsy had flourished at the center, and had proven to have a knack for business, so Lainey had brought her on as a partner and teacher. She had proved indispensable when dealing with some of the language barriers and attitudes from the women on the street. Now that Lainey was about to have her first child, she was leaving Betsy in charge. She had full confidence that the center would flourish under her direction. Still, it was hard for her to leave the center for any amount of time. She and Elizabeth had built this place from the ground up, dealing with the prejudices of men who didn't think women should be in business, or the society folks who thought Lainey and Elizabeth should not be dirtying their hands with work. Lainey didn't give a fig what they thought. This work was as important to her now as it was then, and she had helped countless women find a way off the street and into a safe occupation or a decent marriage. She was proud of all that she had accomplished, and acknowledged that there was so much more to do.

At the time, Lainey's reasons may have sounded impulsive, but she was never so glad that she had followed her heart. After the house party three years ago, the men had made good on their promises of financial support and had donated generously to the cause. It was because of them that Lainey had had a good start, and she was grateful to each one.

She often saw the viscount as social gatherings, and was pleased when he announced his engagement the year after her party. His wife was a lovely woman who was clearly head over heels in love with him, and it appeared he returned the sentiment. Lainey was thrilled to see him so happy after all he'd gone through, and though she knew they would have done well together, Kingston would have been robbed of the second chance at true love, for Lainey's heart would never belong to anyone but her husband.

The handsome devil himself walked in the door, and Lainey's heart automatically sped up. Would she ever stop thrilling at the mere presence of him? She certainly hoped not.

"Hello, my love," he said, kissing her soundly. "I hope you are not overdoing it today."

"I"m fine, Gavin, no need to fret."

He slipped his arm about her waist. "I will always fret over the comfort of my wife," he declared. "Also, I have a surprise for you!"

"Do you?" She smiled excitedly, wondering what it could possibly be. Suddenly, a hand bearing a bouquet of flowers was thrust around the door frame, and a moment later, its owner appeared. Lainey gasped.

"Charles!"

Charles Devereaux walked into the office, looking as devastatingly handsome as always. He and Gavin had put aside their differences long ago, and as it turned out, found they had quite a lot in common. Once Devereaux was no longer seen as a threat, Gavin had found he quite liked the fellow, and they had become good friends over the years. Charles swept into the room, bestowing the flowers upon Lainey. She pulled him into a warm embrace.

"You devil! What are you doing here?"

"You didn't think I was going to miss your send off, did you?"

Lainey buried her nose in the flowers. "These are beautiful, thank you. Tell me, how are things at Thistleview?"

"We are doing well, thank you. I'm in town on business and Gavin told me of your temporary retirement, so I thought I would celebrate your newest accomplishment," he said, pointing to her stomach. "I'm very happy for you both."

"Thank you, we are excited...and nervous."

Charles flashed her a charming smile. "I'm sure you will do well." He leaned close. "Though if it's a boy, promise you'll name him after me," he said in her ear. She let out a laugh and swatted him with her flowers.

"Ah, Charles, I am very glad to see you."

"As am I. You've done wonders with the place since I saw it last."

"My love, perhaps you'd like to show him the improvements you've made?"

"Would you care to see, Mr. Devereux?"

"It would please me greatly, Lady Mayfield."

Charles offered her his arm and led her from the room. Gavin looked at Betsy.

"Is everyone here?" he said in a low voice. She nodded, a sparkle in her eye. They both followed Lainey out of the room and down the hall. Charles swept open the door to the main hall and ushered Lainey in, where she was met with an uproarious "Surprise!"

Lainey stumbled back into her husband's arms in shock. "What on earth is all this?"

"A party for you, my love."

She turned to him. "For me? You did this for me?"

"It's the center's second birthday, you are taking some time off to have our first child…we thought that was a perfect time for a celebration."

Lainey put a hand to her throat, unable to speak. So many of the women she had helped were here, beaming at her. Elizabeth stood in the middle of the crowd, pride and love radiating from her face. Lainey stepped forward to enfold her in a hug.

"This never would have happened without you," she said into her hair. "I love you so much and I am so glad you are my sister."

"And I would never have been here if it weren't for you and Aidan," Elizabeth replied, laying a hand on Lainey's cheek. "I am proud to be both your business partner and your sister-in-law."

Lainey sighed. "We have built something pretty special here, haven't we?"

"We sure have. And I can't wait to see what our future brings!"

"Right now, that's another baby in the family!" The reason Elizabeth wasn't running the center in Lainey's absence was that she had just had her own child a few months ago and was also taking some time off from work. It was an exciting time for both of them.

"Are you going to keep the lady of the hour all to yourself?"

Lainey looked up into Viscount Kingston's gentle face. "My lord! How lovely to see you!"

"And you as well. You are radiant," he replied, bowing over her hand. "The place is looking wonderful. Look at all the two of you have accomplished. You should be very proud."

Lainey blushed and thanked him before getting swallowed into the crowd of well-wishers. Over the next hour, she hugged and laughed and chatted non-stop with the women who had come here to learn and better their lives, and they regaled her with stories and provided updates on how things were going. They were an inspiration to the women who were new here, and gave them hope that they, too, could be successful.

She was beginning to flag when Gavin brought her a glass of lemonade. "Oh, bless you! I haven't stopped talking!"

He chuckled. "I've noticed. Are you ready to go home and rest? It's been a long day and you are looking a little wan."

"I am tired," she admitted. "A cup of tea and a nap sound like just the thing."

"Then let's go home." He put his arm around her and kissed her temple. "You are amazing, you know that? Just look around. All these lives you have changed. You have indeed made your mark on this world, my dear, and it is all the better for it."

Lainey blinked back tears. "This place is my heart. Thank you for believing in me and supporting my dream."

"Always, my love. I will always believe in you." He slipped behind her and wrapped her in his arms, resting his chin on her shoulder. "I love you, Lainey. My heart is here," he said, placing his hands on her belly. "And here." He kissed her cheek. "Now let's go home so I can hold you while you nap. I can't lie and say I won't be happy to have you home more for the next few months…but I'm glad you are continuing to teach your class. This place needs you as much as you need it."

"Ah, you know me so well." Lainey turned in his arms. "I'm very glad you are my husband. Although, thank goodness I had not one, but two back-ups," she teased, nodding her head at Charles and the viscount.

Gavin gave a shout of laughter. "Minx. I should birch your bum for that."

"Mm," Lainey purred, turning to wrap her arms around his neck. "Don't make promises unless you intend to keep them," she said against his lips.

His eyes flared with interest and he took her offered mouth in a quick, hard kiss. "It is most definitely time to go home."

"I couldn't agree more." She smiled up at him, contentment flowing through her veins. She'd come so close to giving up what she truly wanted, to settling for something less than love. And while some women could view marriage as a practical situation, Lainey knew it was so much more. She'd never been able to imagine her life without Gavin, and she was grateful she hadn't had to face that reality.

She swept her gaze over the room, observing the excited chatter, the laughter that flowed between women who lived on the street and women who were wealthy and titled, and suddenly, that gap didn't seem quite so large. She fervently hoped that one day, the differences would disappear completely. Now *that* would be a dream come true.

ACKNOWLEDGMENTS

I would like to thank the Romance Writers of America for giving me the opportunity to learn from some of the best in the industry. I am a writer because of this organization.

Thank you also to my local chapter, CTRWA, and the friends I have made there. Your critiques and encouragements help me produce a better book every single time.

But most of all, thank you to my beloved late husband, who spent years encouraging me, yet did not live to see my name in print. There was no truer romantic hero than you, my love. I do this in honor of you.

ABOUT THE AUTHOR

Grace Hartwell is a lifelong resident of Connecticut and has been crafting stories since she knew how to hold a pen. A sucker for happy endings, Grace began reading romance at age 12 and has never looked back. She lives in her "castle" with her four cats, and the occasional squirrel. When she's not writing, she spends her time on stage pursuing her other passion, or making jewelry and historical fashions. Grace loves tea and travel and would move to England in a heartbeat if her family would let her! Find out more (including cat photos!) at www.gracehartwell.com